[redacted]

UPSTAI

John Hawkesworth

It is the beginning of the twentieth century. The sun never sets on the British Empire and in the streets of London horse-drawn carriages jostle for space with the new-fangled motor cars. Henry Wood conducts at the Albert Hall and in Piccadilly the flickering images of the bioscope draw gasps of delight from servant girls on their afternoons off.

Under the surface new tensions stir: Balfour's Conservative government is swept from office by an overwhelming majority; unemployment spreads a cancer of poverty among the working classes; and a parlour maid in Eaton Place works a ten-hour day for £20 a year.

Such is the background to John Hawkesworth's fascinating novel of life – above and below stairs – in an Edwardian household.

The Bellamys reside at 165 Eaton Place. Above stairs Lady Marjorie gives the orders. The daughter of an Earl, she has only two ambitions: to smooth her husband's path into high office and to find a suitable match for her unconventional daughter, Elizabeth. She regards her servants as possessions: their sole function is to ensure the smooth running of the house.

Below stairs is the domain of the butler, Mr. Hudson, as staunch a champion of the established social order as his employers. Under his stern eye the footman, Albert, Mrs. Bridges the cook, Lady Marjorie's personal maid Miss Roberts, Mr. Pearce the coachman, and Rose the parlour-maid, pursue their ordered rounds . . . at least until the arrival of a cheeky waif named Sarah, under house parlourmaid and self-styled gypsy princess.

Front cover photograph by kind permission of LWT.

[redacted]

This book is based on the television series, *Upstairs, Downstairs*, produced by the author for London Weekend Television Limited and Channel Four and created by Sagitta Productions Limited in association with Jean Marsh and Eileen Atkins.

Rex Firkin was Executive Producer and Alfred Shaughnessy was Story Editor of the series.

The author wishes to acknowledge the fact that in writing the book he has drawn largely on material from television scripts by the following writers:

Charlotte Bingham and Terence Brady
Maureen Duffy
John Harrison
Jeremy Paul
Alfred Shaughnessy
Rosemary Anne Sisson
Fay Weldon

This book is dedicated to them and to the actors, directors, technicians and all the other people who worked so hard to make the production such a happy one.

Upstairs, Downstairs

JOHN HAWKESWORTH

SPHERE BOOKS LIMITED
30/32 Gray's Inn Road, London WC1X 8JL

First published in Great Britain in 1972
by Sphere Books Ltd.

Reprinted March 1972 (twice), 1973 (five times),
1977, 1983

TRADE
MARK

Printed in Great Britain by
Cox & Wyman Ltd, Reading

CHAPTER ONE

NOVEMBER 1903

'What is your name?'

'Clemence Dumas.'

'French?'

'Half French.'

'You must call me m'lady, when you reply.'

'I'm sorry, m'lady.'

Lady Marjorie Bellamy suspected that the references she held in her hand were false and she didn't believe for a moment that the pert, shabby little cockney girl standing by the sofa in the morning room was telling the truth. But instead of ringing the bell for her butler to dismiss Clemence Dumas from her presence, she hesitated.

In an age when malnutrition caused chronic ill health among the lower classes and tuberculosis and rickets were commonplace, this girl looked remarkably healthy, but quite apart from that important consideration there was something else about her that impressed Lady Marjorie. A sort of style. Lady Marjorie had style herself. It was reflected in the cool elegance of all about her: her house, her clothes, even her voice, all of which seemed perfectly chosen to show off her tall, fine-boned patrician beauty dominated by the great mass of her golden red hair.

But the latest applicant for the post of under house parlourmaid had not impressed the servants at 165 Eaton Place. She had shocked Mr Hudson, the butler, by coming to the front door; she had insulted Mrs Bridges, the cook, by calling her 'cook' in her own kitchen; and she had been cheeky to Rose, the house parlourmaid.

Now dinner time was approaching and the servants were assembling in the servants' hall.

The hall faced south onto the area and was in consequence the least gloomy of all the subterranean rooms in which the servants spent the larger part of their daily lives. It was dominated by a long table covered, at all except meal times, by a cloth of patterned chenille. Round the cast iron fireplace there was an ancient club fender and an assortment of easy chairs, all of which, apart from Mrs Bridges' padded wickerwork basket chair, were cast-offs from upstairs, as was the rest of the furniture and decoration in the room. The velvet curtains, the big oil lamps and the large engravings depicting *'The Battle of Inkerman'*, *'A Meet of the Quorn Hounds'* and a portrait after Reynolds of George the Third were all gifts from the Bellamys. A touch of colour was added to the room by the various boxes, tea caddies and biscuit tins in which the servants kept their sewing and mending things. On the table by the window a large ebony Indian Elephant suported the library, starting classically with the Bible, the Encyclopaedia Britannica (Seventh edition) and Mrs Gurney's *'The Childhood of Queen Victoria'*, and descending through various novelettes of the twopenny variety to *Pearson's Weekly* and *Hilda's Home Companion*.

'Lady Marjorie will never take that girl on,' said Mrs Bridges who resembled a very neat cottage loaf in her pink dress, starched apron and cap. 'Her? Not in a month of Sundays. She couldn't tell a feather boa from a boa constrictor.' Though why that should be a necessary qualification for a house parlourmaid Mrs Bridges didn't explain.

'She's quite unsuitable. She went to the front door,' said Rose with the sniff that she used to underline her opinions.

'You are quite right, Rose. Untrained and blind to all decency,' Mr Hudson remarked from the door. He was watching the serried ranks of bells in the passage waiting for her ladyship to call him to the morning room. She was spending an inexplicably long time interviewing the despicable Miss Dumas who had been late for her appointment in the first place.

Mr Hudson was a craggy square-built highlander tamed by time and servitude into a decent, conscientious and rather humourless butler. He had fair, wiry hair now thinning and going white at the temples, and his sombre uniform was enlivened by touches of gold, a substance of which he was very fond. Gold rims to his spectacles, a gold tooth and the heavy gold chain of his half-hunter watch, a legacy from his father, prominently displayed across his waistcoat. This last was a privilege not always granted to butlers in larger and more particular establishments.

The morning room bell rang and Mr Hudson set off briskly up the dark, curving flight of stone steps that led from the basement to the front hall.

'Well, that's the end of her,' said Rose with some satisfaction. 'Clemence Dumas! How could anyone hope to go into service with a name like that?'

Emily, the little Irish kitchen maid was just finishing laying the long table. She was a poor bedraggled little creature, very shiny and scrubbed and her clothes were much patched and mended which didn't matter as she was never allowed to appear upstairs.

'Well I hope she gets taken on!' she said in her County Claire lilt.

'It's not for you to hope, Emily,' Mrs Bridges retorted, 'or not to hope neither for that matter. It is for you to keep the fire in. You let it out on purpose.'

There had been a running battle on this subject all morning.

'I never did,' said Emily. 'The coal's wet. And that's Alfred's fault; he always leaves the coal-house door open.'

Alfred was hanging up his green tail coat in the corner.

'I'll put you in the coal house, Emily. Ashes to ashes, dust to dust,' he said darkly. Alfred had a long sardonic india-rubber sort of face with sad eyes, the eyes of a clown or a martyr. His limbs seemed uncoordinated, his hands and feet too large for his body and when serving at meals his movements were extravagantly formal.

'Don't pass blame, Emily,' snapped Rose.

'Now you're against me too. You're all against me.' And Emily sighed, for it was nothing more than the truth; being the most lowly person in the domestic hierarchy, she was the natural scapegoat when things went wrong.

Mr Hudson pushed open the swing door, covered with green baize on one side and polished mahogany on the other, and walked across the front hall to the morning room. He opened the morning door without knocking and advanced three paces. 'You rang, m'lady,' he said.

'I mean to engage this young woman, Hudson.'

Lady Marjorie waited for the familiar pause and the ill concealed look of shocked surprise, before Hudson replied, 'Yes, m'lady.'

'She will have her dinner in the servants' hall and fetch her belongings later. Rose will tell her what to do.'

Hudson nodded and coughed. 'And the young person's name, m'lady?'

Lady Marjorie didn't hesitate. 'Sarah.'

Clemence Dumas was startled at this decision which she had in no way foreseen. Little did she know that in choosing 'Sarah' for her name, Lady Marjorie was paying her a compliment. When she was a little girl she had been very fond of a spaniel called Sarah.

'My name is Clemence, m'lady.'

'Clemence is not a servant's name,' Lady Marjorie turned to her desk. 'Go with Hudson, Sarah, and remember you are here on trial.'

In the hall Sarah caught up with the butler at the bottom of the big stairs.

'Mr Hudson.'

'Well?'

'Do I have to be called Sarah?'

'Yes.'

'I don't like it.'

'It's not for you to question your betters.'

'Are you my better?'

She was anxious to keep him talking.

'Indeed I am.'

'What makes you better than me, Mr. Hudson,' she said very innocently. 'I'm not being uppish, I just want to know.'

'I am older than you and therefore wiser. And I have

learned humility.' It was one of his favourite remarks. 'It is a hard lesson but once learned, never forgotten.'

He walked on to the door.

'How did you learn it?' said Sarah. She held the door open for him, almost overdoing her own new-found humility.

'My grandmother was a proud woman, and died of starvation,' said Hudson. 'And remember another thing. Above stairs you do not speak unless you're spoken to.'

And he gave Sarah a sharp look as if to fix the statement in her mind for eternity.

Lady Marjorie leant back in her chair and smiled to herself at the thought of Hudson's face. He never could conceal his emotions which was one of the reasons he would never gain promotion to a grander establishment. Silly old Hudson; sometimes he maddened her by his obstinacy and his slowness, but she wouldn't have changed him. He was loyal and honest and only drank in moderation and that was saying quite a lot for any butler.

Hudson was the son of the head gillie on her father's estate in Perthshire, while Mrs Bridges and Rose had both come from Southwold, her family home in Wiltshire.

That the other servants wouldn't understand why she had engaged Sarah was of no interest to Lady Marjorie. She had been brought up with servants all her life and she took them very much for granted. If they did something silly like stealing or having a baby they were sacked, if they were ill or in trouble they were helped, more from a practical than a humane point of view. If a servant was ill it was a nuisance and the sooner she was got well again and able to perform her duties the better for everyone.

The only time Lady Marjorie really noticed the servants was when they annoyed her, so that she was apt to think of them in terms of their faults and give little consideration to their virtues. When she thought of Mrs Bridges, she remembered the cook's moods and tantrums, not her delicious quails in aspic; when she thought of

Rose, it was her sulky face when she was put out, not the spotless cleanliness of the house; as for Roberts, her lady's maid, Lady Marjorie really couldn't think for the life of her why she kept such a stupid chatterbox of a woman in her house a moment longer.

Unlike a lot of ladies, she found the subject of servants very uninteresting.

It would have surprised Lady Marjorie to find out how much more her servants were interested in her than she in them.

An expectant silence greeted Mr Hudson and Sarah's entrance into the servant's hall. The butler, who had a sense of occasion, didn't at first break it. He indicated to Alfred to fetch a chair and Emily to lay an extra place. Then he sat down, looked round the table, and lowered his head.

'May the Lord bless our endeavours and grant us conciliation to that rank in which, in His infinite mercy, he has seen fit to place us.'

At this point in the Grace, Mr Hudson looked up briefly. Emily was staring at Sarah, and Sarah was studying the servant's hall. He quelled them both with a look.

'And for what we are about to receive, of His great bounty, may we find favour in His eyes, and sit in honour at His table, Amen.'

Mr Hudson began to carve the mutton with ceremony.

'Sarah is joining us as under house parlourmaid, Miss Roberts,' he remarked.

Miss Roberts sat, correctly in order of precedence, on the butler's right and Alfred, his amanuensis, on his left. Mrs Bridges commanded the other end of the table with Rose on her right and Emily handy on her left. The middle places were taken by Mr Pearce the coachman and Sarah.

Miss Roberts regarded Sarah without enthusiasm. She was a small prickly woman with a tight mouth.

'Indeed, Mr Hudson,' she replied. 'On trial, I take it?'

'Yes indeed,' said Mr Hudson as the plates were handed round the table. 'Rose, you are to instruct her in her duties.'

'Yes Mr Hudson,' said Rose in a flat voice.

'With a good heart and a glad will, if you please, Rose.'

'Of course, Mr Hudson.'

Rose gave Sarah a look of pronounced distaste and began to introduce her formally to the others.

'Miss Roberts is her ladyship's personal maid,' she said. 'Alfred is the footman. Mr Pearce is the coachman.'

Mr Pearce, a large hearty man, who, because he lived in a couple of rooms over the stable in the mews behind the house, felt himself to be a man of the world, was about to give Sarah a big smile when it was frozen on his face by Mrs Bridges rapping the table with her spoon.

'Silence, if you please,' she announced.

Rose shut her mouth angrily. She felt that she had been led by Mr Hudson into breaking the rule that only the senior servants might speak before the vegetables had been served.

Emily came hurrying in from the kitchen with the vegetables and they were quickly sent round.

Mr. Hudson looked over his spectacles.

'Vegetables are served, Mrs Bridges,' he said.

'Thank you Mr Hudson,' answered Mrs Bridges. 'You may talk,' she announced to the table at large.

Although the formal opening ceremony was now over there was no immediate outbreak of conversation, only considerable concentration on the caper sauce.

'Mutton again,' said Mr Pearce at last, giving Sarah his smile. He liked the look of the new girl, she had a good bosom, something you could really get your hands round. Bosoms counted a lot with Mr Pearce.

'And what's wrong with mutton, Mr Pearce,' said Miss Roberts, resenting the implied criticism of Mrs Bridges. 'With a nice drop of caper sauce, eh?'

'Nothing, nothing at all,' replied Mr Pearce, already in retreat.

'Perhaps you'd rather eat hay like your horses,' said Mrs Bridges forcefully.

'Forget I spoke, ladies,' said Mr Pearce completely routed.

'Millions would be grateful for what we have, Mr Pearce,' said Mr Hudson to finish him off. 'Don't you agree, Sarah,' he added, looking at Sarah.

Sarah didn't seem to hear him.

Rose gave her a sharp nudge.

'You were being addressed by Mr Hudson, Sarah.'

'Who, me?'

'Yes, you.'

'I'm sorry,' said Sarah. 'The name is so strange. Couldn't I be called Clemence, if only down here?'

'In all my born days, I never heard of such a name below stairs,' said Miss Roberts. 'Whatever was your mother thinking of?'

'You could search the good book from cover to cover,' Alfred remarked with his mouth full, 'and still not find it.'

Mr Pearce winked at Sarah.

'Don't worry about him, he was brought up religious,' he said. 'Clemence,' he added reflectively. 'Good name for a filly, I'll say that. But hardly human.'

'I think it's a lovely name,' said Emily reaching for more caper sauce.

As the subject of Sarah's name now seemed to have been exhaustively covered, Mr Hudson tried again.

'As I was saying,' he addressed Sarah directly, 'millions would be grateful for mutton once a week, let alone once a day. Wouldn't you agree, Sarah?'

Everyone looked at Sarah.

'Yes, Mr Hudson,' said Sarah, humble and waiflike.

Mr Hudson and Mrs Bridges exchanged gratified smiles.

'Did you really live in France?' asked Emily.

'Yes,' Sarah answered very casual.

'Were you in service there?' asked Miss Roberts, hoping to catch her out. She had been to France once with Lady Marjorie.

'No,' Sarah replied. 'I lived in a chateau. Once I had a personal maid. Like Lady Marjorie.'

She gave Miss Roberts the look a very grand lady might give a personal maid.

Miss Roberts gave an angry flounce.

'I think we must learn to take Sarah's statements with a pinch of salt,' she announced with an acid smile.

'I don't lie,' said Sarah, suddenly aggressive.

'We never said you did,' explained Rose sweetly. 'But perhaps you exaggerate.'

Mr Hudson was ready to pour oil on troubled waters.

'If her ladyship finds Sarah satisfactory, I am sure we all do,' he pontificated. 'It is not for us to choose, or to judge our companions in service. As I am sure we all know very well.'

He addressed the last sentence pointedly to Rose who sniffed, furious to be put down a second time in front of the new girl.

She turned on Sarah.

'Say something in French then,' she said.

'Some other time.'

'You're as English as I am,' Rose retorted giving the table a knowing smile.

'I am not,' said Sarah. 'My mother was a gypsy, and I can read hands and tell the future.

She looked round defiantly. 'And put curses on people,' she added for good measure.

Emily gasped at the wonder of it.

'God preserve us, the witch of Endor herself,' said Alfred.

'If my mother was a gypsy I wouldn't speak of it,' said Rose.

Sarah wasn't in the least put out.

'A French count saw her and married her,' she replied grandly, still on the subject of her mother. 'She died giving birth to me. He married again, a very wicked woman. When my father died she made me live like a servant, and in the end turned me out altogether. But I have lawyers fighting for me. One day I will come into my own.' She gave the table a brave look.

'In the meantime,' she added, 'I must live as best I can.'

Nobody said a word. They were bewildered by such invention. They all knew Sarah was lying, all except

Emily, but it was lying on such a grand scale that it went beyond the frontiers of their experience. It seemed pointless to comment.

'It's like a story in a book,' said Emily wonderingly.

'Exactly, Emily,' retorted Miss Roberts, seeing her chance. 'A tale from a penny novelette. All very well for kitchenmaids but not what one expects from house parlourmaids.'

'Wicked nonsense,' said Rose. 'She ought to be locked up.'

Mr Hudson held up his hands. 'Enough Rose; Emily fetch in the roly-poly pudding.'

'Why won't she say something in French, then?' Rose almost shouted. 'Because she can't that's why.'

She turned to Sarah. 'Go on then. If you can.'

Sarah drew herself up and gave Rose a sweet smile, then quite slowly she began to sing,

'Au près de ma blonde,
Qu'il fait bon, fait bon dormir,
Au près de ma blonde
Qu'il fait bon dormir.'

She had a high true voice and a perfect French accent.

Emily crossed herself. She now knew for certain that Sarah was a real gypsy princess.

CHAPTER TWO

Rose was a very good houseparlourmaid. She took great pride in her work, and not being by nature a very sociable person, it tended to fill her whole life.

She never skimped or hurried a job however trivial and there was no nook or cranny that went undusted in the part of the house that was her domain. 'I like to see things done properly' she often remarked.

The under houseparlourmaid was Rose's particular cross. Not only did she have to share the same bed but she was responsible for her work and if the under houseparlourmaid made a mess of things—a not uncommon occurrence—Rose had to take the blame.

When the underhouseparlourmaid was sacked, which was quite often, Rose grumbled that she had too much work; when an assistant was in residence, it was her constant grouse that it was more work than without one.

But although she grumbled, Rose accepted that Lady Marjorie's wishes must be respected. Just as she accepted all the other conditions of domestic service, so she accepted Sarah as a necessary evil. Rose was also a practical person and after Sarah admitted that the belongings which she was to fetch later were non-existent, she asked Mr Hudson if she might have a couple of hours off to take the new girl to the shops to fit her out.

In the general way of things everything in life was found for a servant by the employer, but this did not include clothes except special uniforms, such as Alfred's tailcoat and the housemaid's fancy caps and aprons for the afternoon.

The best bargains in servants' clothing were to be had in Oxford Street. On the way there in the horse bus Rose made a list of Sarah's requirements and as each article was purchased she put the price beside it. When they had finished the list read as follows:

Lisle stockings, black, two pairs	5 5¾d
Ribbed vests, two 3¾ each	7 d
1 pair stockinette knickers	1 6½d
1 pair black boots	3 11d
Aprons (two at 6d)	1 0 d
Caps (two at 3½d)	7 d
Stays (1 pair)	2 11d
Stiff cuffs and collars	
Two sets at 10d	
Two morning dresses (pale lilac)	8 2 d
Two black cotton afternoon dresses	9 6 d
Two nighties (2 1¾d) each)	4 3½d
Total	£1 13 7¾d

Sarah had one pound six shillings and twopence in the world. As she had no small personal possessions worth pawning except a Chelsea dog given to her by her father, Rose advanced the necessary cash to be paid back in weekly instalments from Sarah's wages of fifteen pounds a year.

Sarah was as pleased with her new clothes as a child at Christmas, and although she liked having two sorts of dresses she couldn't understand the need to change until Rose explained to her that they were housemaids in the morning (pale lilac) and parlourmaids in the afternoon (black).

One the way home Rose began to make a list of her duties for Sarah and she found in her new assistant a willingness to learn and a quickness of brain that prompted her to remark to Mrs Bridges later that evening that there was some good to be found in the most unlikely places if you looked for it.

Attic bedrooms in big London houses were very hot in the summer and very cold in the winter, especially at five thirty on November mornings. Or so it seemed to Sarah, waking suddenly on her first day to see Alfred's unshaven face close to her own as he shook the bed. Rose jumped up immediately and pulled the bedclothes off Sarah. There was a film of ice on the water in the ewer and the windows were frosted over. When Rose tried to light a candle the draft blew it out.

'I'm cold,' Sarah moaned trying to rub some feeling into her toes.

'Work will soon warm you up,' Rose answered briskly scrubbing her teeth with a cloth at the basin. 'If we get behind in the morning, there's trouble all day, so up with you.'

'My feet are frozen and my legs won't work,' said Sarah with a huge yawn.

'Oh yes they will. They must,' Rose answered and she began to dress Sarah as if she was a huge shivering doll.

'And when you're dressed and downstairs, what then?' Rose asked.

Sarah rubbed her eyes.

'I must make sure that Emily has the range going properly so that Mrs Bridges can get on,' she recited parrot fashion. 'Then I lay up breakfast in the servants' hall and then there's Lady Marjorie's early morning tray.'

'And don't leave sticky marks on the milk jug like the other girl always did,' said Rose pulling on her own dress and beginning to button it up. Sarah copied her.

'Did the other girl sleep in this bed, Rose?'

'Yes.'

'Was she called Sarah, too?'

'Kate.'

'Oh. What happened to her?

'Curiosity killed the cat,' said Rose, very short. 'What's next on the list?'

'Then there's servants' breakfast, I suppose I'm allowed to sit down and eat that,' said Sarah battling with her stiff collar.

Rose came to her aid.

'After breakfast make sure Emily hasn't dropped off to sleep in the boothole,' said Rose. 'She's like a dormouse that girl. If she has and won't budge inform me, not Mrs Bridges. You'll find me dusting and polishing in the morning room or the drawing room. What next?'

Sarah had to think.

'Upstairs to clean the grates and relay and light the fires,' she said. 'I wish I'd come in the summer.'

'You haven't got a bad memory, I'll say that,' said Rose kindly as she put up her hair with a mouthful of pins. 'Quiet as a mouse doing the grates, then call me to draw the master's bath. You fetch up the hot water; if the big boiler's giving trouble you can try the range or the big kettle.

The plumbing in the house was modern by the standards of the eighteen eighties when the Bellamys had first moved in but had hardly kept abreast of the times. There was cold water on every floor and bathrooms on the main bedroom floors but the hot water had to come up in large copper jugs drawn from the boiler in the basement.

'After the bath,' Rose went on, 'you help me lay the upstairs breakfast, then there's the clean boots and shoes to be taken up, that's if Emily's done them which isn't often. Then there's the master's newspaper to iron for Mr Hudson to take up—and today's the day for fresh bed linen, which is quite a rush because it must be done while they're having breakfast—and Lady Marjorie eats like a bird—and of course, there's the towels to be aired.'

'I'll never remember,' sighed Sarah sinking down on a chair.

'You must,' snapped Rose. 'Anyway you've got your list. Here,' she thrust it into Sarah's hand.

Sarah studied it blankly.

'You've got it upside down,' said Rose.

'So I have,' Sarah answered making a funny face.

'Tsk', Rose sniffed. 'Just look at that cap of yours. Oh dear, I don't know. We're behind already.' And it was still only twenty to six.

Later on in the morning Rose showed Sarah over the house. Behind the servants' hall a passage led to the butler's pantry where the silver and glass were kept; beyond it was Mr Hudson's bedroom and at the end of the passage a mysterious dark door that led to the cellar. Only the master and Mr Hudson had keys to that door.

There was a hatch through from the servants' hall to the huge kitchen where Mrs Bridges presided at the long heavy iron range or the thick wooden table which Emily scrubbed daily white as snow. There were shelves of china and a dresser of copper pans of every description and even an articulated copper turtle for serving soup and so many jars and containers that it was amazing that the cook herself knew what was in them all.

The scullery where Emily slaved for hours and hours at the washing-up led off the kitchen conveniently near the bottom of the lift that led up to a small serving room off the dining room. There was an old fashioned copper in the scullery which was only used once a fortnight when the lower female servants were allowed the luxury of a Sitz bath in front of the servants' hall fire. There was a so-called servants' bath upstairs but only Miss Roberts, Mrs Bridges and Mr Hudson were allowed to use it. The odd thing was that no one ever offered Alfred any bathing facilities whatever, but he never complained and even Mr Hudson's sensitive nose couldn't detect any unfortunate result stemming from this deprivation.

When you went through the green baize door Sarah thought the whole world seemed to change. Here Lady Marjorie's house began. She liked soft greens and greys and browns and she hated too much clutter. Because so much of the furniture and so many of the paintings had come from her family, the feeling in the house was more Georgian than Victorian. People who came to visit the Bellamys often copied Lady Marjorie's ideas and so to some extent she quite unintentionally helped to create the Edwardian style.

Entering at the front door the dining room was on the left and the morning room lay straight ahead at the back of the hall. The stairs on the right lead upwards to the drawing room which occupied nearly the whole of the first floor.

The drawing room was more in the French style of cream and gold. Sarah thought it was like a room out of a palace, which was rather clever of her as the chairs and the sofa had come originally from Fontainbleu and the big screen from the Summer Palace in Peking. Rose explained that the room was hardly used in the winter except when there was a dinner party. If there was a big reception, the double doors were opened to include a gloomy room with stained glass windows known as the music room because it housed the grand piano which Miss Elizabeth used for her lessons.

The second floor was the principal bedroom floor; it contained the Bellamys' bedroom, Lady Marjorie's boudoir, Mr. Bellamy's dressing room, and a spare room, as well as two bathrooms side by side for the convenience of the plumbing, and a water closet of imposing proportions. Sarah had never seen anything quite like it before; the occupant sat on a large mahogany chair with sides and back filled in with cane and the hydraulic mechanism was activated by lifting a large china handle decorated with roses sunk in the polished surround.

The next floor was still called the nursery floor, but

the nurseries had been converted into bedrooms for Miss Elizabeth and Mr James, the Bellamy's son who was twenty-two and an officer in the Life Guards stationed in Knightsbridge Barracks. Miss Roberts had a room on this floor and through a door at the back of the landing there was a housemaid's pantry and linen cupboards. From here the backstairs lead to the servants' rooms and the attics at the top of the house.

Unlike the great houses in Eaton Square to the south and Belgrave Square to the north the smaller Eaton Place houses hadn't room for a back stairs to connect the basement to the attics. And as it was considered a great disgrace for any servant to be caught on the stairs by any of the Bellamys, they were engaged in a permanent game of hide and seek. It was even considered a bad mark to be caught working upstairs by any member of the family, and Rose explained that the correct procedure was either to leave the room quickly or to freeze and become part of the decorations.

Sarah was cleaning the stair-carpet in the front hall when she was caught in exactly this predicament. She had scattered some dry tea leaves on the carpet to give a pleasant aroma as Rose had showed her and was carefully brushing the way of the pile, when she heard voices from above and almost immediately a pair of highly polished shoes appeared, encased in grey spats with pearl buttons and surmounted by beautifully creased striped trousers. She cowered to the banisters as they passed her and were followed by Mr. Hudson's more serviceable footwear. Sarah stole a sidelong glance and caught her first sight of her master, a tall distinguished looking man with hair greying at the temples, wearing a beautiful dove-grey morning coat. He and the butler were discussing whether or not his best silk hat should be sent round to the hatters for ironing before the German Embassy reception.

Sarah remembered that Mr Hudson was not only the butler but also Mr Bellamy's valet, and it seemed to her that such vast duties must be beyond the scope of one human being.

After downstairs dinner and upstairs luncheon a kind

of peace settled on the house for a couple of hours. Mrs Bridges went up to her room for a nap, Emily persevered with the washing up and the housemaids settled to their mending. If the weather was clement, Mr Hudson took a constitutional.

Before setting off he liked to pause a moment to survey Eaton Place. He liked the vista of the ordered rows of creamy white stucco late Georgian houses, all alike, stretching east as far as the eye could see; on sunny days the shiny facades of the houses on the north side of the wide quiet street lit up the faces of their less favoured fellows on the south side with a reflected glory. Mr Hudson was glad that the Bellamys house was on the north side and he liked the thought that all the houses were owned by one great and powerful nobleman.

Every day he went to Hyde Park, allowing himself exactly eleven minutes from Eaton Place to Albert Gate. Once in the park he spent a few minutes enjoying the carriages and horses and all the people in their fine clothes.

Depending on whether his mood was peaceful or warlike Mr Hudson would then turn west or east and walk off at a brisk pace. To the west his goal was the Albert Memorial, to the east it was the statue of Achilles.

From a distance the Albert Memorial seemed to the butler to look like some great exotic tree made of stone and bronze and marble and mosaic, and when he came closer, the view of the huge and peaceful prince surrounded by the sculptured evidence of his queen's vast Empire, gave Mr Hudson the pleasant assurance that here indeed was the very centre of civilization.

If his mood took the butler the other way, the iron statue of Achilles at Hyde Park Corner, erected to the Great Duke by his fellow countrymen, never failed to arouse fierce and patriotic emotions in his breast. He particularly liked the part of the inscription that read: 'Cast from cannon taken in the victories of Salamanca, Vittoria, Toulouse and Waterloo.' A great uncle on his mother's side had been killed at Waterloo, and he was proud of it.

When he had more time on his half day, Mr Hudson's interests lay in sport and the law. Lords cricket ground in the summer, to watch the great Dr Grace or Ranjitsinghi; the Fulham Football Club's field in the winter to see his heroes battling in the mud. But at all times of the year the Law Courts were Mr Hudson's favourite haunt, not, as he was quick to explain, to gaze with morbid curiosity at the faces of murderers, but to hear the great advocates of the day plead their cases.

If he had been born to a different station in life, he felt sure that he could have become a great lawyer, but it was not to be. The Lord above saw to it that every human being was placed in a certain rank at birth, and as far as Mr Hudson was concerned, that was that.

Unlike most of the butlers of Belgravia, Mr Hudson never visited the public houses in the area which were the counterpart for menservants of their masters' clubs in St James's Street. The tittle tattle and gossip over the beer which was the principal food for conversation in such places, he held to be a great cause of scandal in society.

Just before four o'clock the house began to wake up again. Emily was in the kitchen showing Sarah how to prepare Lady Marjorie's tea tray.

Everything was special about Lady Marjorie's tea. The tray, the traycloth, the special transparent oriental cup and even the tea itself which came from China in an enamelled one pound canister and cost the incredible sum of three and eightpence from the Army and Navy Stores.

'What does Lady Marjorie do in the afternoons?' asked Sarah.

'Paying calls mostly or just driving about,' Emily answered, lifting the lid off the kettle which never would boil. 'To while away the time, I suppose, until Mr Bellamy comes back from the Parliament. I wouldn't fancy it.'

'Oh I would,' said Sarah. 'To drive round and round in a fine carriage with a pair of strong horses with everybody looking at me.'

Outside in the street there was the sound of horses' hooves coming nearer and then stopping.

'That'll be her back,' said Emily, thankful that the kettle was boiling at last. 'Always punctual. You could set a clock by her.'

The morning room bell rang. Emily poured the boiling water into the teapot and the hot water jug. Rose came in briskly, picked up the tray and took it upstairs.

'How is the new girl getting on?' Lady Marjorie asked Rose when she had set down the tea tray.

'Quite satisfactory, m'lady,' Rose replied without enthusiasm.

'I hope you are looking after her.'

'Of course m'lady. Will that be all m'lady?'

But it wasn't quite all, for Lady Marjorie had asked Sarah to mend a tapestry cushion without informing the head housemaid.

'She has delicate fingers and nice neat movements,' Lady Marjorie explained.

'Yes, m'lady.'

Rose answered sulkily because she sensed that there was a new favourite at court, and if it was anyone's business to mend tapestry cushions it was her own.

Emily and Sarah were sitting by the fire in the servants' hall drinking their own tea.

'If I was rich I would never lift a finger, except perhaps to adjust a curl,' said Sarah, adjusting an imaginary one. 'And I'd have stage-door Johnnies crowding round outside waiting for me, all black and white like penguins with bottles of champagne tucked away beneath their fine feathers. All for me.'

Emily was shocked.

'That's not proper at all,' she replied, tucking her feet under the bar of her chair. 'You know what actresses are. If I was rich I'd have a little cottage in the country and no one to shout at me and lots of kids. And I'd never forget their names the way our mam did.'

Rose came in through the door very nose in the air.

'Time to chat I see.' She looked at Sarah. 'I thought you were supposed to be sewing Lady Marjorie's cushion. I hope you know it's worth hundreds of pounds,' in this she allowed herself a pardonable exaggeration. 'The least you can do is to get on with it.'

Sarah leaned over and produced the cushion beautifully mended and wrapped in a clean piece of cloth.

'I see,' said Rose, trying to show that she was not impressed. 'Well you'd better take it up to her.'

When she saw the cushion Lady Marjorie was delighted and asked her protegée where she had learnt to sew so beautifully.

'In a convent, m'lady,' Sarah admitted.

'In France?'

'That's right, m'lady.'

'Were the nuns good to you?'

'Most of the time, m'lady. Though sometimes they would dress me in a canvas robe and shut me in a dark cell all day, with no food or water.'

'But why?'

'To teach me to be thankful.'

'What for?'

'God's mercy, m'lady.'

'A strange way surely of bringing you to know it.'

'That's what I said, m'lady, so back I went.'

And Lady Marjorie laughed in spite of the fact that this wasn't the sort of remark under houseparlourmaids ought to make to their mistresses and she strongly suspected that Sarah's French convent was more likely a sweat shop in the East End of London.

'Thank you, Sarah, you may go.' She said.

Sarah moved to the door.

'Sarah!'

Lady Marjorie indicated the tea tray that Sarah had forgotten to take with her.

Sarah came back and took the tray very delicately and then she curtsied as if to say 'I can play charades as well as any of them, m'lady.'

One cold early morning a few days later Sarah came down to the kitchen to find Emily in a dreadful state. She had been frightened half out of her wits in the coalshed by a cockroach with whiskers as long as her arm, and on top of that the fire in the range refused to burn and was smoking like a factory. Which meant that the water wouldn't boil and she was late calling Mrs Bridges with her tea.

Emily dashed upstairs leaving Sarah to struggle with the recalcitrant fire when the backdoor bell went. Outside Sarah found a strange dirty little old woman carrying a basket. It seemed on odd time to call and while Sarah was still trying to find out what the woman wanted, Emily was back and pushing her out of the way.

'Oh, it's you, Matty . . . she's on her way down, I was late calling her and she's in such a wax.' She turned to Sarah. 'You should be laying up the servants' breakfast, go on now.'

There was something about Emily's manner that made Sarah both suspicious and curious. A few minutes later Mrs Bridges came wheezing and grumbling down the stairs and Emily whispered something to her.

Sarah watched from behind the servants' hall curtains as Mrs Bridges took the old woman's basket and disappeared into the larder.

In a moment she was back and when the old woman lifted the cloth on the basket Sarah clearly saw a bowl of dripping and a trussed chicken lying in it; and she also saw money passing between the old woman and Mrs Bridges.

Emily had explained to her that the sale of dripping and bottles was one of the cook's unwritten privileges, but she hadn't mentioned chickens.

That evening the Bellamys went out to dinner.

'It's nice when they've gone out, the whole place to ourselves and no bells ringing,' said Emily. She was sitting in her usual place by the fire in the servants' hall reading a book. Sarah was wandering round the room unable to settle down.

'There's a story in here just like yours,' Emily went on. 'The orphan princess turned out by a wicked stepmother.'

'How does it end?' Sarah answered more for something to say than anything else; she was feeling fidgetty and shut in.

Emily held up the book. 'You can read it if you like.'

'I don't read rubbish like that.'

Emily shrugged her shoulders sadly. 'I suppose you had a good education in your French chateau,' she said. 'No one ever taught me anything. Everyone tries to keep me down. Washing dishes is all I'm good for and stamping on cockroaches.'

But Sarah wasn't listening, she was putting on her coat and hat. Emily was quite startled. 'Where are you going?' she asked.

'Out,' said Sarah crisply. 'It's the gypsy in me. I can't bear to be shut up.'

'Does Mr Hudson know you're going?'

'It's only for a minute.'

Emily was genuinely alarmed. 'You'll have to ask him, or you'll get into trouble.'

'Well I'm not asking Mr Hudson and you aren't going to tell him . . . are you?'

Sarah stood above Emily menacing.

'Are you, Emily?'

'No.'

'Then I'll read your fortune when I get back.'

Emily's funny face broke into a smile of pleasure.

'But if you tell a living soul that I've gone out, Emily,' Sarah stretched her hands in front of Emily's face.

'I'll curse you and the blood will turn to ice in your veins, and you will die horribly within a week.'

Emily sank down in real terror, Sarah walked briskly out of the room through the back door and up the area steps.

For a long time Emily sat huddled and motionless as if the blood in her veins really had turned to ice. When Rose came in she quickly buried her nose in her book.

'You'll ruin your eyes, Emily,' said Rose sitting down and picking up her needlework.

'What does it matter? I won't be needing them much longer,' Emily answered in a tragic voice which made Rose look across at her.

'When I breathe I have a pain,' Emily went on. 'The

good die young they say and I have the impression on my chest.'

'I wish you'd stop reading that rubbish,' snapped Rose.

'It isn't rubbish, Rose. Things like that do happen.' She took in a deep breath obviously in the grip of some strong emotion. 'I think Sarah is more tragic and more romantic than anything in a book. I would lay down my life for her. If I was asked.'

'Would you?' said Rose, looking round and wondering what was up. 'Well, where is she then?'

'I don't know,' Emily replied slowly and dramatically. 'I am silent.'

'What's the matter with you?' said Rose, her suspicions now very much aroused.

The door flew open and Mrs Bridges flew in through it.

"All right,' she shouted menacingly, 'who's been at my larder? Where's Mr Hudson? It's a police matter, nothing less. Mr Hudson!'

Mr Hudson came in putting on his jacket.

'Did you call, Mrs Bridges?' he said.

'I did indeed, Mr Hudson.'

'Why was that, Mrs Bridges?'

'Because a plucked and trussed chicken cannot walk, Mr Hudson. We have a thief in our midst. A two-legged fox. A chicken stealer. And when I find out who it is I'll skin her alive.'

'Or him,' said Emily unwisely.

Mr Hudson sighed; he was always being disturbed by these hysterical females just when he'd got himself nicely settled down to one of Sir Walter Scott's romances and a glass of Mr Bellamy's vintage port.

'How long has the melancholy fowl been missing?' he asked Mrs Bridges resignedly.

'It's not an hour gone, Mr Hudson, since last I saw it lying on the shelf in my larder.'

'In that case we have the staff in question except for Sarah who seems to be temporarily absent,' said Mr Hudson, knowing that Alfred was upstairs tidying the morning room. He still felt disinclined to take Mrs Bridges too seriously.

'You would hardly steal your own bird, and then complain of it,' he said with a slight nod towards the cook. 'We know Rose would not, could not. And if Emily had done it,' Mr Hudson went on in the same vein, 'I swear there would be feathers round her mouth.'

'It was a plucked bird, Mr Hudson,' Mrs Bridges was indignant. 'Not a feather left on it. Even the back fluff had been singed.'

'I was speaking in metaphor, Mrs Bridges,' said Mr Hudson, rather pained that his forensic witticism had fallen on such deaf ears. 'I am led to the conclusion that the guilty party is none other than Sarah, the stranger in our midst. Not a gypsy princess after all, but a common thief.'

'I knew it,' said Rose nastily.

'And what is to be done with a creature so unnatural,' said Mr Hudson in a magisterial voice.

'I stole it. It was me, not her,' pleaded Emily. But no one listened to her. They seldom did.

'All this fuss about a bird.' Mrs Bridges suddenly changed her tune seeing that her business with old Matty might be brought into the open.

'It was you who summoned me, Mrs Bridges,' said Mr Hudson who knew all about Mrs Bridges' illicit dealings.

'Perhaps a rat ran off with it,' Mrs Bridges suggested without conviction.

'Or a team of cockroaches, working in harness, I dare say,' said Rose, afraid Sarah might escape her deserts.

'I'll pay for it out of my own savings,' said Emily to no one in particular.

'Principle is at stake, ladies,' said Mr Hudson now prepared to take the case seriously. 'A chicken today, emeralds tomorrow, and the whole staff under suspicion. It is not, after all, as if Sarah had the privileges granted by custom and common humanity to the cook.'

This diplomatic sop to Mrs Bridges' conscience seemed to put the spirit back in her.

'When she comes back,' she said, 'I'll skin her alive.'

'*If* she comes back,' said Rose meaningfully.

Emily gave a stifled scream and when the others looked round they saw Sarah passing the window.

When she walked into the room pandemonium broke loose, Emily beseeching her to believe that she had not betrayed her, Rose telling her that she was a liar and a slut, walking the streets at night. Mr Hudson had to shout to be heard at all.

'Silence!' he roared. There was a sudden calm. 'Sit down Sarah.'

Sarah sat down at the long table.

Mr Hudson placed an oil lamp where it would light up the defendant's face.

'We have reason to believe that you have stolen a chicken from Mrs Bridges' larder,' he said, looking down at Sarah over his glasses. 'That you have crept out into the night to dispose of your forbidden loot, and have returned with your ill-gotten profits concealed about your person. What have you to say for yourself?'

Sarah looked round defiantly.

'If Mrs Bridges can do it,' she said very cool, 'why the hell shouldn't I?'

Alfred who was listening behind the hatch in the kitchen nearly gave himself away by bursting into laughter.

Mr Hudson now realised that he had a very serious case on his hands. In the silence that followed Sarah's outrageous remark he took several deep breaths, took a firm hold on his lapels and composed his face into a suitably grave expression.

For fully fifteen minutes he pointed out the evils of Sarah's way in language that would not have disgraced the Lord Chief Justice.

'If we fetch the police,' he exclaimed at last to the three ladies who constituted his jury, 'they will take her off and shut her away from decent folk until she is old and grey and can do no one any harm. We will of course be understaffed again and have to put up with Rose complaining, but justice will at least have been done, and we could all perhaps have some peace.'

Sarah began to sob. 'Don't fetch the police, please. Please!' she begged.

'She's scared of the police all right,' Rose remarked. 'Once bitten, twice shy I shouldn't wonder.'

'She's a gypsy princess and she'll die if they shut her up,' said Emily greatly daring. But nobody heard her.

Mr Hudson turned away shaking his head sadly.

'Poor child,' he said. 'One could pity her, I suppose. She is a moral imbecile.'

'What have I done to you?' said Sarah suddenly rather defiant.

'You pretend to be something that you are not,' snapped Rose. 'You make yourself out to be better than us.'

And in those two sentences Rose stated the real charge on which Sarah stood indicted that evening.

They were all looking at Sarah as she raised her head with a sad pleading smile.

'Not better, Rose,' she said, 'but perhaps more interesting. It cheers everyone up, it's only a bit of fun.'

'How can lies be fun?' asked Rose.

'Not lies. Make believe,' Sarah explained.

'You can't escape from what you are, none of us can, and to be an under houseparlourmaid isn't so terrible.'

'I think it would be wonderful,' said Emily dreamily.

'In a minute I'll remember you're here and send you to bed,' warned Mrs Bridges.

'Please not, Mrs Bridges. Nothing exciting ever happens. Why can't I watch the police take her off?'

'Because the police may not be coming, Emily,' said Mr Hudson quietly and he looked at Sarah. 'Not if Sarah chooses to confess her faults.'

He turned to Mrs Bridges inviting her to commence the cross-examination.

'You are an ignorant, common, worthless girl, Sarah. Do you deny it?'

Sarah was downcast. There was a terrible silence in the room.

'No,' Sarah whispered.

It was Rose's turn.

'And a liar and a thief.'

'Yes.'

'You are an ordinary person, Sarah,' from Mr Hudson. 'Like the rest of us.'

'Yes.'

'And you told lies to Lady Marjorie. You lied your way in where you had no right.'

'Yes, Mr Hudson.'

'And you have no French blood in you, let alone noble blood.'

'No.'

'Is she not a gypsy princess at all then?' cried Emily, unable to believe that her idol had such feet of clay.

'Keep quiet will you,' hissed Mrs Bridges.

'And you are lucky to have found this home here with us,' Mr Hudson went on steadily.

'Yes,' said Sarah and Mrs Bridges almost looked pleased.

'Very well,' said Mr Hudson. 'The police need not be called.'

'Thank you,' said Sarah.

'But upstairs must be told.' Rose wasn't having the new girl getting away scot free.

'I don't want Lady Marjorie to know. I'd be ashamed,' Sarah's voice had the ring of the true penitent.

Mr Hudson nodded.

'She's not all bad, you see. She is capable of remorse.' The butler frowned to himself, something in the trial scene was missing. It came to him that it was the ritual act of the penitent.

He turned and picked up the Bible from the table near the fire. With great deliberation he opened it and ceremoniously placed it in front of Sarah.

'Take this Bible, Sarah,' he commanded. 'You will find here the Ten Commandments. Take note of the Sixth Commandment. "Thou shalt not steal." Repeat it to yourself.'

'Make her write it out like at school,' said Mrs Bridges inspired by a distant memory of her youth.

'She shall write it out a dozen times in her best hand,

Mrs Bridges. Just to please you,' said Mr Hudson graciously. 'Rose fetch pen and paper.'

Rose fetched the necessary implements from the drawer in the table under the window and laid them carefully before Sarah.

'Take the pen,' said Mr Hudson, 'and write for Mrs Bridges . . . Thou . . . shalt . . . not . . . steal.'

Sarah picked up the pen slowly and awkwardly.

'I can't, Mr. Hudson.'

'Write, girl. Mrs Bridges waits for proof of reformation.'

'Please no,' Sarah pleaded in genuine alarm.

'What new depravity is this?' Mr Hudson sounded almost godlike.

They all waited.

'It's just . . . it's just. I can't write, Mr Hudson. I don't know how.' And she burst into pitiful tears.

'You can't write?' Rose sensed another lie.

'Not even my own name, Mr Hudson.'

Sarah rightly believed she would get more sympathy from the butler.

'Weren't you sent to school?' Rose inquired.

'I was needed at home.'

'Didn't your mother teach you?'

'I didn't have a mother. I was everyone else's mother from when I was five. They went to school, I stayed at home and kept house.'

Here was something they all could understand. A wave of sympathy seemed to flow out towards Sarah.

'I'm sorry,' she said.

Remorse, apology, confession. Now the battle was won Mr Hudson felt he could afford to be magnanimous.

'I don't think that there is any necessity to tell them upstairs about this unfortunate incident,' he announced. 'A chicken, a dog, a cat, who's to say? These things will happen even in the best regulated households.'

The implication was unmistakeable, that this particular household was extremely well run.

Mr Hudson smiled, Mrs Bridges smiled, even Rose

smiled. On that satisfactory note Sarah was bidden to go up to bed.

As she was creeping mouse-like up the front stairs a shadowy figure emerged from the shadows on the half landing causing her to jump and stifle a scream. It was Alfred.

'So they've let you go,' he said, his long white pasty face near to hers. 'Been a bit of trouble down there, raised voices and that.'

'Oh that,' Sarah replied, very casual as she pulled herself together. 'Bit of an argie-bargie. A contreetemps you might say.'

'They're all hypocrites, the lot of them' Alfred answered darkly. 'Write out the sixth commandment. "Thou shalt not steal".'

He made a noise somewhere between a snort and a sniff.

'How do you know then? You weren't there,' Sarah retorted.

'I know everything that goes on in this house.'

'Listening at the keyhole, wasn't you?'

Alfred suddenly seized her arm in a tight grip.

'There's a vileness and sin in all of us. Filth and degradation' he hissed at her.

'Let go my arm, Alfred.' Sarah could fend for herself when it came to most men but she'd never come across one quite like this. She was really quite alarmed.

'Beware the lusts of the flesh.'

'Stop it and let me go up to bed.' She snatched her arm away and ducked past Alfred up the stairs.

'Kate was the same,' Alfred said darkly.

Sarah stopped. 'What did Kate do then?'

But Alfred had turned away and was walking down into the hall. He was intoning to himself. 'Lust not for thy neighbour, for the wrath of the Lord will surely be visited on you . . .'

A few minutes later Sarah was safely tucked under the blankets on her side of the old hard, brass-knobbed double bed that she shared with Rose, thinking to herself what a lark it all had been. 'What new depravity is this?'

she said to herself, imitating Mr Hudson's voice exactly and giggled. If he could have seen his own face. Poor Mr Hudson, she thought, soft as cheese and easy to play as a penny pipe. And that strange Alfred. She wouldn't fancy him in that bed. Sarah shivered and suddenly wished Rose would hurry up. Emily had said that Alfred was just a bit touched but there wasn't any harm in him, but Sarah wasn't so sure. And she wondered about Kate and the lusts of the flesh.

'I daresay she just withered up,' she said to the empty room. 'I'll find her in a corner all dried up like a dead insect.' She shivered and wondered suddenly how long she would be able to stick being a servant before there was a bust-up. Sarah's life seemed to consist of a series of bust-ups. A friendly parson at an East End Mission had once said to her, 'You are born to trouble, as the sparks fly upward.'

Sarah often thought of herself as a spark flying upward, like when a chimney was on fire. After a bit the spark died out but there was always another one following. And as she was still thinking about the sparks she dropped off to sleep.

Two floors below Lady Marjorie, returned from her dinner party, was being undressed, layer by layer, by Miss Roberts. As she was put into her night clothes and sat by the dressing table for her hair to be brushed, Mr Bellamy knocked on the door, and being granted entrance, came in.

He was still in his stiff shirt and white tie and evening trousers. When he reached his wife he held his wrists out for her to remove the cufflinks.

It was a ritual that had developed over the years.

'Strange to see Archie Hislop across a dining table again,' he said. 'And that new wife. But I see why it happened. What eyes that woman has!'

'More charming than the original Mrs Hislop, I admit,' said Lady Marjorie. 'She was a very irritating woman. But one can hardly excuse it. It was not so much strange, Richard, as surprising.'

She gave him one cufflink which he put in his waistcoat pocket where Hudson would find it in the morning.

'It is the thin end of the wedge,' Lady Marjorie continued. 'Soon we shall have divorced couples everywhere and be obliged to chat and smile as if it were nothing unusual.'

Mr Bellamy smiled affectionately. 'In a minute, I'm afraid you will say "and the old Queen hardly cold in her grave".'

'It's true. I don't like change. Once started, it goes too fast. It becomes not progress but disintegration.'

And by progress Lady Marjorie meant some advance which she and the class to which she belonged could control.

'Spoken like a good English woman and a good wife for a Tory politician,' Mr Bellamy teased her.

Lady Marjorie handed over the other cufflink. 'Fetch me a clean handkerchief, Roberts,' she said and took over the hairbrush herself.

All Lady Marjorie's dressing table articles were made of silver and decorated with embossed angels.

Mr Bellamy sat down in the bergère chair. 'Tomorrow doesn't bear thinking of,' he said. 'Joe Chamberlain on Tariff Reform again and the Front Bench shuffling in its shoes.'

Lady Marjorie had lived all her life in the heady air of politics and liked to talk about them.

'The Prime Minister should be more firm with him. My father would never have endured it,' she said.

Her father, Lord Southwold, had often held high office and had indeed been strongly tipped for Prime Minister if the Conservatives had won the election of 1885.

'Your father,' Mr Bellamy said smiling, 'would have run England single-handed if he could.'

'He knew the value of firmness and resolution.'

'And you are your father's daughter.'

'I hope so,' said Lady Marjorie. 'You may go to bed, Roberts.'

'Yes, m'lady,' said Miss Roberts.

Miss Roberts disliked these intimate bedtime moments

between husband and wife; they somehow diminished her own authority.

'Don't worry your pretty head,' Mr Bellamy continued. 'These are men's matters.'

'Why shouldn't I bother my head? It has precious little else to fill it.'

'But you do so much.'

'What do I do?' It was a favourite grumble of Lady Marjorie's.

She would have liked to have been a great pro consul or a minister. It was her bad luck that she had been born a woman into a man's world.

She remembered a winter's day at Southwold when she was a little girl; the men had all gone off shooting and she had been left behind. She had gone to a secret place behind the greenhouse and cried her eyes out at the terrible realisation that she would never be an earl.

'You run the house most excellently,' her husband remarked in a comforting voice.

'The servants do that—in their own way. Things go on I know nothing about,' Lady Marjorie said, refusing to be comforted.

She sensed that there had been some sort of drama in the servants' hall from Alfred's manner when they returned from the dinner party and wondered if it concerned Sarah. Now it was on her lips to tell her husband about the new maid.

'I'm rather tired,' she said instead.

'Why don't you have some hot milk before you go to bed?' said Mr Bellamy going to the bell.

'No, don't ring,' Lady Marjorie held up her hand. 'Everyone worries too much about me. I don't like the thought of bells ringing late in dark passages. One day, you know, if things go on as they have been, you could ring and ring and nobody would ever come. There will be no one there. Only the empty kitchens, and the old leaves blowing along the passages with no one to sweep them up.'

Mr Bellamy understood this mood. He got up and kissed his wife gently.

'Stay in bed in the morning, my dear,' he said. 'I shall sleep in my dressing room so as not to disturb you. Good night.'

Lady Marjorie smiled at him gratefully. You could not have found a kinder or more thoughtful husband in the whole of London. She was really very lucky.

CHAPTER THREE

During the weeks that followed Sarah settled down better than either Mr Hudson or Rose had hoped. Because she was still amused and interested she did her work really well, and she brought into the servants' hall a sense of gaiety that had been missing before.

Servants in the big London houses were mostly sad, lonely people. They were never able to lead normal lives because, although fed and clothed and generally looked after much better than the poorer classes outside, they were, in return, expected to accept conditions little short of slavery.

A female servant could only very rarely expect to get married before an advanced age, if at all; this was because no mistress wanted a married woman as a servant. In addition their poor pay and limited prospects made servant girls the most ineligible of all females. In the eyes of the predatory male hunting in Hyde Park, they were good for one thing only.

Even when servants became friends within a household they could never get their days off together, so that more often than not the few hours of freedom in the week so looked forward to, were spent in a lonely wander round the streets window-shopping, followed by a solitary meal in a tea-shop.

Emily, who was desperately shy by nature and terrified of strangers, had been warned by her priest that London was a sinful wicked city worse than Sodom and Gomorrah, so that she hardly ever ventured beyond the pillar box on the corner and the paper shop in Pont Street. Emily spent her half-days in bed like a dormouse, putting aside half her tiny pittance towards buying a passage to America to join her brother in New York, and the other half towards the church.

The arrival of Sarah changed Rose's life more than she realised at the time. Because she too was withdrawn and sensitive, she had developed a defensive manner and made few friends. Sarah made Rose laugh and play silly games like snap and spillikins that she hadn't played since she was a little girl, and she would happily sit for hours listening to Sarah's seemingly endless stories made up of her own particular blend of fact and fiction.

Every day Rose gave Sarah a short lesson in reading and writing. Rose wrote the lesson first in her beautiful copperplate on lined paper leaving every second line blank for Sarah to fill in.

One evening Sarah was frowning over a particularly complicated lesson that Rose had put in her copybook.

'To Clean Marble' it read. 'Mix with quarter of a pint of soap lees, half of a gill of turpentine, sufficient pipe-clay and bullock's gall to make the whole into a rather thick paste . . .'

Sarah was struggling away when the pen spattered all over the page.

'Oh Rose,' she sighed, 'this pen doesn't like me.' She put it down and fidgetted. 'Who wants to know how to clean marble anyway.'

'Who wanted to learn to write,' Rose said huffily, looking up from her sewing. 'Anyway you wait for the spring cleaning, there's plenty of everything to clean then—including marble.'

'I used to dream of all kinds of future for myself,' Sarah said miserably. 'I can't think for the life of me why I came into service.'

'It's safe,' Rose replied. 'It's all right. You know where you are and what's going to happen next. It's the outside world that's dangerous.' She thought for a moment. 'Or perhaps it only seems so because we are ignorant.'

'There are so many things I want to do and be, Rose,' Sarah said impatiently, 'and time passes so quickly.'

'You must learn to accept.'

'Like you?'

'Yes.'

Sarah looked at the calm quiet Rose sitting at her work.

'Don't you ever . . . ever think of things outside, Rose?' she asked.

'Yes, of course. I mean I was going to get married once.'

Sarah was suddenly interested.

'Who was he, Rose?' she asked.

'He was called Eddie. He was an under gardener at Southwold.' Rose looked up, remembering. 'He was ever so good looking. When the war in Africa came he went in the Yeomanry like they all did, because his lordship wanted it. Of course he got killed and they gave him a medal—silly bugger.'

'I think that's very sad,' said Sarah.

'I have accepted that now,' Rose replied bravely.

It is also sad to relate, that although Rose was forever picking on Sarah for embroidering the truth, her romance with Eddie was mostly of her own invention.

It was true that Eddie Graves and Rose Barton had known each other for many years, they could hardly have done otherwise being born within fifty yards of each other and sitting together in the village school. It was also true that they took occasional walks together on Sunday afternoons. But in all the hours spent in each other's company, Eddie had never even tried to kiss Rose, far less bring up the subject of matrimony. And it was well known in the village that what had gone on between Eddie and Daisy Newton went a long way beyond kissing.

'Why did you go into service then?' Sarah asked Rose.

Rose pursed her lips and looked up from her work.

'When I was a little girl living in a cottage at Southwold a carriage used to go past our door every Thursday on the way to market. The lady and the gentleman who rode in it had been butler and housekeeper to a great family near there. My mother put me into service so that

I too would ride in a carriage some day. Some hopes. I sometimes wish that carriage had gone a different way to market.'

And that was the nearest Rose ever came to admitting that she was not completely happy with her lot.

The subject of Lady Marjorie's portrait had been rumbling round the family since the previous year like summer thunder. Richard Bellamy had suggested that the portrait would be an appropriate gift for him to give to his wife on the occasion of their silver wedding and Lady Marjorie had been delighted with the idea, but she had been quite unable to choose a suitable painter.

Like many intelligent, sensitive people, Richard Bellamy had no more eye for a painting than he had an ear for music, and on these two subjects he left all the decisions to his wife who adored music, especially the opera, and played the piano with an almost unladylike brilliance, and she had always taken a great interest in painting.

Of course everyone had suggested Mr Sargent, but Lady Marjorie didn't like his style; she found it superficial, and facile, and the very fact that he was so fashionable put her off as much as the fact that he painted so many actresses and Jews.

Early in 1903 Richard Bellamy had been made a junior Minister in Mr Balfour's Conservative Government, a post he filled with quiet ability, although the Liberals had criticised the appointment as being one of the most blatant examples of high Tory nepotism since the eighteenth century.

In the wake of King Edward's triumphant conquest of Paris, the Bellamy's went there early in 1904 for a round of conferences and receptions further to cement the *Entente Cordiale*. It was at one of these receptions that they met Guthrie Scone.

Scone was a young Scottish aristocrat, a cousin of Lord Abercraven, good looking in a rather Bohemian sort of way, of independent means and already making quite a reputation for himself as a painter, having worked in the studios of both Lautrec and Whistler. Lady Marjorie and Scone took to each other immediately and, as he was coming to London to his studio in Chelsea for a few months in the spring, it was agreed to everyone's mutual convenience that the painter should undertake the portrait during that time.

One day early in March Scone came to Eaton Place to make some preliminary sketches and to arrange his composition. He very much liked the Chinese screen from the Summer Palace and he sat Lady Marjorie in front of it on an old Venetian chair near the window. Then he set to work sketching and talking at a furious speed.

'You have beautiful hands,' he remarked at one moment. 'Sargent would make them of wax, gleaming and moulded. I shall make them pieces of mist yet with a hint of the bone underneath.'

It was a fine evening and the winter sun turned Lady Marjorie's hair to glowing fire.

'This is your moment,' said Scone. 'The moment the French call *"sous-feuille"*, those few precious minutes when nature seems to pour back the colours she's sucked up during the day, when a red brick wall throbs like a blown ember and there is an auriole of light round every twig like a vibration.'

Although Lady Marjorie teased him for being more a poet than a painter, she rather enjoyed Scone's gentle flattery and colourful language.

The painter was still at work when the master of the house returned from the House of Commons. This was more by design than luck and Scone had found by bitter experience that it was an essential part of the portrait painter's skill to ensure that the person who was doing the paying was satisfied. Mr Bellamy, seeing his wife's happy smile, was content with everything Scone suggested and the design, the size, even the price, were agreed on then and there in a most civilised manner. On one point only Scone was firm; he insisted on being the sole arbiter of the dress that his sitter would wear for the painting.

Thus it was that Sarah staggered into Scone's studio

the next day under the weight of a hamper full of Lady Marjorie's dresses and dumped it near the door.

She was awed by the size of the studio. Half the ceiling seemed to consist of a great angled window which illuminated a mass of carvings, sculptures, brightly coloured carpets and curtains. There were half finished canvasses and strange bronze figures holding up lamps and bric-a-brac everywhere. Sarah had never seen anywhere in such a mess, as she confided to Rose afterwards; it would have taken a dozen housemaids a week to put the room straight.

Scone was lying on a chaise longue and made no effort to move.

'I'm from Lady Marjorie Bellamy,' Sarah explained and added 'Sir' as an afterthought.

'Put it here,' Scone ordered brusquely, pointing at a large Italian marriage chest.

When Sarah had done as she was told, Scone stood up.

'Now open it,' he said. Sarah opened the hamper.

'Well, hold them up, girl,' the artist snapped, impatient at Sarah's stupidity.

Sarah took out a dress and held it up.

'Looks like a dust sheet,' was Scone's only comment. 'What's your name?'

'Sarah . . . er . . . sir.'

'You can drop the 'sir' with me. You don't like saying it anyway.'

Sarah bridled.

'How do you know what I don't like saying?'

'Next one.'

Sarah held the next dress up against herself.

'The simple milkmaid,' Scone said. 'I thought there'd be one of those. They never learn it won't do over forty.'

'Fair's fair,' said Sarah indignant at this slur on her mistress. 'She's ever so nice looking for her age.'

It may have been the fact that she was not in uniform or that Mr Hudson's ever listening ear was not within range but away from Eaton Place Sarah's accent deteriorated sadly.

'But a tyrant underneath I'll bet. Treats you like dirt,

eight pounds a year, a bed in the basement and a couple of hours off on Sunday.'

'No, Mr Cleverdick, you're wrong. I get all Wednesday afternoon off and twice as much as you said and a nice room in the attic which I share with Rose.'

'Who's Rose?'

'She's my friend. One day when we've made a lot of money we're going to buy a boarding house in Brighton.'

The revelation of Sarah's ultimate ambition made Scone shake his head sadly.

'Next,' he said.

'You'd better fancy this one,' Sarah replied. 'It's the last.'

Scone looked at it and then at Sarah. Taking her by the shoulders he turned her to look into the tall mirror.

'Would you bury all that beauty in a boarding house in Brighton?'

Sarah didn't know what to think of this strange artist. Was he teasing or serious?

'I rather fancy Brighton,' she replied. "All those great balls in the Pavilion and handsome gentlemen to hand you into the water from your bathing machine and then perhaps a drive along the front in a motor car.'

'You've never even been to Brighton.'

Sarah sniffed.

'I've been to Southend. Resorts is all the same.'

After that final pronouncement on the subject Scone told Sarah to fold up the dress and inform her mistress that it was the one she was to wear for the portrait.

The next Tuesday after dinner Sarah burst into the attic room in a state of great excitement as Rose was putting on her afternoon cap and apron.

'I got a letter,' she panted. 'Someone pushed it under the back door. It says 'Sarah. By hand.' I can read that much myself.'

She thrust the letter at Rose who regarded it coolly.

'Read it to me, Rose,' Sarah begged.

'You read it yourself,' Rose answered.

'I can't.'

'You can if you persevere.'

'I can't. It's all squiggly writing. Please, Rose.'

'Well, come on and get changed, or you'll be late downstairs,' Rose replied, very practical, but she took the letter and looked at it.

'What's it say?' Sarah asked, excitedly.

Rose sniffed sourly at what she read.

'If this is one of your games,' she threatened. 'Who did you get to write it for you? The same as wrote your French reference, I suppose.' She folded the letter ready to tear it up.

'Don't,' Sarah yelled. 'It wasn't like that. Honest to God, Rose. Read it, please.'

Rose began to read the letter in a dull flat voice.

'Divine Sarah,' she read. 'There will be a cab waiting for you at the end of Eaton Place where it joins Lyall Street at two-thirty on Wednesday. It will bring you to me. Ask no questions.'

Sarah was thrilled. 'Who's it from?'

'An admirer,' Rose replied, and she put a wealth of sarcasm into the two words.

'Where's it say that?' Sarah asked.

'There,' Rose replied pointing at the page. Sarah took the letter and held it close to her eyes.

'Ad . . . mire . . . er,' she whispered and put the paper against her cheek.

Rose turned away to the mirror, disgusted at the sight. 'And you expect me to believe that?' she asked.

'Why shouldn't I have an admirer?' demanded Sarah.

'Who is he then?'

Lady Marjorie would have recognised the style of the letter and Sarah herself had a fair idea who it was from, but she wasn't going to let on to Rose. Not yet.

'Oh,' she answered vaguely,' 'someone who has seen me about in the park or something.'

'He knows your name though, doesn't he?'

Sarah hugged herself. 'Divine Sarah!' she exclaimed.

'That's an actress, a Frenchwoman,' Rose said. 'He's just laughing at you.'

'I won't sleep tonight for wondering.'

'You aren't going?' Rose was really shocked.

'Course I am.'

'Gentlemen don't make assignations with housemaids for the pleasure of their conversation you know,' Rose said sharply.

'Assignation. That sounds ever so romantic.' Sarah looked dreamy.

Rose adjusted her cap. 'Well it isn't ever so romantic when you're turned off in disgrace and he won't marry you,' she replied. 'They never do. When it's all over you're thrown in a corner like a rag doll the moths have been at.'

'Like Kate?' asked Sarah.

'Yes. Like Kate. She went with guardsmen in the park and caught scarlet fever. And that was the end of her.'

Sarah sat on the bed.

'Sometimes girls don't come back at all,' Rose went on, rubbing it in. 'They end up on a slab in the morgue.'

'Don't say that, it makes me feel all . . . all goosey,' Sarah shivered.

'Well then,' said Rose ready to go, 'I don't know how you can even stand the thought of someone pawing you about.'

'It's only you says he will, Rose. If he's a gentleman . . .'

Rose cut in. 'If he's a gentleman he'll paw you about. Now come on or we'll be late downstairs.'

Nevertheless the next day when Sarah set out to keep her assignation she was very much on her guard just in case the painter started to get fresh with her. She was miserable that her old coat and skirt were so shabby and spent fourpence on an imitation rose to brighten up her hat.

When she got to the studio Mr Scone treated her quite formally which allayed her suspicions. But they were immediately aroused again by the sight of a large double bed in the middle of the room which certainly hadn't been there on her previous visit.

'Here. What's this supposed to be doing?' she enquired suspiciously.

'Oh models . . . posing. Sometimes I sleep on it myself.'

'I'll bet.'

Scone opened a bottle of champagne with a pop that made Sarah jump. He offered her a glass and raised his own in a toast.

'To the Divine Sarah,' he said. 'I have a proposition to make to you.'

'I'm sorry. I only take propositions from gentlemen,' Sarah replied haughtily. The effect was rather spoilt by her choking on the champagne.

'And how do you know I'm not a gentleman?' Scone asked, rather put out.

'You're a painter.'

'I'm cousin to an earl.'

Sarah thought of Rose's warning. How ridiculous if of all the painters in the world this one really did turn out to be a gentleman.

'Prove it,' said Sarah.

'I'm damned if I will. Finish your champagne and I'll call a cab to take you home to Rose.'

Sarah realised that she'd gone too far. She smiled at him and winked over her glass as if it had all been meant as a joke.

'Rose said if you turned out to be a gent, I wasn't to trust you,' she said winningly.

'Rose is a wise girl,' Scone replied.

'Now this proposition.'

Sarah was quickly on guard again. 'Well,' she said. 'All right. What is it?'

'I want to paint you,' said Scone simply. At that very moment, as Sarah told Rose later, you could have knocked her down with a feather.

'Paint me,' she exclaimed. 'Like Lady Marjorie?'

Scone nodded. It sounded very fishy to Sarah.

'Why?' she asked.

'Your face interests me.'

'My face!' Sarah put her hands to her face. 'Well I must say'—a new thought struck her—'I can't pay, you know.'

'It won't cost you a farthing.'

Sarah looked at Scone and at the bed, trying to come to a decision.

'Well, all right,' she said at last. At least it's warm in here.'

Scone went into action.

'On the bed with you,' he ordered, and before Sarah had time to complain, he lifted her onto the bed, taking off her jacket and hat like a conjurer.

'Here, what are you up to?' Sarah said rather breathless as Scone unpinned her hair.

'That's how I want to paint you, in bed, your frail white face against the shadows.'

'Well, I don't know . . .'

'Take your blouse off.'

When Sarah hesitated to obey, Scone unbuttoned her blouse and had it off in no time.

'That's better,' he said.

'Now look here I'm not standing for much . . .'

'Stop talking, Divine Sarah, and stay still.' Sarah got up on one arm.

'I said still!' Scone roared. Sarah subsided, deciding to compose herself and look beautiful.

For the next few weeks Lady Marjorie Bellamy visited Scone's studio every Friday morning and her under houseparlourmaid every Wednesday afternoon. When Lady Marjorie was sitting for him it was Scone who did most of the talking, but when it was Sarah's turn it was she who prattled away, telling Scone all the silly details of her life at Eaton Place. While Lady Marjorie was allowed to see and comment on her portrait, Scone never allowed Sarah so much as a glimpse of the canvas he was painting of her.

One evening when the light was almost gone, Scone allowed Sarah to relax her pose.

'What colour is Rose's hair?' he asked.

'Well that's a funny question I must say,' Sarah replied. 'Sort of dark mouse. She hardly talks to me these days. She doesn't like me coming here.'

'Jealous?'

'Oh, do you think so?' Sarah answered. She hadn't

thought of this before and it rather pleased her. 'She still doesn't trust you,' she added.

'People like Rose never trust anyone,' Scone replied beginning to clean his brushes. Sarah wriggled round on the bed to face him.

'Rose says,' she said deliberately, 'Rose says, if you was honest you would pay me.'

Scone laughed.

'Do you think I should?'

'Well models get paid, don't they?'

'So do prostitutes.'

'Here . . . ' Sarah was indignant.

'How much do you think you're worth?' Scone asked her.

'Keep your money—I'm not like that,' Sarah answered very huffy.

Scone got up and put the canvas away face to the wall.

'Rose is right,' he said. 'I ought to reward you. What do girls like?'

'You should know,' Sarah replied with meaning. 'What do French girls like?'

'It's what English girls like. You'll have to help me. What's it to be?'

'Anything?'

'Well, in reason.'

'The bioscope then,' said Sarah greatly daring.

'The bioscope?' Scone looked bewildered.

'The Daily Bioscope in Bishopsgate. That's in reason,' she pleaded.

Scone seemed to be quite shocked.

'Moving pictures are the enemy of creative art and artists,' he explained to her gravely and continued to pronounce on the terrible effects the photograph was having on the artistic imagination, working himself up into quite a fury on the subject. 'We will soon be so sickened by those pictures that ape photographs that we shan't be able to paint a human being at all,' he raged at her. 'And it'll all be your fault with your naïve demand for the truth.'

He pointed his brushes at her in an accusing way.

'It's not my fault,' said Sarah indignantly.

'Get dressed,' Scone replied.

'Can we go then?' There was hope in her voice.

Scone raised his hands in a very French way. 'Who am I?' he exclaimed, 'to hold back the march of civilisation. Au Bioscope!'

The Bioscope was more wonderful than anything Sarah could possibly have imagined. There was a film of a train being ambushed by Red Indians somewhere in America, and when all seemed lost, the Indians were driven off by a handful of brave cavalrymen. But the most extraordinary thing of all were some moving pictures of King Edward actually shaking hands with Kaiser Wilhelm of Germany.

Sarah couldn't believe it; it was just as if they were there actually in the same railway platform with the monarchs and their entourages. The painter was greatly depressed by his young model's enthusiasm, it only made his conviction even more certain that the birth pangs of the cinema heralded the death throes of creative art.

Richard Bellamy didn't like the painting of his wife very much; but he hadn't expected to. The colours seemed too bright and the brush work decidedly blurry. But he didn't say so: the portrait pleased his wife and that was what mattered. Lady Marjorie had met him at a ball at the British Embassy in Paris when he had been a brilliant but impoverished second secretary and his diplomatic training had stood him in good stead many times since those days. When Scone asked permission to submit his painting to the hanging committee of the Royal Academy Bellamy was privately rather surprised but he raised no objection; he really didn't understand these things.

Sarah's reaction to the first view of her painting was less restrained.

'Cheeky sod!' she said, acknowledging the fact that the part of her body visible on the canvas was completely naked whereas she had never exposed herself beyond her underclothes.

The painting showed Sarah lying in bed with another

girl sitting on the other side with her back to the viewer, wearing only a pair of long black stockings.

It was not the bed in the studio but exactly like the double bed in the housemaids' attic in Eaton Place. Indeed Scone had managed a remarkably accurate reproduction of the whole room.

'That's our room all right,' Sarah went on. 'When did you get up there?'

'I didn't,' Scone replied.

Sarah pointed at the naked girl on the far side of the bed.

'That's Rose?' she asked in wonder.

'Yes. Is it like her?'

'Yes,' Sarah replied, rather confused. 'When did you . . . I mean, has she been . . . ?'

'No,' Scone explained, very pleased. 'I saw her through your eyes, Sarah.'

'You're a bloody magician,' Sarah said admiringly. 'There's my things hung over the screen where I always throw them. Rose folds hers up. She's the tidy one.'

They looked at the painting for a moment in silence; if Sarah had known it owed a great deal to the Count Toulouse-Lautrec.

'There *is* one thing,' said Sarah, 'if you'll excuse me saying it . . .'

'Go on,' said Scone.

'Well there should be a sort of little framed picture just here on the wall. It says, "To Work is to Pray".'

Scone thanked her and made a note of it.

'What you going to call it?' Sarah asked.

'The Maids.'

It didn't appeal to Sarah as a title.

'I don't think much of that,' she said. 'Why not something nice . . . like . . . like 'Waiting for the Dawn".'

Scone cast his eyes to Heaven to pray for mercy on the girl.

'What are you going to do with it now?' Sarah asked him.

'Sell it,' he replied.

'Sell me and Rose?' Sarah sounded quite wistful.

'You won't want me any more now, will you?'
Scone shrugged.
'Not now you've finished your rotten old picture. Cast off like an old shoe, that's me.'
Scone took the picture and put it against the wall.
'You've used me!' Sarah said indignantly warming to her theme.
'Art has used you, Sarah,' Scone answered. 'Art has used both of us.'
'Why aren't I your mistress then? You haven't even asked. What's the matter with me. Only good enough for your bloody picture I suppose.'
Scone threw up his arms in mock horror.
'Madame Bernhardt,' he replied. 'What language!'
'Damn you!' Sarah shouted at him and picking up a pillow began to belabour him in earnest.
'I wouldn't be your mistress for all the crown jewels in Europe. But you should have asked me. It's only decent!'
Scone fell on the bed laughing helplessly and defended himself as best he could with his arms.
'Go on, laugh then,' Sarah shouted. 'Ha, Ha, Ha! What's so funny?'
'Your idea of decency,' Scone answered and pinned her to the bed by her arms. Sarah wondered what he would do next. She had heard of girls who had become famous through being painted by famous artists and began to regret her remark about all the crown jewels in Europe. Here she was almost in his arms. If she gave herself to him then and there would he take her to Paris and set her up in an apartment to herself and take her out in a carriage to show her off to all the other ladies of the half world? After all he was an aristocrat and the cousin to an earl. Or would he discard her like a rag doll? The trouble with Scone was that you could never tell if he was joking or being serious.
He leant down and kissed her on the lips.
'Remember Rose's awful warning,' he said. 'Never trust a gent.'
He kissed her again. 'Come on we'll go to the Bioscope

and then I'll take you home safe to Rose in a cab.'

That was the last Sarah saw of Scone and for some weeks she found her Wednesday afternoons very hard to fill. Once she went by herself to the Bioscope but it was not the same without him and besides it cost sixpence to get in and she hadn't all that much money to throw around.

CHAPTER FOUR

One bright morning in June Sarah was clearing up the servants breakfast and Mr. Hudson was having his last cup of tea and reading the newspaper before ironing it and taking it upstairs.

'I don't know what the world is coming to,' he said to Rose who was looking out a clean duster. 'Alf Common, the Sunderland centre-forward; transferred to Middlesborough for a thousand pounds!'

'Well I never did,' Rose replied politely not really understanding a word.

'No footballer's worth that amount of money,' Mr Hudson went on to the world in general as Rose went out. 'It's not a game anymore. It's a blooming trade.'

'I quite agree, Mr Hudson,' said Sarah.

'I didn't ask your opinion, Sarah,' said the butler getting up and turning over a page. 'Now you just get on with clearing this . . .'

He stopped in mid sentence, horror and amazement on his face.

'Sarah,' he asked in a dreadful voice. 'What have you done?'

'I ain't done nothing,' Sarah replied automatically just as the morning room bell began to ring.

Mr Hudson jumped up and to Sarah's amazement tore a piece out of the paper, stuffed it in his pocket, crumpled the rest into a ball and thrust it into her hands.

'Mr Hudson,' Sarah exclaimed, 'That's today's paper.'

'Burn it,' he replied dramatically, as he put on his tail coat. 'All of it. In the kitchen range. No one must see it.'

At the door he turned. 'And you wait here until I return.'

Sarah went slowly into the kitchen and stuffed the paper into the range. If Mrs Bridges had been in the kitchen at the time she wouldn't have approved. Burning paper made clinkers.

It was one of Mr Hudson's faults that if anything upset him he was apt to fly off the handle and do something he regretted later, and even now as he handed Mr Bellamy his hat and gloves and blurted out a story of idle delivery boys and lazy newsvendors, he wished he had not ordered the paper to be burnt.

Fortunately Mr Bellamy took the news of the missing newspaper with equanimity. It was Private View Day at the Royal Academy and he seemed more concerned that Mr Pearce should have the carriage ready at two o'clock precisely.

Sarah was folding the table-cloth and wondering what on earth she had done to get Mr Hudson's goat when the personage in question descended on her once more, if anything more agitated than before.

'Now my girl,' he proclaimed thrusting the piece of torn newspaper in front of her nose. 'What's the meaning of that?'

Sarah took the piece of paper and looked at it.

There were two small reproductions of paintings on it. The one of herself in bed and Lady Marjorie's portrait.

Sarah was pleased. 'It's me,' she said. 'It's my painting in the paper, fancy that.'

'Fancy that indeed,' Mr Hudson replied, eyes raised in supplication. 'Read what it says . . . read!'

'I can't, it's too small.'

Mr Hudson had forgotten that the wretched girl couldn't read. He snatched the paper from her and put on his gold-rimmed spectacles in one swift movement.

'The twin sensations of this year's Academy,' he read with feeling, 'are undoubtedly the two striking paintings by Guthrie Scone . . .'

'Pronounced Scoon,' Sarah corrected.

'Shut up!' Mr Hudson continued reading. 'Artist nephew of the Countess of Abercraven. Hung side by side in fascinating counterpart are the mistress and the maids, as this pair of canvasses are already being called, are both set in the house of Mr Richard Bellamy, M.P. Under Secretary of State at the Admirality.' Not coming from a seafaring family Mr Hudson always slipped an extra syllable into the word. ' . . . and set a new fashion for home portraits! He continued. 'A piece of artistic radicalism we wouldn't have expected from a junior minister in a Conservative Government!'

Mr Hudson took a deep breath and gave Sarah a wild look that nearly made her giggle out loud.

'When asked to name the model of the scantily clad maidservant in his canvas, Mr Guthrie Scone referred our reporter to the servants' quarters at 165 Eaton Place.'

'What cheek!' Sarah said. 'Typical of old Scone,' she thought.

'You've been up to your tricks again, haven't you, Sarah? What's been going on in this house behind my back. How dare you allow this man up to the maid's quarters . . .'

'But he never did, Mr Hudson.'

'Don't lie to me, Sarah. Look . . . look at that picture. You didn't paint it, I'm sure of that.'

'But Mr Hudson, I went to his studio . . . on me days off.'

'And took your bed . . . and everything else with you . . . oh very likely.' Mr Hudson wasn't in a mood to listen to unlikely explanations. He wagged his forefinger at Sarah.

'I can tell you one thing,' he said. 'There's going to be hell to pay in this house before the day is out. You mark my words.'

With that dire threat he marched off to his pantry leaving Sarah looking at the paper. She couldn't see for the life of her that she was in any way to blame, whatever the ruddy hell there would be to pay, it certainly wasn't her fault.

'Good old Sarah,' she said out loud to herself. 'You've got your face in the papers at last.'

When they arrived at Burlington House that afternoon the Bellamys went directly to Room 4 where Lady Marjorie's portrait was hanging. Near the door they encountered Mrs Graham, the wife of one of their neighbours in Eaton Place.

'My dear Marjorie,' she said. 'Quel courage!'

Even then Lady Marjorie thought she must be referring to the modern style of the portrait and she led her husband through the passage in the crowd that opened in front of her as if by magic, not realising it was as good as to the guillotine.

Husband and wife saw the two paintings hung 'in fascinating counterpoint' at the same moment. They turned to each other in silent dismay as a hush fell upon the room.

With a sang froid reminiscent of her ancestor, the second Earl of Southwold, when led to the scaffold, Lady Marjorie smiled.

'My dear,' she said quietly, 'would you please take me home.'

Richard Bellamy had never liked Scone; he had always found him conceited and self opinionated, and now he raged against the little swine who had had the impudence to make his wife the laughing stock of London. He thought of consulting his lawyer.

Lady Marjorie had the greater cause for anger. It was she who had chosen the painter and in doing so greatly enhanced his reputation. She had offered him the hand of friendship only to have it bitten without any good reason.

But Lady Marjorie was a realist; she kept calm. To take vengeance on Scone would be difficult, expensive and to some extent pointless and might well make matters worse. The best way to spoil his sport would be to let the world know that the Bellamys were quite impervious to such childish behaviour.

Instead Lady Marjorie reserved her anger for her servants whom she felt had been guilty of gross disloyalty. Action must be taken—and taken swiftly—or the discipline of the whole household would collapse.

Mr Hudson had been dreading his employers return all afternoon and when at last his turn came to be summoned to the presence to explain himself he was, according to Mrs Bridges, 'in a proper dither.'

The butler was not seen at his best in these circumstances. He blustered and stammered and blew and excused himself, blaming the maids for letting him down. It was clear to the Bellamys that however negligent and stupid he had been in the matter, Hudson was not a party to the plot and was as shocked by it as they were themselves.

Rose and Sarah were the guilty ones. Sarah was new to service and inexperienced and therefore far less to blame than Rose. That Rose, who had been so long in their service and who owed so much to the Bellamys, should stab them in the back was betrayal indeed and deeply hurting.

Sarah and Rose were already waiting in Mr Hudson's pantry when he came down.

'You're to pack your bags tonight and be gone in the morning, the pair of you,' he said. 'They'll pay you a month's wages, which is generous in my opinion. I doubt they'll want to set eyes on you again. They were to have gone out to dinner tonight. Now they've cancelled it.'

Rose sank down on a chair and began to sob. She was completely shattered by this terrible and sudden catastrophe, and the thought that the Bellamys had actually cancelled a dinner engagement because of her behaviour was almost unbelievably shocking.

'It's not fair,' Sarah said defiantly. 'We haven't done nothing wrong.'

'Nothing wrong you call it,' Mr Hudson shouted at her. 'You don't know right from wrong, never have, that's your trouble. Only made this household the laughing stock of London. The master's in a proper rage and who's to blame him?' He drew himself up.

'"I don't know how you could". Those were the master's words to me,' he added dramatically.

'But what have you done?' Sarah said, despair in her voice. 'What have any of us done?'

She went to Rose and put her arm round her.

'Oh Rose,' she whispered. 'I'm sorry.' She sighed, and looked at Mr Hudson.

'What did you say to him then?'

Mr Hudson looked slightly uncomfortable. 'I told him I didn't know anything about it and what I didn't know I couldn't be responsible for,' he answered. '"Ignorance is no excuse in law," he said to me. "It's your job you know. It's what you're paid for".'

Mr Hudson sniffed and grew suddenly fierce again. 'I told him there was no knowing with you modern girls,' he ranted. 'Not like in my young day when girls were properly brought up and glad to get a good place; I said I couldn't be held responsible for the changing times and that you were all as deceitful as a waggon load of monkeys.'

Sarah counterattacked angrily. 'You mean you let him think what he liked and put the blame on us?'

'I've got my own position to think of. And the family's. Now out with you. Out!'

Sarah got up and went out followed by Rose. Outside they stopped.

'Stupid old windbag; all he thinks of is his own precious skin,' said Sarah angrily, putting her arm round the sobbing Rose. 'I don't see why you should suffer. You didn't even have the fun of it.'

Suddenly she had an inspiration.

'They can't blame you if I tell them the truth,' she exclaimed. 'Come on.'

'Where to?' Rose asked weakly.

'Upstairs,' Sarah replied, and although it was the last thing she would normally have done, Rose allowed Sarah to lead her upstairs and into the front hall.

'We can't go in there without being sent for,' Rose said as they approached the morning room door.

'Oh yes we can,' Sarah replied, and opened the door and went in still holding Rose by the arm.

Lady Marjorie was sitting on the sofa, her husband standing with his back to the fire.

'Excuse me, m'lady,' said Sarah and curtsied.

'Send them away, please Richard,' said Lady Marjorie in a tired cross voice.

'But, m'lady, it wasn't our fault,' Sarah persevered.

Lady Marjorie got up and swept to the door.

'I really don't think I can listen to any more excuses,' she said to her husband. 'I am going to my room to lie down.'

Rose automatically opened the door for her and got a withering look in passing for her trouble.

Left alone Mr Bellamy faced the two servants.

'Your mistress feels betrayed in her own house by people she trusted,' he shrugged in a way that conveyed the fact that Lady Marjorie was more sorry than angry. 'That is all there is to be said.'

He went to the bell by the fireplace and rang for the butler, then taking up the *Illustrated London News* sat down and began deliberately to read it.

Sarah knew she had to act quickly, it was her last chance and like as not Mr Hudson was already running up the backstairs.

'Beg pardon, sir, but it isn't,' she said, and greatly daring went over to her master's chair and tapped the arm.

'It's not just, sir. Not to Rose. She never done nothing, never even seen him, Scone I mean. It was all me.'

'It's no good, Sarah,' Rose sobbed from behind.

Mr Bellamy looked up at her in astonishment.

'Yes it is,' Sarah went on quickly. 'Mr Scone asked me to go to his studio. I went every Wednesday. He never came up to our room. He never even saw Rose. I swear it on the Bible. You're fair, sir. You wouldn't want to see an injustice in your own house.'

Richard Bellamy looked round at the door hoping

for the butler to relieve him.

'I will not be badgered by my own servants in my own house,' he said.

At that moment Mr Hudson came in and ushered out the two maids with a brow of thunder.

At the door he caught Mr Bellamy's eye and gave a small shrug of apology as if to say 'now you see the sort of girls I have to deal with'.

Left alone, Richard Bellamy frowned unhappily to himself and poured out a whisky and soda. He disliked nothing more than a row, especially at home. The servants were always the concern of his wife and the butler until there was any trouble and then they landed him with it. He began to feel rather resentful. It also annoyed him that he was definitely being assailed by a sense of guilt.

Mr Hudson sent the girls up to their room in disgrace. They sat on the bed in silence. At last Rose went wearily for her valise.

'I'll go round to Scone. I'll make him explain,' said Sarah, but her voice lacked conviction.

'What's the good,' Rose answered bitterly. 'No gentleman would ever stand up for a couple of servants, no matter what the truth was.'

'He isn't like that,' Sarah replied. 'In Paris . . .'

'Paris!' Rose sounded quite savage. 'Who cares what they get up to over there! This is London. Gentlemen can marry chorus girls—that's romantic. But if they carry on with skivvies they don't announce it in the papers. He got what he wanted. More fool you . . .'

'He didn't.' Sarah was near to tears now. 'I tried to make it all right, but don't be angry with me, Rose.'

Sarah was determined not be beaten. She put on her outdoor clothes and went out into the passage. At the end there was a key in a little glass case on the wall. The glass case was open although it was meant to be locked because a notice below it read, 'Break the glass. Only to be used in an emergency.' If ever there was an emergency, Sarah thought, this was it. The key opened a small door that led onto the iron fire escape which zigzagged all the way down the back of the house till it finished in the little back-yard and the mews.

Sarah looked down. In the mews far below the coachmen and the grooms were cleaning their carriages and their horses and some of the brasswork glinted in the evening sun. She felt dizzy and began to creep down the iron steps one by one as if each was her last. When she came to the mews she hugged the wall for fear of being seen by Mr Pearce until she came at last to the arch that led into Lyall Street, then she began to run and she didn't stop until she was safely across Sloane Square and halfway down the King's Road.

Scone was reading when Sarah arrived. He was annoyed at being disturbed and told her to run away and stop bothering him. He was surprised to find that she wasn't after money.

'All I ask is that you should tell them the truth,' Sarah pleaded with him.

'Oh for God's sake, what truth?' he replied brusquely.

'They think we let you up into our room and you painted us both naked in bed,' she answered.

Scone stood and laughed. This aspect of the affair hadn't occurred to him and it somehow made the whole joke richer.

'What's so funny, Mr bleeding Scone?' Sarah shouted at him.

'The bourgeois mind,' he replied. 'I think that's really quite delicious.'

'You don't care if me and Rose gets chucked out on the dust heap just so you can have your little joke. Do you? Do you?' she snarled at him.

'Oh for goodness sake,' he answered. 'You have lost a rather dreary job with rather dreary people; go off and find another one. Personally I'm going back to Paris in the morning where the air is rather fresher than in this dull city.'

There was a silence. Sarah suddenly felt at the end of her tether. She knelt beside him.

'Look,' she said quietly, 'I'll come and live here and

look after you and you needn't pay me anything. I'll do anything you like . . . anything at all. I swear it.'

Scone put his hand out and held her chin and looked at her. For once she seemed to be telling the truth.

'Anything at all?' he asked.

'Anything at all,' Sarah repeated. 'Only get Rose off.'

'You'd really do that for Rose?' he asked. Sarah nodded. Scone considered the tear-stained little face; was this girl really capable of such a noble gesture, he wondered. He would see.

'Take your clothes off,' he said. 'All of them.'

Sarah began to undress and Scone watched here in silence.

There was a knocking on the door. He stood up angrily.

'Damn it,' he said. 'You'd better get behind the screen.' As Sarah carried her clothes behind the screen, Scone went to meet his visitor. It was Richard Bellamy, the last person he wished to see.

Bellamy explained his reason for the visit. He had not come to have a shouting match or discuss the affair of the painting, he had merely come to ask Scone a simple question; had he, or had he not gone upstairs in Eaton Place to the servants' bedrooms?

'Why the devil should I give you an answer?' Scone demanded rudely.

'Then on the evidence I take it you did,' Bellamy replied.

'You politicians are all the same,' Scone retorted, beginning to enjoy himself. 'You twist any fact to suit yourselves. Good Lord, man, do you think I haven't the imagination to paint an attic bedroom . . .'

'You give me your word as a gentleman?'

'My word as a gentleman!' Scone spat out the words. 'As you can't revenge yourself on me, I suppose you'll take it out on your wretched servants.'

This was too near the truth for Bellamy's liking and Scone saw it.

'I give you my word as a gentleman,' Scone said in a teasing voice. 'I never went beyond your drawing room in my life. I'm afraid you'll have to keep your two servant girls.'

'That depends on my wife's attitude,' Bellamy replied rather haughtily. Scone went up to him.

'Think of the ammunition it would give the Liberals if it were known that a junior minister, a member of the Committee of Imperial Defence, had dismissed two of his servants unjustly just because his wife's vanity was a little ruffled,' he taunted. 'Victimisation! The Radicals are very fond of that word.'

'You talk like a blackmailer, Scone.'

'You sound rather frightened to me, Bellamy. And I don't blame you. Good-day.'

There was a noise from behind the screen. Bellamy looked up.

'I leave you to your . . . your work,' he said with a cold bow and a nod towards the screen. 'Thank you for receiving me.'

As soon as he had gone Sarah came out from behind her hiding place. She went up to Scone and kissed him on the lips.

'Thank you, Mr Scone,' she said.

He smiled at her and began doing up the little buttons on the back of her blouse.

'You'd better get back,' he said, 'and tell Rose the good news.'

In accusing Richard Bellamy of twisting any fact to his convenience Guthrie Scone had done him an injustice. When Sarah had said that he was a fair man she had been nearer to the truth. It would have been perfectly simple and much more convenient for him to take the easy way out and to do nothing. The two girls would have gone to be replaced by two others. But Sarah's words had continued to prey on Bellamy's conscience, and had finally forced him to take the unusual and disagreeable step of paying the painter a visit.

To be fair to both men, it is true to say that in spite of all Sarah's pleadings, Scone would never have undertaken the journey in reverse.

As it was Bellamy was now faced with the delicate and

difficult task of explaining to his wife and his butler why the two girls had to be retained. They didn't understand him and they didn't agree with him, but sometimes, when he considered something really important was at stake, Richard Bellamy was adamant, and on those occasions, and this was one of them, he got his way.

Mr Hudson was furious. He felt he had been let down by his employer and he had certainly lost face with the servants and his authority had diminished accordingly.

He was honest enough to admit to himself that he had badly botched the whole business and the knowledge that he could have easily saved himself and his employers a great deal of embarrassment did nothing to improve his mood. In the next few weeks hardly a word passed between the butler and the two house parlourmaids. It was a considerable relief to all the servants when the summer holidays arrived and the Bellamys set off to Southwold to join the house party for Goodwood taking Mr Hudson and Miss Roberts with them. Mrs Bridges went off for her annual two weeks in a boarding house at Eastbourne kept by Mr Hudson's married sister. As usual she went in company with her dear friend Amy, once cook to Lady Wallingford, and now living in retirement in Pimlico.

Rose, Sarah, Alfred and Emily were left behind in Eaton Place on board wages to do the summer cleaning.

CHAPTER FIVE

All day the four servants worked in the big empty house. Alfred went through every bit of silver in the cupboards, some of which had not seen the light of day since the previous summer, and he repolished every piece till it shone gleaming white and then wrapped it up in special black paper or a green baize bag.

Emily delved deep into grim unexpected places like the back of the stove and the corners of the larder sometimes singing strange Irish songs to herself, sometimes squeaking as she unearthed a mouse or a cockroach.

Rose and Sarah went through the whole of the upstairs part of the house systematically. One day it was the turn of the paintwork and Sarah learnt that no scrubbing brush should ever be used on paint. First she had to blow off the dust with a pair of bellows, then wash the paint with a sponge dipped in pearlash and water, and finally wash it all off again and dry it. Where there was wall-paper the walls were swept with a soft feather broom.

There were all the carpets to clean and the muslin curtains to take down and mend and launder, and all the soot and dirt of London seemed to have been trapped in their folds although they had only been hanging on the windows since April. London was one of the dirtiest cities in the world which was why the fogs in winter were such a deep dirty yellow and killed so many old people and also why the outside of the houses in Eaton Place had to be washed every year and completely repainted every five years.

Before his departure Mr Hudson had made a list of all the work that was to be done by outside contractors. One day the sweep and his boy came to make sure all the chimneys were clean for the winter and that all the bird nests were removed; for good measure he cleaned out the gutters while he was up on the roof. Next it was the turn of the carpenter and the glazier who went round all the windows replacing cracked glass and mending all the broken window cords. For weeks the decorators were in Miss Elizabeth's room completely repainting it against her return from Germany in the spring. The mess they made was nearly the death of Rose.

It was tiring work and Rose saw to it that nothing was skimped but Sarah found it more interesting than ordinary housework because it was different. There was a sense of being free from ordinary routine and a relaxation of the strict discipline that was usual when the Bellamys were at home The servants didn't have to get up so early in the morning or wear uniform, and when work was over and they had washed and changed, they could do what they liked with their evenings as long as one of them stayed in the house. That one was usually Emily, although one evening Sarah managed to induce her to venture as far as the park to hear the band. Alfred kept himself to himself and spent most of his time and wages in 'The Grenadier' or 'The Star' getting quietly pickled.

One day Rose and Sarah were working in the morning room. Rose had gone round all the paintings rubbing them with a slice of potato damped in water and then polishing them with a piece of silk. She then brought up a hot shovel from the kitchen and poured carbolic into it. This was to kill the flies that plagued London in August.

Sarah's task was to clean the big chandelier, unhooking each piece of crystal and washing it in soapy water. As it was dreadfully fiddly work putting all the hundreds of pieces together again Sarah was working late.

At last it was done and she took a proud look at the sparkling crystal before she covered it up in its cotton bag and pulled the blinds and the curtains. It was like a ghost house with all the furniture covered in dust-sheets and Sarah felt a sudden panic as she picked up her ladder and bucket and half ran across the hall for the safety of the backstairs.

To her surprise she found there were visitors in the servants' hall, in the shape of Enid, house parlourmaid to the Grahams, and the footman from the same establishment, a humorous man called Henry.

Rose was sitting mending a dress.

'Finished Sarah?' she asked.

'Yes. All done,' Sarah replied.

'Sarah has been cleaning the chandelier in the morning room. First one she's ever done,' Rose explained to Enid.

'Oh,' Enid replied, 'we have a special firm comes in to do our chandeliers.' She gave the impression that there were at least half a dozen to every room in the Graham household. 'I mean once one of those drops is lost or broken—well there you are.'

'I hope you haven't broken anything,' Rose asked Sarah, suddenly worried.

'I was extra careful,' said Sarah, undoing the duster and releasing her hair.

'Mr Hudson's very queer about breakages,' Alfred chipped in. He was playing pontoon with Henry at the big table, with a jug of beer between them, and Emily was watching them entranced.

'So you see, Sarah, just how careful you've got to be,' Rose added, really to show Enid that she was in charge.

'Our old Mr Blacker couldn't give a hoot,' said Enid pouring a drink from the gin bottle she carried.

'Does most of the breaking himself,' Henry added. 'Up to here in port, he is.' He held his hand across just below his eyes.

'Can't leave it alone. You know what some butlers are,' Enid explained to Rose.

'Lady Marjorie wouldn't stand for that sort of thing,' said Sarah sitting down. Enid made a face at her behind her back.

'Be that as it may we're quite happy,' Enid remarked. 'Glass of gin, Sarah?'

Sarah looked at Rose who nodded dispensation.

'Enid brought it with her. It's all right,' she explained.

'Don't they ever miss it?' Sarah asked in wonder.

Henry laughed. 'Captain Graham's too busy turning the blind eye,' he said.

'To everything mostly,' Enid added. 'Particularly to Mrs Graham!'

'Mr Bellamy isn't like that at all. He's very particular,' said Rose.

'Not about his wife being made the laughing stock of London apparently,' said Enid and Rose and Sarah both started to bristle like angry terriers.

'You should have heard the Grahams when they got back from the Academy that day,' Enid went on. 'The Captain said . . .'

'Enid!' Henry interrupted, not wanting the peace and quiet to be broken by a female row.

'Well, Perhaps it is better not spoken of in the present

company,' Enid went on, putting special emphasis on the last two words.

Rose contained her temper with difficulty.

'It would take a great deal more than something so . . . so . . .' Rose searched for the 'mot juste' '—so trivial to upset Lady Marjorie,' she said with enormous dignity. 'This is a respectable household.'

'Oh how dreadfully dull for you, my poor dears,' Enid taunted in her best imitation of Mrs Graham. 'Oh of course I forgot, Henry,' she went on in her usual voice, 'this is the household who keep their old bones and give the bottles back. The rag-and-bone man don't call here.'

'So what do you then?' asked Sarah.

'What do we do?' Enid jeered. 'Where do you think I came by this hat?'

Alfred pursed his lips.

'Let not thy sins nor thy evil doings be revealed to the children of God in their innocence,' he said thickly, giving Enid a beery wink.

"All right Alfred,' said Rose sharply turning to Enid. 'Nothing like that goes on in this house, Enid,' she remarked definitely.

But Alfred was in no mood to be silenced.

'I say put thine own house in order,' he said pointing his finger at Rose accusingly like an Old Testament prophet. 'Our Mrs Bridges isn't above losing a bit of lard now and then—or the odd chicken, eh, Sarah?'

'That's quite enough from you,' said Rose and Henry winked at Enid.

'Let's drink up; it's holidays,' said Enid, replenishing the glasses.

'Is that yours?' she asked feeling the material of the dress Rose was mending.

'It's Lady Marjorie's,' Rose answered, knowing that Enid knew that fact just as well as she did.

'Not very fashionable . . . you people,' Enid replied.

'Then Lady Marjorie's hardly Mrs Graham, is she?' Rose retorted with a sweet smile. 'I mean she has no *need* to be fashionable.'

Enid sniffed.

'So we hear,' she replied nastily.

'Your meaning exactly?' asked Rose.

'We hear that Lady Marjorie's appearance at a certain ball wasn't all that it should be.'

'Which ball?' Rose and Sarah were simultaneous and defiant.

Enid was really beginning to enjoy herself.

'Apsley House.' She paused for effect. 'We heard the dress had been seen before.'

'Never,' said Rose emphatically.

'It was a new dress,' Sarah added, backing Rose up, although she hadn't the least idea of the true facts.

'Never,' Rose went on even more emphatically. 'She'd never wear a ball gown *twice*.'

'It was new. I saw it arrive,' Sarah chimed in. 'From Paris,' she added for good measure, her gift for invention coming to her aid.

'That's right. From Paris,' said Rose, perfectly prepared to back Sarah's invention in a good cause.

'In France,' Sarah explained. 'It had a lovely train.'

'Not so long as Mrs Graham's,' Enid answered, fighting back.

'It was long,' Sarah went on. 'We all saw it. It was ever so long. Wasn't it, Emily?'

'I'd never seen a dress like it,' Emily answered loyally.

'Shouldn't think you'd ever clapped eyes on a pair of shoes till you came over here,' said Henry.

'It really was long,' said Sarah emphatically, sticking to the point.

'Mrs Graham's train was so long,' Enid groped for words to describe its length, 'as she came down the stairs . . . it just . . . well it just covered all the stairs. Didn't it, Henry?'

'Yes,' said Henry unwisely changing from beer to gin. 'Yes. It was really long.'

'Well, Lady Marjorie's was so long,' said Rose, refusing to be beaten, 'it was so long that as she stood in the hall, well, Miss Roberts her personal maid was still picking up the end in her boudoir.'

The thought of Lady Marjorie's train extending for

two storeys was a little too steep for belief and Rose regretted the remark as soon as she had made it.

'Oh yes, I'm sure,' Enid answered, as cutting as she could manage.

There was a silence. Rose was being challenged.

'I can show you if you like,' said Rose quietly. 'If you've eyes large enough to take it in.'

The drink had made Rose bold and Enid's eyes flashed at the prospect of adventure. She downed her gin in one gulp.

'Lead on,' she said to Rose.

'Follow me,' said Rose to the company.

They all got up except for Emily.

'Do you think we should?' she said nervously.

Sarah looked at her contemptuously. 'Mouse,' she said.

The atmosphere of the dim hall seemed to damp their ardour.

'I don't know what we're all standing about for,' said Rose. 'It's not going to bite us.'

'Our hall's twice as big as this,' said Enid predictably.

'Would you follow me, please,' said Sarah grandly taking on the role of hostess and starting to sweep up the stairs. The other ladies followed.

Not wishing to poach on what was undoubtedly a strictly female preserve, Alfred and Henry had the notion to play a game of cricket, being a very upper class sort of sport.

As for little Emily, she never dared to come further than the green baize door before scuttling back to the safety of the servants' hall.

Everything had been carefully put away in Lady Marjorie's boudoir by Miss Roberts before her departure and Rose and Sarah found some difficulty in finding the dress. There were so many cupboards and so many dresses, all carefully wrapped in cotton covers.

At last they announced they had found it. The dress they brought out was indeed one of exceptional beauty. It was made of heavy cream satin and embroidered with hundreds of flowers in coloured silks, liberal use being made of semi-precious stones in the design. Actually it was not the one that Lady Marjorie had worn at the Duke of Wellington's ball at Apsley House, but the one she had worn at King Edward the Seventh's Coronation.

Enid concealed her admiration with difficulty.

'Not bad. I don't think much of it really,' she said, feeling the material. 'It's not a patch on the one . . .'

'Not a patch,' Rose snapped furiously.

'Mrs Graham's really was something,' said Enid.

'I could well imagine,' Rose replied sniffily. 'But, my dear Enid, something you probably haven't realised. The secret of a really beautiful gown is the cutting. Isn't that correct, Sarah?'

'It's the subtlety of the cutting,' Sarah repeated dutifully. 'I mean a dress like this has to be seen on.'

'I'm sure,' said Enid continuing to provoke.

'There simply is no other way of judging it,' Rose added grandly.

There was a silence. Enid smiled.

'Well, put it on then,' she said.

'You're mad,' said Rose.

'We heard it fits where it touches. If that.'

'Wouldn't fit me anyway,' said Rose, refusing to be drawn out.

'Oh I see,' said Enid scornfully. 'Oh well. It'll be nice to tell the rest of our staff I saw it. And everything.'

Sarah could bear it no longer. She began to take off her apron.

'Good girl,' said Enid.

'Well if you're going to put it on you'd better have the proper underclothes,' said Rose with typical thoroughness as she warmed to the game.

Rose and Enid searched all the drawers and cupboards until they found the things they needed, while Sarah took off her clothes and sat at the dressing table as God made her, brushing her hair luxuriously with Lady Marjorie's beautiful brushes.

The height of the ambition of most housemaids was to become a lady's-maid, and Rose and Enid were no exceptions to this rule. They had both of them acted many times as personal maids to visitors and they now vied with each other in dressing Sarah up in Lady Marjorie's finery, as happy as a couple of little girls with their first doll.

First a pair of silk and woollen combinations, so fine that they could be pulled through a wedding ring; next the corsets, whalebone covered in silk and decorated with ribbons and bows. They were the latest thing and had four elastic suspenders to which were attached the fine white silk woven stockings decorated with butterflies and birds right up to the top of the thighs. Next a pair of linen drawers which buttoned at the side, costing over four pounds, according to Rose, and then the French petticoat, an elaborate confection trimmed with insertions and edgings of real Valenciennes lace.

Lady Marjorie had taken her jewellery with her as there were always many grand parties during Cowes Week but they were able to find a Victorian paste tiara and some diamanté drop earrings to add lustre to their achievement. Finally Sarah held out her arms for her two minions to draw on the long cream kid gloves which had six buttons each.

In the hall, Alfred bowled a full toss on the leg stump which Henry despatched with casual grace to the boundary.

'Gone for six,' he shouted triumphantly. 'Into the pavilion. That's a century for good old Ranjit!' . . .

The words died on his lips at the sight of the vision descending the stairs. Sarah's two ladies-in-waiting had also raided Lady Marjorie's cupboards and were now equipped with huge hats and fans.

The two men went to the downstairs cloakroom and emerged with opera hats and red-lined cloaks worthy of the occasion.

Sarah received her guests in the morning room, the dust sheets having been hurriedly thrown aside. Naturally the conversation turned to topics of the highest importance.

'I hear Mrs Graham has caught the highest eye,' Sarah remarked to Alfred.

'My dear!' said Enid in her role as Mrs Graham, 'at

Ascot this year, don't you know, the King come right up to me himself and says, "You are the prettiest thing I've seen since the flowers in my garden".'

She took a sip of neat gin from her champagne glass.

'I hope you're serving the Voove Clickotte,' she enquired of Alfred.

'Use it for shaving water, don't you know,' he replied blandly and they all laughed in a very high society sort of way.

'Such fun,' said Enid. 'Deevy,' said Rose, not to be outdone.

Alfred found a gramophone and they all enjoyed themselves, talking and singing and dancing and imitating their betters with horribly cruel accuracy, until the gin ran out.

'Richard,' Sarah said to Alfred in her role of Lady Marjorie. 'Be a perfect dear and ring for Hudson to bring up some more refreshments. We're clean out of gin.'

Alfred made an elaborate charade of ringing the bell by the fireplace which had so often summoned him to the presence.

'Oh really, where is that wretched Hudson. Ring the bell again,' Sarah commanded. 'Really I don't know what servants get up to nowadays. They're never here when you want them.'

Suddenly, as if losing her patience, she stood up.

'Hudson!' she roared in her best Billingsgate voice. 'Hudson, where is Hudson?' Alfred began to chant and the others all joined in the chorus stamping their feet and clapping.

'Hudson, Hudson, where is Hudson?' they shouted.

The door from the hall opened to reveal a tall elegant young man in full evening dress. Silent and expressionless, he surveyed the pantomime scene while the voices died and a terrible silence followed.

'You rang, m'lady,' said the newcomer with a slight bow to Sarah. Nobody said a word. The young man walked over to the gin bottle and turned it upside down on the tray.

'Perhaps you will be requiring something more to drink,' he said, and went out closing the door behind him.

'Who was that?' Henry broke the silence.

'Mr James Rupert Bellamy, the Life Guards. The bleeding son and heir, that's all. Come on. Quick,' said Rose and they all made for the door. It was locked.

'Gone to fetch the police,' said Henry gloomily.

Enid sat down and began to cry.

'He'll tell Mrs Graham. We'll all be ruined.' Even in their half sozzled state they all knew that any revelation of their evening's play must lead to one thing. Instant dismissal. The best a housemaid without references could expect was to become a maid of all work to some tradesman in the suburbs, and as for a footman fallen from grace, his future didn't bear thinking about. Only Sarah seemed cool and unmoved. Rose turned to her.

'What are we going to do, Sarah?' she asked.

'What can we do?' Sarah replied. 'Wait. We shall simply have to wait, that's all.'

She sat down and began to fan herself, cool as a cucumber, just as if she really was Lady Marjorie.

When James Bellamy came back into the room he was in his shirt sleeves and wearing Mr Hudson's green baize apron and carrying the tray with three bottles of champagne on it.

He opened one of the bottles and came up to Sarah.

'Champagne, m'lady?' he said. 'Nothing like champagne to make a party go.' He began to go round with the bottle.

'No thank you, Hudson," said Rose when it came to her turn.

'Yes please, Hudson,' James replied. 'It's a party and we drink at parties.'

He filled her glass and went on to Alfred.

'Mr Bellamy won't say no,' he remarked. 'Mr Bellamy enjoys his champagne.'

'On top of gin,' said Alfred sadly with a hiccup.

'On top of everything. Everything's tops. What a charming party.'

And refusing to let them escape, James went round

and round the sickening, silent group refilling their glasses until all the bottles were empty. Only Sarah stayed sober, pouring her champagne into the flower pot on the table beside her chair when her tormentor's back was turned.

At last James Bellamy left them and Sarah was able to hustle her stumbling giddy crocodile across the hall and down into the basement. Here she left them to their own devices and returned upstairs slowly and sadly to Lady Marjorie's boudoir to take off her finery.

It was quite a formidable task for no Edwardian lady would ever think of undressing without the help of her maid and the fastenings were accordingly mostly inaccessible to the wearer.

She was struggling to unlace the corset when she saw something move in the long oval cheval glass.

It was James Bellamy, bottle and glass in hand, standing watching her from the doorway.

CHAPTER SIX

James Bellamy was very tall with a pale complexion, dark hair and a silky moustache. He had excellent manners when with people of his own sort and was always perfectly turned out. In every way he seemed to be the archtype of conventional Edwardian gilded youth. He was a good shot and went hunting in the winter and played polo in the summer, and enjoyed musical comedy and staying in the country at the weekends and parties of any and every sort.

Sometimes he ran into debt through gambling or betting on horses and his mother paid up because that sort of thing was almost expected of a young officer in the household cavalry. Lady Marjorie was proud of her son although they didn't know each other very well as he had spent most of his life away from her company either in the nursery or at school or at Sandhurst and now in the army. He only rarely came to Eaton Place to tea or dinner or to collect something from his room.

The other servants were proud of the young heir because his name was often mentioned in the weekly gossip columns always associated with the very smartest young set. Above the fireplace in the servants' hall there was a framed drawing taken from the Illustrated London News showing him riding near the Coronation Coach in the Sovereign's Escort.

Before that evening Sarah had only seen Lieutenant Bellamy half a dozen times at the most and had never exchanged so much as a word with him.

She wondered how to deal with the situation. James Bellamy was still a little drunk but he was definitely dangerous as he had shown down below.

'You can't come in here,' Sarah said quietly and firmly. 'The party's over, Hudson.'

'Not Hudson anymore,' he replied as he crossed the room. 'Mr Bellamy, Sarah.'

She was surprised that he even knew her name. He sat on the chaise-longue and poured himself a glass of champagne. Sarah didn't move. It was up to him to show his hand and if he proved friendly Sarah thought she might get a promise of silence from him.

'Your friends are going to feel a bit rough in the morning,' said James.

'Make a nice story for *your* friends,' Sarah replied, carefully adding a 'sir' at the end.

'Serve you all damn well right,' James gave a shrug. 'Gallivanting all over the house.'

Sarah wondered if this could mean that he thought they had already been sufficiently punished for their sins.

'A perfect end to a perfect evening,' James went on, putting his feet up. 'I don't think.'

'Someone let you down, sir?' Sarah asked, as James seemed to want to talk.

He looked up at her wondering if she was being impertinent or just percipient.

'Yes, Sarah,' he replied. 'Someone let me down.'

'What a shame!'

Was this dangerously cheeky, Sarah wondered, watching him closely. Nothing venture nothing gain. It didn't seem so.

'Yes,' said James. 'One of my best friends. Last time I shall tell him anything.' He paused thoughtfully. 'She was an absolute corker.' He got up and went to Sarah.

'Are you an absolute corker, Sarah?' he asked.

Sarah remained silent and motionless while James walked round her inspecting her.

'Would you have liked to be taken to the Savoy, Sarah? To have danced all night? To have been given expensive French perfume?'

Sarah suddenly thought what a lot of nice things seemed to come from France and she looked wistful because the things James had mentioned were exactly the things she had always dreamed about.

'What a delightful little waist.' James put his hands round Sarah's waist and his fingers touched. He kissed her on the shoulder.

'Would you like fine clothes?' he asked, and stepping back as if he had suddenly lost interest studied his mother's underclothes lying on the dressing-table stool.

'Take those clothes off. All of them,' he said.

Sarah had dealt with many men in her time but never with one who could be classed in the general category of an officer and a gentleman. She knew Rose's views on the subject and from what she had read in the weekly magazines it seemed highly likely that James Bellamy would throw her on the large fur rug in front of the fireplace and assault her maidenhead then and there. She considered a clip across the ear but it hardly seemed to suit the circumstances.

'Would you undo the laces, please sir?' She asked. He came over and undid the laces. He waited until she had removed the corset. There was still the silk and wool combinations.

'Now put on your own clothes.'

He walked across towards the door. Sarah went quickly behind the screen and blew her cheeks out in relief. Clearly gentlemen were not all as predictable as Rose would have them. She put on her coarse linen knickers, cringing at their roughness and took off the combinations. Her dress was still lying on the dressing table stool. When she went to get it James Bellamy was standing laughing. He had tricked her and Sarah covered her breasts with her hands.

'Oh God, is that what you wear,' he said, and as Sarah made a dash forward to get her dress he pulled it away towards him.

Sarah kept her temper.

'Can I have it back, please sir?' she asked, icily polite. 'Please.'

He held it out to her, snatching it away at the last moment pretending to be a bullfighter.

'Please!' she begged. She grabbed at it again and got hold of the sleeve. They had a brief tug-of-war and the dress split down the back.

Sarah took the torn dress and sitting down began to sob. James looked at the pathetic dishevelled girl and seemed suddenly horrified at the humiliation he had caused.

'I'm terribly sorry,' he said weakly. 'It was meant to be a joke. I didn't know what I was doing.' He went over to her. 'Look, Sarah. How can I make it up to you?'

'You can't make it up,' Sarah replied bitterly through her tears. 'People like you can't make it up. Not to people like me.'

He made as if to comfort her and she cringed away. He dropped his hands and shrugged hopelessly.

'I really am terribly sorry. I just didn't think.'

'Of course you didn't,' Sarah answered looking up at him. 'But then you don't have to think with people like us. We don't feel.'

It was near the truth and James knew it. He went over to his mother's big cupboard and took out a silk robe.

'Here, put this round you,' he said to Sarah.

'It's not mine,' she replied.

'You can't stand there like that.'

'It's what you wanted, isn't it?'

He offered her the robe again. 'Oh for goodness sake, take it. Keep it. She won't miss it,' he said.

'I'll wear it next time the King calls,' Sarah answered with a touch of her old spirit, and allowed him to put the robe round her shoulders. James looked relieved.

'Is there anything else I can do?' he asked.

'No,' Sarah replied. 'Well. You could say nothing about our gallivantings.'

'Gallivantings?' He had forgotten.

'About what you found when you got home,' Sarah went on. 'We'd all lose our jobs, you see. And you know what getting jobs is like.'

James didn't. He regarded Sarah for a moment thoughtfully.

'Bad, is it?' he said.

'Yes, it's bad.'

'Then I won't say a word.'

'Oh, thank you . . . I don't . . .' Sarah broke off, remembering her pride. 'Thank you, sir,' she said quietly and walked towards the door.

'I wasn't going to anyway,' said James.

Sarah stopped, surprised.

'I'm afraid I was avenging myself on all of you for my rotten evening,' he went on. 'Taking it out on you.'

'Yes,' said Sarah.

'It hasn't been much of an evening all round, has it, Sarah?'

Sarah was near the door. How strangely things had turned out, she thought, James Bellamy wasn't at all the arrogant young cad he liked to pretend to be; underneath he seemed lonely and in need of friendship. Or was it just another of his tricks?

'I don't suppose it has, sir,' she replied. 'Except it was a lovely dress.'

'You'd like a lovely dress,' it was a statement of fact.

'Yes.'

'Then you shall have one.'

'No.'

'Why not?'

'No.'

'No favours asked, Sarah.'

'I shall get one my own way, thank you, sir.'

James smiled at her.

'If not a dress, some clothes. I mean, well, some nice things.'

'I don't have much occasion to wear nice things.' She looked at her torn dress. 'But I shall—one day.'

James stood near her looking down at her. He was a clear foot taller than Sarah.

'You're not happy—with your lot?' He asked slowly and seriously.

'No,' Sarah replied. 'Are you? What do you want?'

'What should I want? I want for nothing.'

'You are happy being a soldier?'

He looked surprised and put out by this question which no one had ever asked him before, so that Sarah added quickly, 'Begging your pardon, sir.'

James thought for a moment. 'I am happy doing what is expected of me,' he answered rather pompously.

'So you're happy,' said Sarah.

'I don't see what any damned business it is of yours,' he replied rather petulantly. 'Nobody ever asked what I wanted,' he went on with a little shrug.

'They never do,' Sarah answered quietly. 'You just get put into things. Just so long as they can fob you off. Any old how.'

James looked at her intently as if he suddenly realised that even under houseparlour maids were human.

'That's right,' he said.

'One day,' Sarah said very quietly.

'You mustn't think so much,' James answered very gently. 'It's bad for people like us to question things.'

'People like us?' Sarah questioned.

'Must remember what we've been taught. Everything has its place,' James answered.

'Depends what your place is,' Sarah remained defiant.

'Yes,' said James. He looked at her for a long time in silence, studying each part of her face and neck. Sarah knew what the look meant.

'Sometimes I think we might have got it all wrong,' he

muttered and suddenly laughed. 'A thinking officer is cannon fodder,' he quoted to himself as if in warning. 'I shouldn't have come home this evening, you know.'

It was too late now. Too much had happened.

'That's what Mr Hudson always says,' said Sarah laughing.

James' thoughts were elsewhere.

'What?' he asked.

'About thinking,' she explained.

'Damn Hudson,' said James. He took her hand and looked at it, and let his fingers go slowly up her arm. Sarah didn't move. He gently put his arms inside the loose robe and took her body in his arms.

'To hell with the regiment?' said Sarah and smiled at him. He wanted her and she wanted him. She suddenly wanted him more than she'd ever wanted a man.

'To hell with everything,' James whispered in her ear. 'Vive la Republique!'

He let his lips just touch hers. She put her arms round him and pressed their bodies hard together.

'Come on,' he said. 'Let's go to my room.'

They kissed again.

Somewhere downstairs there was a shout immediately drowned by the horrible crash of breaking glass followed by smaller tinkling crashes.

James jerked his head up like a startled animal. He frowned angrily. Sarah still held him but he tore himself away from her and ran out of the room.

Sarah stood quite still. She could just hear his footsteps on the stairs. She could imagine that it was Alfred who had dropped a tray in a drunken attempt at clearing up. But what did it matter. She stamped her foot in fury, cursing her luck. Slowly she walked out of the room and went quickly downstairs. From the drawing room landing she could see James in the hall, the broken champagne bottle and glasses at his feet, and Alfred crawling to the green baize door like a whipped dog.

She shivered as she waited, watching. James didn't move for a long time. Then he put out his foot and turned over a piece of broken glass in disgust as if he had suddenly realised that the mess and the muddle were all his fault.

Then he turned and walked slowly into the morning room. Sarah knew that the sensible thing was to go to bed. If James had wanted her he would have come back to her. But curiosity mixed with hope forced her downstairs.

The morning room door was ajar and he was standing in front of the fire smoking a cigar.

She went in quietly and smiled at him.

James looked at her.

'Don't stand there,' he said. 'Go and get a brush and a dustpan and clear up that mess.'

Sarah's first thought was to give this arrogant bastard a few choice East End phrases that he wouldn't forget in a hurry. But she held her tongue. Experience told her that although it might relieve her own feelings it wouldn't help the situation and might change James's mind about telling his parents, if only to revenge himself on her. The James Bellamy she had seen a few minutes before was gone, the arrogant boy had taken his place.

Alfred had shattered the tenuous web of intimacy that they had begun to weave together as surely as he had smashed the contents of the champagne tray.

She turned and went out without a word. In the servants' hall, Alfred was sitting at the table moaning, with his head in his hands. Rose was trying to break a raw egg into a tea cup. Sarah thought they looked disgusting and degraded. She was tempted to break the whole bowl of eggs over their silly heads.

When she went upstairs with the cleaning things, James had gone and the lights were out in the morning room.

In a sullen fury of self-pity Sarah cleared up the mess and then took Rose up to bed. Rose, sodden and drunk, was something she found sickening. Oddly she remembered a fat spaniel that the men at the pub where her father went used to make drunk on beer. On top of it all Rose began to snore. She heard Alfred staggering and cursing on the stairs, but she didn't stir to help him. For hours Sarah lay awake thinking. She was born to trouble as the sparks fly upward. This was it, the next bust up.

When the dawn came she got up and began to pack her belongings. She tried to be quiet but after only a few minutes Rose woke up.

'What's happening?' she said, moaning. 'Ooh. My head.'

Sarah ignored her. Rose sat up.

'Sarah,' she said hazily. 'What are you doing?'

'I'm off,' Sarah answered coolly. 'Isn't that obvious? Even in your state.'

Rose took in the valise and the outdoor clothes.

'But Sarah. He mightn't . . . he may not . . .' Rose groped back to the world of reality. 'He may not tell on us, you never can tell . . . anyway . . .'

Sarah interrupted her crisply.

'He isn't going to. He promised me,' she said. 'You can tell the others. But personally I'm not staying here anyway. Not after last night.'

'You're cuckoo,' said Rose.

'Maybe,' Sarah picked up the boots Rose had lent her. 'Here you are.' She put them on the bed.

'You can keep them,' said Rose.

'I won't be needing them, not where I'm going.'

'Where are you going?'

'To my cousin—in Ilford.'

'I didn't know you had a cousin in Ilford.'

Sarah was at the mirror putting on her old tweed hat.

'Why should you? You don't own me?'

'But what are you going to do, Sarah?' Rose rubbed her eyes to try to make more sense.

'I don't know.'

'You can't just waltz out of here with no references—I mean no proper ones—and just get a job.'

For Rose the world was bounded by the four walls of 165 Eaton Place.

'I mean, look at Katie,' she went on. "I can look after myself"—that's what she said to me in this very room. Well, the baby died, and now she's on the street. Looking after herself.'

'I'm not pregnant,' Sarah answered, refusing to argue, as she packed her underclothes and nightdress.

'That's all you know,' Rose answered.

Sarah still refused to be drawn.

'You'll never get another job. Never,' said Rose after a moment.

'You've got it wrong, Rose,' Sarah replied. 'I'm not interested in jobs. I'm interested in something happening.' She turned and leant over the rail of the bed.

'I'm not interested in the kind of life we have here!' she said. 'Living everything through *them*, as if we weren't flesh and blood. As if we're some sort of vegetables that don't have feelings, that depend on them for everything. Talking about them all the time, sticking their silly letters together again just so as we can read them and get a thrill.'

This was a common practise among the female staff aided and abetted by Alfred but much frowned on by Mr Hudson.

'Dressing them hand and foot,' Sarah went on. 'Admiring their finery, wearing their clothes.' She put her afternoon uniform neatly at the foot of the bed. 'I don't want a second hand life. I want a real life of my own.'

She began to put on her coat. It suddenly struck Rose that Sarah was really in deadly earnest and it wasn't just one of her more elaborate jokes.

'Look, Sarah,' she said, getting up, and a desperate tone creeping into her voice, 'just because James Bellamy made love to you doesn't mean you're going to have the doors of society flung open, you know.' She sniffed. 'Nobody would look twice at you,' she went on. 'I mean look at you.'

'A famous artist painted me and I got hung in the Royal Academy; he looked at me more than twice,' said Sarah. 'James Bellamy looked at me. James Bellamy thinks a lot of me.'

'Enough to make a fool out of you.' Rose retorted.

'He thinks a lot of me.' Sarah repeated.

'Then why are you leaving?' Rose asked.

'Because,' Sarah answered. 'Because of the circumstances.'

'What circumstances?'

'Really there are some things I prefer not to discuss,' said Sarah leaving Rose to imagine what she liked.

She had finished packing and now she picked up Lady Marjorie's robe that James had given her. The feel of the soft and beautiful material suddenly brought back the memory of the boudoir very vividly.

'Put that back in Lady Marjorie's wardrobe,' she said to Rose. Rose took the robe and looked at it.

'Did he make love to you?' she asked quietly.

Sarah turned away.

'Fact or fiction?' she said, trying to make a joke of it.

'Did he make love to you?' Rose persisted.

'That's not the point, Rose,' Sarah replied. 'That's nothing to do with it, don't you see!'

Suddenly something snapped in Rose's head. She seized the old magazines from the top of Sarah's valise and tore at them furiously throwing them on the floor as if she could thereby destroy Sarah's fantasy world for ever.

Sarah knelt down and began to gather the pieces up. After a moment Rose knelt beside her and began to help.

'Why did you do that?' Sarah asked. 'You knew what they meant.'

'Can you piece them together?' Rose asked in a small voice.

'Should think so,' Sarah answered putting all the pages in her valise.

Sarah stood up. She was all ready to go. Rose began to clutch at straws.

'Don't go yet. Let's have a cup of tea,' she begged hopefully still on her knees. 'I'll make it.'

'No thank you, Rose,' Sarah replied.

'It won't take a jiffy. We can have a talk.'

Sarah wasn't to be tempted.

'I must be off,' she said firmly.

'Please. Please stay. I don't know what I shall do.' Before Sarah could move Rose put her arms round her legs. Sarah helped her to her feet.

'You're all I've got,' said Rose. 'You're all I've got—anywhere.'

It was very difficult for Sarah.

'You know I've got to go, Rose,' she said carefully. 'You'll just have to get on.'

She pulled herself away from Rose and picking up her valise walked quickly out of the room without turning back.

Rose sat on the bed in dumb misery for a full minute before she began to weep.

Sarah walked down the stairs and into the cold empty hall. At the foot of the stairs she halted as if she had suddenly thought of something. She cocked her head with a defiant smile and instead of going down through the servants' door went straight across to the front door and opened it.

Emily was on her knees scrubbing the front steps. She looked up at Sarah in wonder.

'Sarah!' she said, 'wherever are you going?'

'Out through the front door. The way I almost came in,' Sarah replied.

She walked past Emily and turned left along Eaton Place, on past the milkman and the baker and the countless other kitchen maids all scrubbing their own front steps until she was lost to Emily's view in the early morning haze.

When the Bellamy's returned from Scotland in mid-September and Lady Marjorie was told that Sarah had left of her own free will she was not in the least surprised. She had always realised the girl was unsuited for service and had only taken her on in the first place in a capricious mood. After the Royal Academy affair Sarah had ceased to amuse her. Mr. Hudson was openly delighted at the news.

Poor Rose took it very badly. For a few weeks she refused to believe that Sarah wouldn't come back, but as the evenings began to draw in and still no letter or message of any kind arrived, she began to give up hope. On one of her days off, she went to Ilford only to find it was far too big a place to search singlehanded. As she trudged the suburban streets, she became disheartened at the thought that the cousin in Ilford was probably only another of Sarah's sudden inventions.

At night she lay awake worrying, putting Sarah into all sorts of terrible situations and in need of her help; sometimes she blamed herself for letting Sarah go and at other times she was seized with fits of bitter anger.

One day before Christmas she was polishing the handrail of the stairs when James Bellamy came in from riding and asked her if she had seen or heard of Sarah.

His inquiry at least answered one of the questions that played on Rose's mind. If James Bellamy didn't know where she was, he certainly hadn't set Sarah up as his mistress. On the other hand, Rose reflected, he was clearly still interested in her. Was it that he was worried that he had put her in the family way?

Rose grew thinner and thinner and black shadows began to form under her eyes. Lady Marjorie and Mr Hudson became seriously worried that she would have a breakdown. In the servants' hall she hardly ever spoke a word. She refused to agree to any suggestion that a new under houseparlourmaid should be engaged to replace Sarah.

It wasn't until the early spring of 1905 that Lady Marjorie had her brainwave. Her daughter was due back from finishing school in Dresden to spend her debutante year in London, and she would need a maid to look after her. During the ten years Rose had been in service with the Bellamys, she and Elizabeth had become very fond of each other. Rose having often acted as nursery maid on Nanny's day off, and had helped Elizabeth with her clothes and even her lessons during her schoolgirl years.

When Lady Marjorie put the suggestion to her, Rose appeared to be delighted with it and raised not the slightest objection when a quiet girl called Ivy with adequate references was engaged as under houseparlourmaid.

It was a relief to everyone in the house that Sarah's ghost seemed to have been laid once and for all.

CHAPTER SEVEN

There had been a telegraph from Dresden and now Lady Marjorie awaited her daughter's imminent arrival with feelings of trepidation.

Elizabeth had never been an easy child. At a very early age the Bellamy nanny had described her as 'wilful' and there were some days when she had to admit she could do nothing with her young charge. Lady Marjorie had longed for a gentle girl imbued with a natural ability to sew and paint and dance, whose charm and beauty would be the envy of other mothers.

Alas, Elizabeth had grown into a rather gawky tomboy who didn't seem to care a jot about her appearance and who, because she was really very shy, could give the impression of being rather sullen and sulky at parties. She had always been happiest down at Southwold messing about with the keepers and the grooms, or riding her pony round the estate.

After a succession of governesses had come and gone declaring her beyond their control, the Bellamys had decided to send Elizabeth to Frau Beck's finishing school in Dresden, as much for its reputation for discipline as its other well-known virtues.

As she waited Lady Marjorie prayed that Frau Beck's magic wand might have changed her daughter from a goose, if not into a swan, at least into a cygnet.

Downstairs in the kitchen Mrs Bridges was putting the finishing touches to a chocolate cake. 'Now Emily,' she said, 'get out from under my feet and give Rose a hand with the cucumber sandwiches. And remember, you're not making them for elephants.'

'Nice thin slices,' Rose explained to Ivy and Emily,

'and always cut off the crusts. Don't put in the cucumber till the last minute or they'll go all soggy.'

'What a funny notion to have cucumbers at all,' Emily remarked.

Mrs Bridges brought over the cake.

'I don't suppose you ever heard of such a thing back home among the heathen,' she said to Emily.

'No, I never did,' Emily admitted tasting a piece of cucumber and making a face.

'The Irish eat nothing but tatties,' Ivy informed the others.

'So they do,' Emily agreed.

'Fat lot of Heaven you'll see,' said Mrs Bridges with her own brand of logic.

Alfred came in pulling on a clean pair of white gloves.

'Spark up girls,' he said. 'We're all alive in this house. I wonder if we'll notice the difference, now that she's done her schooling and that.'

'I'm sure nothing could change Miss Elizabeth for the worse, anyhow,' said Rose loyally.

'She's all right,' Alfred admitted. 'Not one of your hoity toity ones.'

'Finicky with her food ever since she was a little mite,' said Mrs Bridges voicing a personal opinion.

'Oh you must be able to say better than that,' Rose exclaimed, neatly overlapping the sandwiches in a circle on a folded napkin.

'I speak as I find,' Mrs Bridges replied conclusively.

Rose added parsley as a finishing touch.

'You can tell Mr Hudson we're ready when they are,' she said to Edward.

The front door bell rang, but it wasn't Elizabeth; it was Lady Marjorie's Aunt Kate, a formidable person of great presence who had consented to help launch her great niece into Society. Being a marchioness as well as the sister of an earl she could take on any duchess at equal weights and usually won.

Sailing into the drawing room Aunt Kate found Lady Marjorie, James Bellamy and a friend, Billy Watson of the 'Blues', all waiting for Elizabeth.

'James, you've put on weight,' Aunt Kate announced and sat down. 'Well,' she continued looking round, 'a tea party to welcome Elizabeth with no tea and no Elizabeth.'

James went to the window at the sound of a carriage approaching and was able to announce the good news that at last Elizabeth had arrived.

Rose was waiting in the hall and Elizabeth ran straight into her arms and hugged her.

'We've all missed you so much,' Rose exclaimed.

'I've missed you too, Rose. Terribly,' said Elizabeth tearing off her hat and flinging back her rather wild locks. 'I've got so much to tell you.'

Rose helped her off with her coat. Elizabeth twirled round.

'Gosh,' she said, 'I'm in a whirl. London's all noise and bustle after sleepy old Dresden.'

'They're waiting tea in the drawing room, Miss Elizabeth,' said Rose.

'Oh Lor' ' cried Elizabeth and ran upstairs three at a time.

Elizabeth's explosive entrance into the bosom of her family was followed by so much kissing and hugging that it was some time before Billy Watson could be brought from the shadows to be presented to the prodigal.

'What do you do, Mr Watson?' Elizabeth asked as they shook hands.

'I . . . I ss . . . soldier actually,' Mr Watson explained rather diffidently. He was never much at ease with young ladies.

'How disappointing,' Elizabeth replied making a sad face. I'd quite made up my mind that you were a poet.'

This statement reduced Mr Watson to silence and Lady Marjorie and Aunt Kate exchanged a despairing glance. Elizabeth had certainly not yet acquired all the social graces.

While Rose and Edward were going round with sandwiches and cakes and Mr Hudson was supervising the infusion of the tea, Lady Marjorie began to outline to Elizabeth the plan for the coming summer.

She had already received a great many invitations and the culmination of the Season would of course be the evening party at Buckingham Palace in July, but for the moment the most important thing was to get ready for the great ball at Londonderry House. This was to be held in only three weeks' time and the Prime Minister himself had asked the Bellamy party to dine at Carlton Gardens. Aunt Kate took the opportunity to remark that few girls had the chance to make such a suitable and exciting debut into society.

'Yes. Aunt Kate,' said Elizabeth dutifully. 'I just wish . . . I just wish it wasn't so soon.' She made it sound like an appointment with the dentist.

Billy Watson tried again. He waxed enthusiastic about the German army, but Elizabeth had found German philosophers and musicians of more interest; he asked her hopefully if she liked tennis but Elizabeth confessed she preferred the piano; when he tried polo Elizabeth told him frankly she found it a boring game.

Mr Watson put down his cup and picked up his hat and gloves and stick and took his leave having stayed the requisite fifteen minutes demanded by etiquette.

'I don't think you made much of a conquest there, Elizabeth,' said her mother when James had escorted his friend outside.

'Should I have done?' asked Elizabeth, as she took two cucumber sandwiches at once in a very unladylike manner. 'Really, mother, I'm only just off the train. In any case he seemed a very wooden young man.'

Aunt Kate raised her lorgnettes and gave her great niece the famous look that had many a time reduced a front bench of cabinet ministers to silence.

'A man of wood can be very dependable,' she pronounced. 'Your late great uncle was a man of wood. You must listen to your mother, Elizabeth. She is wise in the ways of the world. German philosophy will not help you to fill your dance programme at Londonderry House. Remember that my girl and be humble.'

Elizabeth looked suitably chastened.

'Yes, Aunt Kate,' she said. 'Sorry mother.' And immediately attacked the chocolate cake.

'Really Elizabeth, don't gobble so,' said Lady Marjorie. 'Have they starved you at Frau Beck's?'

'No, mother,' Elizabeth replied with her mouth rather full. 'We always had tons of scrumptious food. I think it's made my tummy bigger.'

Aunt Kate shook her head.

'I'm afraid Germany has not done much for Elizabeth,' she said.

Mrs Bridges was the only person who detected a positive improvement.

'Well I must say travelling in foreign parts has given the girl a healthy appetite and that's something,' she remarked as she put away the ruins of the chocolate cake.

After tea Rose received urgent and secret instructions from Lady Marjorie to try to do something about Elizabeth's appearance before her father's return from Westminster, so when the general unpacking was finished she sat her young charge at the dressing-table and went to work on her hair. It wasn't easy as Elizabeth kept fidgetting.

'Fidgetty Phil could never keep still. Do try, Miss Lizzy,' Rose begged.

'Oh wretched, wretched hair,' cried Elizabeth, and put up her hands and tousled it again. 'Why can't it just hang down or be cut off or something! Why can't one live just like an ordinary person?'

'I don't know what you mean by that I'm sure,' Rose replied tight-lipped as she started again. 'Every shopgirl is just as particular about her hair.'

'The difference being that shopgirls do it themselves, like I did in Dresden!' Elizabeth retorted making a face at herself in the glass.

'We need no ghost from the grave to tell us that,' Rose replied, her mouth full of pins.

'What a funny expression. Where did you hear it Rose?'

'I don't know. Now that's better.'

And just as Rose had restored some sort of order to

the erring tresses, Elizabeth jumped up and began searching among the pile of newly unpacked books like a terrier after a rat.

'Bartlett's Familiar Quotations' was at the bottom.

'Here it is,' Elizabeth shouted triumphantly. 'Hamlet. Oh Rose, you are clever.'

Rose thought she *would* have to be clever if she was ever going to control this young lady, and before she could say another word Elizabeth had disappeared down to the drawing room to practise on the piano.

James found his mother on the stairs listening.

'Elizabeth really plays very nicely,' she said.

'Yes,' said James, whose own appreciation of music didn't go far beyond the songs of Marie Lloyd. 'I just wish she had become more . . . more sensible.'

'You can't expect eighten-year-old sisters to be sensible, James.'

'Perhaps I don't mean sensible. I just wish she was a bit more like other girls. A bit more stunning.'

'I thought she stunned us all completely at tea,' Lady Marjorie replied with feeling.

'I am very fond of Elizabeth,' James remarked with a sigh and a shrug. He had been looking forward to having a sister in London that he could introduce to his friends, but Elizabeth was clearly still quite unpresentable.

'You weren't so very polished yourself at that age,' his mother reminded him with a fond smile.

'No, I suppose I wasn't,' James admitted, remembering the bumptious spotty Etonian. 'What a pity we can't send Elizabeth to Sandhurst!'

Elizabeth Bellamy and her father understood and loved each other in a very special private way. Bellamy knew exactly why she didn't want to go to the Londonderry's 'beastly ball looking like a stuffed peacock and jig around the floor with a lot of vapid young men with monocles.' He knew she genuinely thought that sort of thing a complete waste of time and that she was really terrified of the whole business.

He understood because he had felt exactly the same at

her age and still found meeting a lot of strangers a great strains on his nerves. He also knew that if she was to succeed in the hard world into which she had been born Elizabeth must face up to the tortures ahead and conform.

'You see, Elizabeth,' he explained to her sitting in the little chintz chair in her room later that evening, 'there is hope of a Cabinet post; and the terrible thing is, whether one likes it or not, a great deal depends on one's family in these matters. The kind of impression we all make on Mr Balfour.'

'Oh father, no!' Elizabeth replied, unbelieving. 'Everyone knows how important you are.'

'No politician ever gets to the top alone,' Bellamy went on not quite truthfully and disguising this rather pompous statement with a little smile. 'A brilliant wife, an enchanting daughter. Very important, believe me.'

'I don't promise to have much skill as an enchantress,' Elizabeth answered doubtfully.

Bellamy leant forward and kissed her. 'For my sake then.'

'Yes, father.'

It was an argument to which she had no counter.

Every morning when she had finished her daily conference with Mrs Bridges on the subject of meals, Lady Marjorie gave Elizabeth instruction on etiquette.

First Elizabeth had to balance a book on her head.

'Now walk towards me Elizabeth. Turn. Walk away. Turn. Smile. Extend your hand. Two fingers for an acquaintance, three for family friends. Now that's much better. Right, now sit.'

Elizabeth collapsed across a chair.

'Sit, darling, not flop,' her mother scolded. 'Now conversation. Remember German philosophy is out. The weather is always safe; but always follow your partner's lead. If he wants to talk about racing, you are interested in racing.'

'But I'm not,' sighed Elizabeth.

'Don't be silly. You can read about it in the papers.

One important rule. No personalities, no politics.'

'Not even to politicians?'

'Especially not to politicians. They want to enjoy themselves.'

Elizabeth suddenly laughed.

'Do you know what James told me, mother. They're not allowed to talk about women or money in the mess because it always used to cause duels. Isn't that funny?'

'It's very sensible,' Lady Marjorie replied.

'Well, I don't expect any young man will come within miles of me anyway,' said Elizabeth making a face.

'Of course they will. Every girl thinks that. But if you are a wallflower don't sit there staring hopelessly—talk in an animated way to your chaperone. And don't stop immediately when a young man approaches—keep talking and smiling—use your fan.'

Lady Marjorie demonstrated the gentle art of not being a wallflower with an expertise and an elegance that had aways ensured that she never had been one herself.

'Make him feel that he is interrupting an amusing conversation, that you had quite forgotten that you were engaged for the dance, hadn't even heard the music begin. Then accept him with delighted surprise as if he was the most important person in the room.'

'Oh mother!' Elizabeth gave a deep sigh.

'Yes, Elizabeth.'

'What is the difference between being a debutante and an actress?'

Lady Marjorie wasn't amused.

'Don't be deliberately shocking, my dear,' she said.

One day Richard Bellamy came in to tell them the great news that he had just met Sir Francis Knollys, the king's private secretary and that Elizabeth's name was on the short and very exclusive list of lucky young ladies who were to have the honour to be privately presented to their Majesties at Londonderry House.

The effect of this news on Elizabeth was to send her into a fit of depression.

On the night of the ball Mr Hudson asked permission for the servants to be allowed to watch the departure in the hall.

To go to a great ball and to be presented to the King and Queen was as near to a real life fairy tale as could be imagined, and the fact that their Miss Elizabeth was actually about to do this wonderful thing made the servants feel that somehow they themselves were involved.

When Elizabeth came downstairs she looked so beautiful in her white dress and her feathers that Emily burst into tears at the sight and had to be hustled quickly down the backstairs by Mrs Bridges.

Shortly after eight fifteen Aunt Kate sailed in looking like a battleship topped by the Castleton tiara and under her flag the whole family embarked on the voyage to Carlton Gardens.

The dinner party could have been worse. Aunt Kate, who had been known to announce that she considered Mr Balfour the most ineffectual prime minister since Lord North, sat next to him and wisely confined her conversation to the Italian Gardens at Southwold.

Lady Marjorie's heart nearly stopped beating when she heard Elizabeth quoting Hegel to Lord Hugh Cecil, but the brilliant young minister seemed more amused than otherwise by his precocious neighbour.

When they arrived in Park Lane the whole street was jammed with fine carriages setting down the guests and as Elizabeth followed her mother and Aunt Kate through the crowd that filled the hall of the great house she began to feel the first butterflies fluttering in her stomach at the sigh of so many awesome strangers.

A liveried footman gave her a small folded card for Elizabeth to write down the names of her partners, and after the Londonderrys had received them at the top of the staircase, Richard Bellamy led her off into the first dance and James claimed the second. All went so smoothly that Elizabeth almost began to enjoy herself and the duchesses, quizzing the young entry like a row of gorgeously dressed vultures, were agreed that 'the

Southwold gal', as they called her, made a better impression than gossip had led them to expect.

Billy Watson had politely requested the third and fourth dances thinking that dancing would cut the need for conversation to a minimum. The third was a polka and could only be accounted a disaster. Billy was no great hand at dancing and the polka was altogether too new and fast for him. He trod twice on Elizabeth's toes and once on her dress, tearing the hem slightly, and finally collided with a powerful hussar.

By the end of the dance Elizabeth felt that everyone in the room was talking about them and her confidence was rapidly evaporating. They had hardly sat down when the music began again and Billy Watson was on his feet proffering his arm.

'I think this is our waltz,' he said.

Elizabeth quite forgot the animated smile and the elegant sparring with her fan.

'I'm still giddy from the polka. Please excuse me,' she replied. 'And do feel at liberty to find another partner!'

'Well, if you absolutely insist,' Billy bowed with unfeigned relief and took his leave.

Sitting alone watching the simpering girls and the asinine young men eating ices and drinking champagne looking as if they were thoroughly enjoying every minute of it, Elizabeth began to feel increasingly tense and desperate.

She saw James but didn't go over to join him because he was positively drooling over a doll-like girl called Cynthia Cartright who Elizabeth had cordially disliked for years.

Elizabeth knew no one else in the room and decided she didn't want to. When she heard the national anthem playing in the ballroom she suddenly had a vision of herself being dragged out in front of the king looking like a prize filly and her nerve went completely. She ran out of the nearest door.

When a royal equerry came to call Aunt Kate and no one could find Elizabeth there was terrible consternation in the Bellamy camp. Between them the family searched the place but in vain and at last Aunt Kate had to go forward and explain—with profound apologies—that her great niece had been taken with a fainting fit.

Mr Hudson, Miss Roberts and Rose were waiting in the hall when the Bellamys returned but none of them had seen or heard of the missing girl. The master didn't see fit to enlighten them as to what had happened, sending the butler to bed and telling Rose to wait up, he went into the morning room for a family conference. As they were all very upset this quickly developed into a family row.

'How could she let us down like this? How could she? Lady Marjorie exclaimed. 'After all you've done for her, Richard, to behave like this.'

Thus she neatly made Bellamy the most injured party.

'Never mind that now,' he said pouring out a much needed brandy and soda. 'An innocent eighteen-year-old girl loose on the streets of London!' He was beside himself with worry.

'Should we notify the police?' James suggested trying to be helpful.

'What a perfectly dreadful idea,' his mother said. 'What if the newspapers get hold of it? I mean it will be all round London anyway.'

'Has it occurred to you that something might have happened to the girl?' Bellamy retorted sharply. The shock had revealed a side of his wife's character that was, happily, usually concealed.

'She's simply done this to spite us!' Lady Marjorie began to shed tears of fury.

There was an awkward silence.

'Pretty bad show I must say,' said James unhelpfully. 'I shall be the laughing stock of the mess.'

"I think it would be best if you both went to bed,' said Bellamy icily, trying to keep his temper.

When they had gone he sat down in the big wing chair and dozed fitfully; in the servants hall Rose was doing exactly the same. Two o'clock struck; then three; then four.

A few minutes later Rose was startled awake by a scurry of steps outside in the area.

It was Elizabeth, her beautifully arranged hair loose and bedraggled, her dress covered in mud.

'Where have you been, Miss Elizabeth?' said Rose, cross and still half asleep. 'Your father's half out of his mind!'

Elizabeth went into the kitchen and sat down on a chair by the table. She looked worn out.

'Oh Rose, it was awful,' she said.

'There, there, poor thing,' said Rose comforting. 'All those awful streets and you lost.'

The streets between Park Lane and Eaton Pace had been wet and muddy but not really awful at all, not half so awful as the turmoil in Elizabeth's mind where guilt at her behaviour and fear of the consequences had created a fury of self pity that she had been forced to make such a fool of herself and to go to the hellish ball in the first place. She would have welcomed sneers and derision as she walked through the streets in her fine clothes but crossing sweepers, prostitutes, streets traders and policemen all vied with each other in offering help and sympathy and their subservience and friendliness only added fuel to her rage.

'Oh not that,' Elizabeth now replied to Rose, shaking her head. 'The ball!'

Rose didn't understand.

'What do you mean, Miss Elizabeth?'

'It was sickening,' Elizabeth said fiercely. 'Sickening! All those repulsive flirting, simpering females. What do you think of the weather? What do you think of the floor?' She gave an angry sniff. 'What do you think of the band? Flutter your fan like youve been taught there's a good girl. One two three, one two three! Oh Rose. It was more than I could stand. So I ran away through the front door. You should have seen the footman's face!'

Elizabeth laughed rather hysterically.

'The shame of it,' she said. 'The shame of all that extravagance and waste when outside there is so much poverty and hardship.

'Shame indeed,' Rose replied putting a very different

meaning to the word. 'Your father's waiting up for you.'

'I can't face him now,' Elizabeth answered affecting extreme exhaustion.

'Coward!' said Rose quietly. Elizabeth couldn't believe her ears. She raised her head and looked at Rose.

'What did you say, Rose?' she asked.

'Coward!' Rose repeated.

Elizabeth opened her eyes wide.

'I shall slap your face!' she said.

'I shall slap yours,' Rose answered, thoroughly roused.

'Rose!'

'Don't Rose me!' the housemaid snapped back. 'You sit there in all your finery—looking a proper mess and all—and everything we've done for you turned to ridicule. Don't you Rose me!'

Elizabeth turned her head away with a pitying shrug of her shoulders.

'You don't understand what you're talking about,' she said.

'No, I'm ignorant, no doubt. I didn't go to Germany. I only know that your father and mother are worried out of their minds while you sit there moaning because you were lucky enough to be invited to the grandest ball of the season that most girls would have given their right arms . . .'

Elizabeth interrupted.

'The Season!' she exclaimed. 'What season? All seasons are alike to the poor and the needy.'

'What do you know about poor people?' Rose's contempt was a great deal more effective than Elizabeth's. 'You only care about yourself. You're a coward and ran away. You'll break your father's heart.'

Because this was true it really angered Elizabeth. 'Hold your tongue,' she half shouted. 'My father will understand. I should think I know him rather better than you do.'

'Of course he will,' said Rose more calmly, 'because he loves you. He may even forgive you in time, though I doubt your mother will.'

Though normally Rose would never have dared make

such an insubordinate statement it showed how well she knew her master and mistress. Lady Marjorie had been brought up in a strict society with clear-cut rules; now she was one of the arbiters of that society. Elizabeth had broken one of the rules and could expect no mercy.

'I'm not going to argue with you,' she said rather grandly. 'It's not my place.'

Rose wasn't going to be silenced so easily.

'Oh no,' she went on, 'you don't like a few home truths. You're more spoilt than any of those other young ladies—you're the most spoilt of all!'

'I won't be able to keep my hands off you much longer!' Elizabeth shouted.

'What a lady!' Rose taunted.

Elizabeth made a lunge and Rose caught her arm and twisted it behind her back forcing her to sit down. Housework had made her wiry and strong.

'You're hurting,' cried Elizabeth, annoyed at her impotence. 'I'll tell.'

'I bet you would and all,' Rose retorted sitting down opposite her. 'Now you shut up and listen to me . . . I get up cheerful at six o'clock and go to bed dead beat at eleven,' she began. 'I do my work as best I can and one day I might be a proper ladysmaid to a proper lady—not a spoilt brat.'

Elizabeth got up but Rose pushed her down again.

'Just sit still and listen!'

And Elizabeth sat still and listened.

'Right. Mr Hudson makes the house run like clockwork and Mrs Bridges may be an old cow sometimes but she cooks a dream and her meals are a pleasure to put on a tray.' Rose's grammar became more haphazard as her passion increased. 'We're the wheels of the cart and we're content it should be so; because the master's a proper gentleman what we're proud of, and does his work right in the House of Parliament and my lady is beautiful and genteel from a great family. We feel . . . we feel that we—this whole house—is part of London Society.'

Elizabeth listened, half amused, half serious.

'London Society,' she taunted. 'More like the parrot house at the zoo.'

'London Society, I said, London Society I mean,' Rose went on. 'The hub of the Empire isn't it? The Empire on which the sun never sets, and if you can't feel some of the glow of that like I can, I'm sorry for you.'

The Empire had always been very dear to Rose's heart and now she went on to avow how proud she was to be part of it, and how she could feel its great heart thumping when she went up Piccadilly on a bus, and Elizabeth thought to herself what a dear silly faithful thing Rose was and how she was really very fond of her.

'How would it be if I was to come singing and dancing into the drawing-room? Or sliding down the bannisters?' Rose asked. 'No more must you step out of line, Miss Elizabeth. If you're not a proper lady then I don't want to be your maid. And that's all I got to say and more than enough already, I know. So now you can have me turned out.' Suddenly she began to cry.

'Oh dear,' said Elizabeth laughing. 'I wish you would slide down the bannisters.' She put her arm round Rose. 'Rose, I love you very much and I'm sorry I was rude. It wasn't fair. I know what I've done was horrible for father and I'll try to make it all right. But I'm not going to be cowed for ever Rose. But there is something wrong and there are new ideas, new people about who want to try to put it right. I don't understand it all, I'm muddled and uncertain and I don't really understand it. But I mean to one day.'

'I'm sorry Miss Elizabeth for overstepping my place,' said Rose apologetically. She hadn't heard a word Elizabeth had said.

'Oh damn your place,' said Elizabeth crossly.

'Miss Elizabeth!' Rose exclaimed.

'And now,' Elizabeth went on with a smile, 'just for your sake I'm going to be brave and face up to father. Now kiss me and say we're friends again.'

She hugged Rose and kissed her which only set the housemaid crying again.

'Dry your eyes, Rose, and lead me to the slaughter.'

They went upstairs together hand in hand. When they came to the morning room door Rose opened it.

Richard Bellamy was awake. Elizabeth ran into his arms and Rose shut the door.

She stretched her arms and yawned. She felt as if she had been awake for a week.

CHAPTER EIGHT

It was not unusual for young ladies in their first season to be taken with a fainting fit at a dance, not yet being accustomed to the combination of hot rooms and tight corsets, so that when this reason was put about as an excuse for Elizabeth's conduct it was readily accepted.

Naturally there was a great debate about it in the family and the only person who was not consulted was Elizabeth herself. Bellamy blamed himself and his wife for forcing their daughter into a situation before she was ready for it or able to cope with it and refused to take Elizabeth to task for her behaviour. Lady Marjorie didn't subscribe to this opinion considering that her daughter was spoilt and self opinionated and needed nothing so much as a good spanking. In the privacy of her boudoir she shed bitter tears that she of all people should have been saddled with such a tiresome ungracious misfit of a girl.

They called in Aunt Kate to mediate and to Lady Marjorie's chagrin her aunt took Richard Bellamy's side and advised them to put Elizabeth out at grass for a year to let her grow up a bit.

On one point they were all agreed, although for very different reasons, and that was that they couldn't risk another disaster like the Londonderry House Ball. So Elizabeth was sent off to spend the rest of the summer with her cousins, the Dunmantons, who lived a gloriously semi-barbaric life in a castle on the West coast of Ireland.

There, riding and fishing and swimming and going on long picnic expeditions, she spent a few blissful months with the wild Dunmanton children and harmed no one with her German philosophy.

When she returned to London in the autumn all was forgotten and forgiven and Elizabeth seemed to her mother to have turned over a new leaf. She filled in the days reading, playing the piano, visiting museums and going to concerts.

As young ladies couldn't go to public entertainments unchaperoned, Elizabeth obtained permission to take Rose with her on these occasions. As long as she was allowed to take some sewing with her Rose was perfectly happy to sit through hours and hours of Beethoven quartets and took a perverse delight in Mr Hudson's disapproval of the arrangement.

That autumn there was change in the air at Westminster. The Conservative Party, led by Mr Balfour, had been long in power, and during 1905 there were more and more signs that public opinion was swinging towards the Liberals. The Conservatives had lost a series of important by-elections and Mr Winston Churchill had taken his celebrated walk across the floor of the House to join the Liberal benches.

The General Election was due to take place early in 1906 and Mr Balfour, being a very cunning politician, decided that the only hope his party had of re-election was to give the country a taste of Liberal rule for a few months first.

Balfour left his resignation rather late because he was determined to hand over the country in a proper state of defence. The strong and growing fear that Germany was becoming too big for her boots had been strengthened by the Kaiser's threatening attitude to France at Tangier earlier in the year. This was one of the reasons Balfour had strengthened the Committee of Imperial Defence by the addition of the formidable fire-eating admiral, Sir John Fisher.

Richard Bellamy was already a member of this committee, and had been very much concerned with the estimates and design for the first of Fisher's great battleships, *The Dreadnought*. By early December she was nearly completed, with three of her sisters under construction, and Mr. Balfour felt it safe to resign. The King sent for Mr Campbell-Bannerman, the Liberal leader, and asked him to form an interim administration, and although this meant that Richard Bellamy no longer held ministerial rank he still remained on the Committee of Imperial Defence.

One cold afternoon, unconcerned by the momentous events taking place a mile away in Westminster, Elizabeth and Rose came back from a Leider concert given by the celebrated German singer, Elena Gerhardt.

When she went into the drawing-room she found a very polished and elegant young man taking tea with her mother. He was introduced as the Baron Klaus Von Rimmer and wasted no time in reminding Elizabeth that they once met at a party given by the Wintersteins during her stay in Germany.

It appeared that the Baron, who came from a banking family, was over in London for a few weeks to study methods of business in the City of London. He was full of apologies for being so presumptious as to call without a formal introduction.

'It's no presumption,' Lady Marjorie told him with a gracious smile. 'We are delighted to receive you, aren't we, Elizabeth?'

She gave her daughter a little nod of encouragement. 'My mother,' thought Elizabeth, 'would be delighted to receive anyone in trousers however oily and boring, as long as he is rich and eligible.'

'We should be more than delighted, mother dear, we should be deeply honoured,' she answered out loud, 'that of all the people the Baron must know in London he should have singled us out. We scarcely exchanged six words if I remember at the Wintersteins . . .'

There were times when Lady Marjorie could have cheerfully strangled her daughter.

'Elizabeth!' she said frowning.

'No please,' said the Baron, holding up his hand and

apparently not the least offended. 'Unhappily I have very few friends in London. I confess I was feeling rather lonely in my lodgings when I remembered that among the six words I exchanged with a certain charming and beautiful fraulein Bellamy were included the names of Schubert and Goethe, who between them produced some of the finest Lieder sounds.'

Elizabeth was surprised.

She said, 'But isn't that funny—I have just been to . . .'

'I was telling the Baron' Lady Marjorie interposed. 'Quite a coincidence.'

Elizabeth realised too late that she had fallen into a trap carefully prepared by her mother and the Baron and shut up like a clam. It was only towards the end of the meal when the Baron mentioned in passing that he knew Elena Gerhadt personally and had actually studied under her at one time that Elizabeth gradually began to warm towards him.

Leaving Alfred to preside over the final stages of the drawing room tea and clear it away, Mr Hudson retired to the servants hall to partake of his own refreshment. Rose had left the programme of the concert on the mantlepiece and he picked it up and studied it with distaste.

'I hope you weren't fooled into thinking it was the cat's whiskers in musical entertainment,' he said to Rose.

'I've got a mind of my own, thank you,' she answered.

'I hope it stays your own, Rose,' Mr Hudson answered, looking at her over the top of his gold-rimmed glasses. 'There are dangers in being a maid to a headstrong young Lady like Miss Elizabeth.'

'What's she done to upset you now, Mr Hudson?' Rose asked, knowing that Mr Hudson strongly disapproved of Elizabeth's behaviour since her return from Germany.

'Nothing,' Mr Hudson went on drily. 'Nothing in particular. I'm referring to the matter of respect. It has to work both ways . . .'

'I know it does,' Rose replied cautiously.

'All very well packing young girls off to foreign parts to advance their education,' Mr Hudson went on, 'but it's not altogether a good thing in my opinion. They get taken advantage of.'

'Silly old fuddy-duddy what does he know about it?' thought Rose.

'In what way?' she asked.

Mr Hudson rubbed his hands together thoughtfully. 'Oh,' he went on, 'heads filled with new-fangled ideas; manners forgotten, loyalties questioned. Don't think it's not calculated by foreign teachers.' He held up his finger in warning. 'There's a name for it,' he leant forward and spoke the next word very low and distinct.

'Subversion,' said Mr Hudson. 'If you want to know. That's a deliberate pulling at the roots of the country, through its young men and women, twisting their minds, so that in a time of crisis . . .'

He paused dramatically leaving Rose to imagine the worst.

'Really Mr Hudson, you're not suggesting that our Miss Lizzy . . .' Rose couldn't help laughing, it was so preposterous.

'I'm not suggesting anything,' Mr Hudson went on in his best preacher-in-the-kirk manner. 'I'm simply giving warning. The signs are all there. Pray God I am wrong.'

Alfred came in with the tea tray from the drawing room.

'What signs, Mr Hudson?' he asked.

'Mr Hudson has some funny notions,' Rose explained.

'Going on about them dirty foreigners again, are you, Mr Hudson?' Alfred asked with a lugubrious wink at Rose.

'That's enough from you, Alfred,' said the butler.

'If it only were, Mr Hudson,' Alfred answered triumphantly. 'But her ladyship asks me to inform you that the Baron is staying to dinner.'

Mr Bellamy was not present at that meal being detained in the House of Commons, but during the course of it the Baron so delighted his hostess with his charm and with and good manners that she asked him to move forthwith into the spare room at Eaton Place for the remainder of his stay in London. The fact, shyly admitted by the Baron, that he was distantly related to the royal family might also have influenced Lady Marjorie's decision.

As was usual when there were male visitors to stay at Eaton Place, Alfred took over the duties of the Baron Von Rimmer's valet. The footman was deeply impressed by the quality of his new master's clothes, especially the shirts and the underwear, all of which were hand-made in Paris of the finest material and embroidered with a coronet. With his head house-parlourmaid and his footman away half the day on other duties and Christmas fast approaching, Mr Hudson continued to consider the Baron's presence a confounded nuisance, but the foreign visitor gained an admirer in another quarter. One day he made a point of visiting the kitchen to congratulate Mrs Bridges on her quails 'en croute'. As Mrs Bridges admitted afterwards it wasn't a thing an English gentleman would have done, but after that nobody—not even Mr Hudson—could say some foreigners didn't have good manners.

In the larger world of Society the Baron made an immediate and favourable impression with his beautiful manners and impeccable breeding easily verified in the Almanach De Gotha. Luckily his duties at the bank did not preclude him from accompanying his hostess and Elizabeth to several pre-Christmas parties and it was soon noised abroad in Mayfair and Belgravia that Lady Marjorie had captured a potential lion for her daughter's hand.

Lady Marjorie was naturally quick to put the damper on any such rumours. When Lady Prudence Fairfax, her most intimate friend, asked her outright if the Baron was in love with Elizabeth, she pooh-poohed the idea absolutely, saying that it was much too early to talk of such things.

'Actually I think it is rather the opposite,' she confided, 'Elizabeth doesn't seem the least impressed.'

'In that case,' Lady Prudence replied, 'you must bring him to dine with us without delay. Agatha is at home and looking ravishing.'

Agatha Fairfax was a tall friendly girl of twenty-three summers but in spite of her mother's untiring efforts, no gentleman had yet come forward to ravish her.

Of course Lady Marjorie had absolutely no intention of having her capture stolen from under her nose and was secretly delighted that the Baron was in fact making an impression on Elizabeth. He was making a far greater impression on that unimpressionable girl than any young man had done before in her life.

Their first point of contact was music. The Baron sang and played the piano quite brilliantly and soon he and Elizabeth were playing duets together. Lady Marjorie waived the need of a chaperone when they went to the Albert Hall to hear Henry Wood conduct a British masterpiece, *The Dream of Gerontius*. Afterwards they inspected the wonderful memorial to the Baron's connexion, Prince Albert, and this led in the days that followed to a further exploration of the sights of London.

Everything about the great city pleased and excited the Baron and he knew far more about its history (thanks to Herr Baedeker's Guide) than Elizabeth did herself and she found herself becoming so infected by her companion's enthusiasm that the dull old town she had always taken so much for granted became a place of fascination.

Richard Bellamy had been much too deeply involved in all the handing over and clearing up and general confusion that accompanied the change in government to be able to give the foreign guest under his roof more than the most formal greeting.

The only time during the day when the two men were in each other's company was at breakfast, never a meal at which conversation sparkles in an English dining-room. Nevertheless Bellamy formed an impression that his daughter and their guest seemed to be getting on very well together and that Elizabeth was in gayer and happier frame of mind than she had been for some time.

One morning he mentioned the fact to his wife and she admitted to having noticed something of the same thing.

'He is a Junker, you know,' said Lady Marjorie as she straightened her husband's tie before his departure for the House. 'One of the best and worthiest families. She could do worse.'

'Oh quite,' Richard Bellamy replied. 'It could be a tradesman's son, with radical views.'

He smiled and kissed his wife goodbye.

As the carriage turned into Birdcage Walk a cold east wind sweeping across St. James's Park made Mr Pearce blow out his cheeks and pummel his shoulders. Victoria Street would have offered a shorter and more sheltered approach to the House of Commons but Mr Pearce couldn't abide the trams, the new electric monsters with their clanging bells and narrow steel rails exactly designed to trap the wheels of a carriage. On the square of Wellington Barracks the new guard were already lined up in their grey greatcoats and a thin powdering of snow was whitening the side of their bearskins. They looked as cold as he felt, thought Mr Pearce, and longed for the time when the Bellamys would buy a motor car. Inside the carriage Richard Bellamy's mind was on other matters. Though he had concealed the fact admirably, the knowledge that his daughter and the Baron were becoming more than just friends had shaken him considerably and that his wife was encouraging the relationship even more so. He tried to bring his impressions of the visitor into focus and found that on the whole they were rather disagreeable. Bellamy's intuition told him that there was something fishy about the Baron Von Rimmer. With the political wind blowing the way it was it would be only common sense to make some enquiries. Richard Bellamy pulled out his beautifully folded silk handkerchief and tied a knot in it.

In the servants' hall there were no such doubts about the Baron. Alfred came down from seeing Mr Bellamy into his carriage in a merry mood.

'Oh take me, take me, take me to the Houses of Parliament,' he sang, horribly improvising tune and words.

'You're very pleased with yourself this morning,' said Rose, who was ironing one of Elizabeth's dresses.

'We're in love,' said Alfred.

'Who is?' Rose answered sharply.

'We is,' Alfred went on sweetly. 'In a manner of speaking.'

'Speak for yourself,' said Rose.

'Being but the reflections of our masters,' Alfred replied, and swept Rose into his arms iron and all and twirled her round.

'Put me down this instant, Alfred! What are you thinking of?' Rose exclaimed, very put out. Mr Hudson was standing watching them in the doorway looking as if he had just discovered a bad fish in his pantry.

'What's the matter, Mr Hudson?' Alfred asked him gaily. 'Don't you believe in love?'

'If it's kept in its place,' Mr Hudson replied without enthusiasm.

'But not between them and us, eh? Foreigners,' Alfred teased him. 'Here do you want to know something,' he went on to Rose, sitting down in the easy chair. 'Germany's beginning to appeal to me. A schloss in Bavaria, a palace in Dresden, a town house in Berlin . . . twenty gardeners and a powdered flunkey behind every chair . . . what about that, eh?'

'Why don't you go there then?' Rose asked tartly as she folded the dress.

'I might and all,' Alfred answered, sticking his chest in Mr Hudson's face and flashing a large diamond pin.

'What's this?' asked Mr Hudson tilting his head up.

'Well, I never did!' exclaimed Rose.

'I was wondering when you'd notice,' Alfred answered. 'Like it?'

'Where did you get it?' Mr Hudson was suspicious of a hoax.

'A present,' said Alfred grinning like the Cheshire Cat. 'From my master.'

He watched delighted as Mr Hudson and Rose exchanged amazed glances.

'What's wrong? No law against getting a present is there?' He deliberately made a face at the butler. 'It's Christmas, Mr Scrooge!'

And before Mr Hudson could reply Alfred waltzed out of the room.

Elizabeth had arranged to take Klaus to the House of Commons. They listened to several rather boring speeches about deep sea fisheries before going out onto the terrace overlooking the river to wait for Bellamy to collect them for tea.

'Well you wanted to come,' said Elizabeth apologetically. 'I'm afraid it was terrible boring.'

'I was spellbound,' Klaus replied seriously. 'Such pomp and tradition.'

'Grimsby trawlermen!' said Elizabeth and they both laughed.

The afternoon sun shone through the light mist giving the river and the bridge the enchanted look of a painting by Monet. Klaus waxed lyrical about the great British Empire at whose epicentre they were standing and it made Elizabeth think about Rose. If Rose and Klaus were both to get onto the subject of the Empire together, she thought, what a bore they would be.

'And the men your country produces; incorruptible, not like in Germany. Men like your father.' Klaus went on and couldn't understand why Elizabeth was smiling.

'Father's a clergyman's son,' she explained. 'It must show. He won't thank you for it. Makes him sound like one of the diehards.'

'Diehards!' Klaus repeated the word as if he liked it. 'But surely your father is more Liberal.'

'Careful! That's a dangerous word here,' Elizabeth said, laughing again. 'Well, shall we say open-minded. Flexible.'

'Flexible?' Klaus didn't understand.

'What you have to understand about father is that he married into the party,' she elucidated. 'He was very clever and he went to Cambridge and things, but he owes his career entirely to mother's family.'

'Diehards?'

'Yes. Very.' They laughed again.

'I suppose from what you say that he is dependent on your mother's family financially?'

'Oh yes. Everyone knows that.'

They were interrupted by the arrival of the subject of their conversation, full of apologies for keeping them waiting.

When she was changing for dinner that evening Elizabeth suddenly couldn't bear it any longer. She was bursting with love; she had to tell someone. So she told Rose.

'It gives you such a pain,' she said.

'Whereabouts?' Rose asked, never having felt it herself.

'Oh all over,' Elizabeth answered, stretching and hugging herself. 'It's rather delicious.'

She was suddenly reflective.

'The funny thing is, Rose, that I still don't like him very much. Can you believe that? I love him. I think. But I don't like him.'

Her puzzled look vanished and she suddenly seized Rose and hugged her. 'Oh Rose, isn't it marvellous? Aren't you happy for me?'

'Yes, Miss Lizzie. I am happy for you.' She didn't sound very enthusiastic as she held out Elizabeth's petticoat.

'But someone isn't?' Elizabeth asked suspiciously. 'Who is it, Rose?' She was intensely curious to know.

'Well, I shouldn't say it really,' Rose admitted. 'But it's Mr Hudson.'

'Hudson!' said Elizabeth unbelieving.

'It's nothing against the Baron personally,' Rose explained as she did up Elizabeth's petticoat. 'But he's got this dislike of foreigners in general, and he will go on about it. He's heard there are thousands of Germans already in this country on the South Coast, working as waiters and hairdressers, but they're really trained soldiers, and if ever there was an invasion, they'd all join up and slaughter us in our beds.'

Elizabeth broke into a smile and then into a laugh and Rose caught the infection and soon they were both doubled up in helpless giggles.

It was really quite ridiculous that in spite of the fact

that Britain had far the largest navy in the world there should always be men like Mr Hudson obsessed by the fear that the country was about to be invaded at any moment.

After dinner, when the port had gone round once and the ladies had retired, Richard Bellamy asked the Baron Von Rimmer if he would join him in the morning room for a private talk. He remained behind a moment to give the butler Mr Pearce's instructions for the morning and when he rejoined his guest he found the Baron standing in front of the fire smoking his cigar, legs wide apart very much in the usual position of the host.

'I expect you are wondering, sir,' Klaus began, 'why when I say I am a banker, I am in fact no such thing.'

Bellamy stopped. As this was the precise question he was about to put to his German guest, it rather took the wind out of his sails.

Klaus stepped forward and with a little bow presented his card. Bellamy looked at it. It stated that Baron Klaus Von Rimmer was the private representative of the director of a very famous German armaments firm.

'So they are employing young barons to look after their sales these days,' Bellamy remarked, more for something to say than anything else. 'Some brandy?'

Klaus accepted the brandy. 'I thought you might have known that, sir,' he said. 'I am a man of peace,' he went on, 'but all countries have the right to protect their shores. And the stronger everyone is protected, the less possibility of war.'

Bellamy laughed. 'You can spare your breath, Baron, I know the story.'

Throughout the world the fear of war was inducing countries to arm almost to the point of panic; the big international arms firms, Vickers, Krupps, Skoda were all booming, and their wheeler dealing agents were fast becoming millionaires.

'Mr Bellamy,' Klaus said in a very serious voice. 'There are many of us in my country—artists, musicians, philosophers and ordinary people—who are appalled at the upsurge of nationalism, who seek only to live their lives in a peaceful and united Europe.'

'And some of them work for armaments firms?'

'And why not?'

Bellamy smiled.

'Come on Baron,' he said. 'We both of us know about the gentlemen who sell arms to both sides and then stand back and watch them engage. What is it that *you* have to sell?'

Without hesitation Klaus felt in his inner pocket and pulled out a fat envelope.

'It is a new form of gun mounting for your Dreadnoughts. These are some preliminary specifications and estimates. You will see as you study them that the mounting is far superior to anything Vickers have to offer at the present time.'

The young baron's forthright approach astonished Bellamy.

'How do you know?' he asked.

'We know,' Klaus replied.

'Why didn't you aproach our government through the proper channels?'

'I am sorry,' Klaus answered with a smile. 'You are a former junior minister at the Admiralty and a member of the Committee of Imperial Defence. Are you not a proper channel?'

'I was referring to your befriending my daughter in Germany, and your subsequent manoeuvrings in my household.'

Klaus frowned.

'My dear fellow,' Bellamy continued. 'I don't particularly mind. I'm just curious to know how you chaps operate these days.'

'I admit, sir. I had to gain access to your confidence.'

'Using Elizabeth?'

'Yes.' Klaus shrugged again and smiled. 'It was my method, but it was in your best interests too. But I would like to say this, as for the feelings that have developed between Elizabeth and myself, that is a separate matter and will remain so.'

'I don't see how you can exactly divorce the two things.' It was Bellamy's turn to shrug. 'I've no doubt she can look after herself.' He held up the envelope. 'What do you expect me to do with this?'

'When you have satisfied yourself that it is genuine,' Klaus explained, 'to use your influence and persuade your government to enter a contract with my company. Perhaps I should add that the contract should be made for obvious political reasons through a Swiss subsidiary which my company controls.'

'I see,' said Bellamy feeling somewhat bewildered, but Klaus wasn't finished.

'It goes without saying,' he went on smoothly, 'should you be interested in a substantial shareholding in this Swiss company—I mean you personally, sir—it can be arranged.'

The openness of the bribe almost took Bellamy's breath away. Diplomatic methods had changed since his day.

'Such financial interlocking between our two countries can only enhance the prospects of peace,' Klaus added to end his oration.

Bellamy was tempted to say 'Amen' but restrained himself.

'Well,' he said, 'perhaps we should join the ladies.'

'Yes sir,' Klaus replied. 'And perhaps it would be more . . . more tactful if for the moment they continued to know me as Klaus Von Rimmer, the banker.'

The next day Richard Bellamy asked Admiral Sir Adam Blake to have lunch with him at his club. Sir Adam was something deep in naval intelligence and like so many senior officers in the services concealed a shrewd sharp brain behind a rather idiotic manner.

Bellamy's main concern was that Von Rimmer's armament story might really be a cover to set up a spying organisation right in their midst.

'Quite possible, old boy,' said Sir Adam gaily. 'On the face of it, it looks too genuine. I mean they really seem to have something to offer and it's politically sound vis a vis the election and the Liberals.'

'I suppose we could whip up a scare about Tirpitz and his ever-growing fleet,' Bellamy agreed.

'Course you could. A.J. would lap it up,' Sir Adam replied.

Those close to Mr Balfour commonly referred to the great man by his initials.

'On the personal front,' Sir Adam proceeded, 'I take it you've been offered a pretty hefty bribe?'

Bellamy looked rather guilty.

'Well, haven't you?' Sir Adam asked again.

'Shares in a Swiss subsidiary,' Bellamy admitted.

Sir Adam didn't turn a hair.

'Standard procedure,' he said. 'Of course I forgot. You're new to this game.' He sniffed thoughtfully. 'So personally,' he went on, 'we'd stand to gain.'

'We?' asked Bellamy in surprise.

'You'd count me in wouldn't you? You'd have to you know. The price of silence. Cry Tally Ho, and all for Peace, and away we go.'

Sir Adam made it all sound like some sort of children's game.

'A couple of shifty profiteers,' said Bellamy with a wry smile.

'Will you never learn?' asked Sir Adam.

'I can't escape my humble and pious origins,' Bellamy admitted.

'I know, Dick,' said Sir Adam fondly, 'and that'll be your epitaph.'

In the meantime they agreed to lay a little trap for the baron.

'We can't move against him till we've actually agreed to be corrupted,' Sir Adam explained to Bellamy. 'These people usually have a few incriminating documents they like you to sign. You'll see!'

Christmas was only a week away and Von Rimmer was due to leave London on the following Tuesday to join his family for the festival.

Lady Marjorie had already talked to her husband

about a farewell dinner party for their German guest on the Monday evening and it was therefore quite easy for Bellamy to introduce Sir Adam as one of the party without arousing anyone's suspicion.

The prospect of Klaus leaving for Germany made Elizabeth almost desperate with misery. On the Monday of the dinner party they spent the afternoon walking in the Park and Elizabeth showed Klaus all the places so beautifully illustrated by Arthur Rackham in a book she had just been given by him as a parting present, *'Peter Pan in Kensington Gardens'*. She showed him the balloon lady, and St Govor's Well by the Broad Walk and the Round Pond and the island in the Serpentine where the birds are born that become little boys and girls; then they went to tea at Gunter's, Elizabeth's favourite place.

Klaus was describing Christmas in Germany when Elizabeth reached across and took his hand impetuously and told him that she loved him.

Up to that moment neither Klaus or Elizabeth had spoken of love or of marriage or even any kindred subject. Considering the conventions of their class it was hardly likely that they would do so after such a short acquaintance, but Elizabeth was no child of convention. Klaus concealed his surprise in a masterly fashion, and whereas most young men would have been frightened to death by Elizabeth's revelation, he smiled gently back at her and told her that he was very much honoured. On reflection Elizabeth thought he had treated her as her grandfather dealt with his over affectionate spaniel when it jumped up and licked his face.

When Rose came into her young mistress's bedroom to lay out her dress for dinner she found her in a thoroughly miserable mood.

'He's leaving and I want to go with him and he won't take me,' she said to Rose.

'I should hope not,' Rose replied. 'Now look at the way you've scrumpled up your bed.'

She began to straighten it. 'He'll come back,' she added hopefully.

'I don't see why he should, since he doesn't love me,' Elizabeth said tragically.

'Of course he loves you. Whatever makes you think that?' said Rose.

'I don't know,' Elizabeth moaned.

'Well you'd better have your bath before he comes up to change for dinner. It's terrible the way Alfred takes all the hot water for him.'

Elizabeth rolled over on the bed.

'I shall go and step into the bath with him,' she said dreamily.

'Miss Elizabeth!' Rose was really shocked.

'Don't be so shocked!' Elizabeth teased her. 'We live in modern times.'

A few minutes later when Rose went into the Baron Von Rimmer's bedroom to deliver clean towels she was truly shocked.

There was a little ante room outside the bedroom and when Rose entered she could see through the half-open door. Inside the Baron and Alfred were together on the bed, both half-dressed, and apparently locked in a passionate embrace.

Once when she was very young Rose had seen two people lying coupled in the corner of a hayfield near the wood behind the cottage in which she was born. But nothing in her narrow experience of life had prepared her for the shock of seeing two men in the act of love. For a moment she thought they were playing some childish game, ragging together like schoolboys, but a long horrified look convinced her that this was certainly not the case. She let out a stifled sob. Alfred looked in her direction and Rose fled, scattering towels as she went.

She ran to her room and jammed a chair in front of the door, thanking God it was Ivy's night out. Then she sat on the bed for a long time feeling sick and faint, clenching and unclenching her fingers.

She heard the front door bell ring far away downstairs and knew the guests were arriving and she would be missed by Mr Hudson. So she washed her face in cold water and steeled herself to go down.

Mr Hudson was in a great flurry and flap. 'Just for once try and remember that Miss Elizabeth is not your only responsibility in this house,' he snapped at her. 'Now go up to the drawing-room and help with the drinks.'

The sight of Alfred cool as a cucumber, pouring champagne into the Baron's glass was enough to make Rose tremble again. She managed to get to the door but Mr Hudson, already suspicious, noticed something was wrong and cornered her in the passage outside, demanding an explanation. Once informed of the situation Mr Hudson lost no time in informing his master of the strange goings on under his roof. Richard Bellamy was put in a dilemma: he and Sir Adam had their quarry in their sights and if all went well he might be in custody by midnight. Any new diversion might rob them of their prey. He told the butler to carry on as usual.

When he returned to his guests Bellamy found that the Baron had been called away to the morning room to take an urgent telephone call from Berlin.

When dinner had been announced some minutes Bellamy grew suspicious and a search was made for the missing guest of honour. He had gone, bag and baggage, and he had taken Alfred with him. Sir Adam and Bellamy held a brief counsel of war and decided in view of the circumstances that pursuit would be unproductive. Elizabeth was allowed to retire to her bedroom where she lay for hours sobbing uncontrollably, wondering what on earth had happened to cause Klaus to run away in such mysterious fashion. She came to the conclusion that it was her sudden declaration of love that must have frightened him off.

After as difficult a dinner party as the Bellamys and their servants could remember and the guests had mercifully departed, Bellamy explained the situation to his wife.

She took the news very calmly; it was accepted in society that many well born Germans were pederasts.

'If Alfred was like that then we are well rid of him,' said Lady Marjorie sensibly enough. 'They probably deserve each other. But what I can't forgive is the way Klaus has treated our poor Elizabeth. She was so in love with him. What am I to tell her? She is far too young to be exposed to such things.'

'I want you to leave this to me, my dear,' Richard Bellamy kissed his wife tenderly. 'And trust me.'

When Rose came into Elizabeth's bedroom later that night to tidy up and say good-night she herself had quite recovered her composure and her worry now was for her young mistress. But Elizabeth seemed quite calm and unconcerned. It was she who brought up the subject of the Baron.

'He was a spy,' Elizabeth explained. 'Do you know about spies, Rose?'

'Yes, Miss Elizabeth,' Rose answered, not wanting to say too much.

'An agent who sells deadly weapons . . . using me to get to father and compromise him. Isn't that awful?'

Rose was folding up Elizabeth's clothes. She said nothing.

'But father was too clever,' Elizabeth went on. 'He got hold of Sir Adam, who is a celebrated spy catcher for the Navy. You'd never think it, would you?'

Rose was thinking that Elizabeth's father really had been clever—very clever indeed.

'They were probably going to arrest him. He must have found out. That's why he ran away without saying goodbye. To get home for Christmas. Better than a cell in Brixton.'

Elizabeth yawned and was asleep before Rose had opened the window and turned out the light.

As she walked slowly downstairs Rose let her mind dwell for a moment on the subject of young love: Cupid's sharp arrow had certainly not left in Elizabeth's heart the desperate and long healing wound described so often and so vividly in Hilda's Home Companion.

Whether the Baron Klaus Von Rimmer was a genuine agent for an armament firm or a professional spy they never found out as Richard Bellamy decided for private reasons to wash his hands of the whole business. Alfred's fate was a subject of whispered speculation in the servants' hall for years to come but no word ever came back from him and in time he was forgotten.

CHAPTER NINE

As Mr Hudson stood watching the Daily Mail magic lantern projecting the election results onto a huge screen in Trafalgar Square, it seemed to him that the end of the world had come. The Liberals were in with the unbelieveable majority of three hundred and fifty-seven. Two hundred and fifty Conservatives had lost their seats, Mr Balfour among them. For the first time twenty-nine Labour candidates had won seats in the House of Commons and Mr Hudson could almost smell the scorching wind that had produced the massacres in St Petersburg.

The only saving grace was the fact that Mr Bellamy had held his South London constituency, even though his majority was reduced by two thousand votes.

For many weeks after the election one hundred and sixty five Eaton Place was like a house in mourning; dinner parties invariably developed into post-mortems and the ladies who came to tea discussed the losses among their friends on the field of battle in solemn tones.

Elizabeth found it all very oppressing and she began to have headaches and attacks of dizziness. Though she would have denied it, Doctor Foley, the Bellamy family doctor, diagnosed the symptoms as the after effects of Elizabeth's unhappy love affair. The Bellamys had great friends called De Tocqueville who lived near Bordeaux and it was tactfully arranged that Elizabeth should spend the Spring and Summer helping the De Tocqueville children to master the English tongue.

When the new parliamentary session began Richard Bellamy found that many of the new government's ideas for reform rather appealed to him. He was strong for the control of sweated labour and had often felt that his own party had shelved educational reforms for far too long.

Lady Marjorie did not agree with her husband. For her Liberals had always been and would always remain the enemy. A strained atmosphere developed between husband and wife and for days they hardly spoke a word to each other.

One of the main sources of friction was Mr Augustine Birrell's Education Bill that began to make its slow way through the Commons in the early summer. At breakfast one day Bellamy mentioned quite casually that he favoured one section of the Bill and might well abstain from voting against it.

His wife's fierce condemnation of the idea surprised Bellamy and he was persuaded to promise that he would not make up his mind until he had had a word with one of the Conservative leaders, preferably Lord Southwold.

When he came back at teatime Lady Marjorie was waiting in the morning room.

'Well, how did you vote?' she asked immediately and it was clear it had been on her mind all day.

'My dear, there's no chance of a division for days,' said Bellamy, and smiled in a concilatory fashion.

'Did you talk to father?'

'He is still in the country.'

'Or Arthur Balfour?'

'No.'

Lady Marjorie made a noise in her throat that expressed displeasure.

'You promised you would,' she said.

'I said I would, if I met him, which I did not!' Bellamy replied rather losing his calm. 'Really, Marjorie, I don't think you realise the position now that we are in opposition and there won't be another election for at least four years. I am a perfectly ordinary common or garden backbencher.'

'A conservative nevertheless,' Lady Marjorie interposed.

'Yes. But backbenchers are supposed to show some

independence—to express their own opinions. I could quote Disraeli on the subject.'

Lord Southwold had been a backbencher himself in Disraeli's time.

'Anyway,' Bellamy went on, 'my own personal opinion is that this Bill is a good one in most respects. I've always been far from convinced that education should be a party political issue.'

'I know father has always thought that far too much time and money was spent on education,' Lady Marjorie retorted. 'Especially for working-class people, it can be a positive disadvantage.'

'Fine,' Bellamy replied, refusing to be taunted, 'he's entitled to his opinion. I'm entitled to mine. It's just that I don't happen to think it fair that Catholics and nonconformists should be excluded from Church of England schools.'

Lady Marjorie shrugged angrily. Catholics and nonconformists were nothing to do with the argument and her husband knew it.

'Please ring for tea, Richard,' she said stiffly. Bellamy rang the bell.

'All I am proposing to do is to abstain from voting against one small section of the Bill—a small personal gesture,' he explained with a cross shrug.

'It will be taken as a gesture of defiance against your own party,' Lady Marjorie replied.

Bellamy blew out his cheeks.

'Whatever happens, the Lords will throw the whole Bill out of the window, lock, stock and barrel. Your father and Lansdowne will see to that.'

It was quite true but hardly the most tactful moment to mention it.

Edward, Alfred's replacement, came into the room and Lady Marjorie asked him to bring up the tea. There was a shortage of footmen in London that spring and Edward, a cocky young man with doubtful references from rich trades people in Putney, had been engaged very much as a last resort.

Storms in the upper regions invariably produced similar weather in the servants' hall. The ladies in particular were never shy of voicing their opinions in the most definite terms.

'Well I think after all her ladyship's done for him it's disgraceful,' said Mrs Bridges as she sat down to eat her tea. 'There's some as got no gratitude.'

'Well I think she's cracked the whip once too often,' said Rose who usually took Mr Bellamy's side. 'And now the worm's turned.'

'There's little enough we can say or do will make any difference,' said Mr Hudson, the peacemaker, from the head of the table.

'She wants her tea,' said Edward from the door.

'Who's she, the cat's mother?' Mrs Bridges enquired sharply. She didn't like Edward.

Mr Hudson got up to put on his tail coat.

'They're still at it hammer and tongs,' Edward announced to the company.

'You show some respect my lad, or you won't last long in this house,' Mr Hudson warned him. 'And get the tray.'

'In my last place it was served by the parlour maid,' said Edward unwisely.

'The less we hear of your last place the better—from what I hear of it,' said Mrs Bridges.

Edward made a face behind her back.

'I suppose in your last place you didn't wear gloves!' Mr Hudson remarked as they went out.

The male servants out of the way, the ladies could really get down to it. Miss Roberts poured herself another cup of tea.

'I remember when Lady Marjorie first brought Mr Bellamy to Southwold; before they were even married,' she said confidentially. 'I said then there would be trouble one day; and I say it again now.' The ladysmaid leant back with a prim expression on her face.

'And that wasn't yesterday,' Mrs Bridges explained to the younger maids. 'I was a kitchen maid then like you are today, Emily.'

Emily was listening open-mouthed.

'Shut your mouth, you'll catch flies,' said Mrs Bridges before returning to the main theme. 'I remember old Nanny Lucas saying as she'd heard Lord and Lady Southwold weren't over pleased at all.' She lowered her voice as if the noble earl and his countess might be eavesdropping in the kitchen. 'In fact quite the opposite. And they had no cause to be neither. A parson's son when all's said and done. And that's not much catch, not for the eldest daughter of an earl and as lovely as any girl in England.'

'Oh she really was a picture in those days!' Miss Roberts agreed enthusiastically.

'But Lady Marjorie would have her way,' Mrs Bridges continued. 'Always has, always will I've no doubt.'

'You could say he wasn't really her class!' said Miss Roberts.

Rose wouldn't allow this slur.

'Mr Bellamy's a perfect gentleman,' she exclaimed indignantly.

'He wouldn't have got far without his Lordship finding him a safe seat I can tell you,' said Mrs Bridges.

'And this house and everything,' Miss Roberts added and tossed her head. 'Mr Bellamy hasn't got a penny to his name.'

Rose glared at the ladysmaid.

'I think sometimes the poor man's more of a servant than we are,' she said. 'I wouldn't blame him if he did turn Liberal—like Mr Winston Churchill. I mean after this election the Tories are finished anyway.'

'I'm Tory and proud of it. Don't you start telling me my party's finished,' Mrs Bridges warned Rose.

'It's not me that's joining the Liberals,' Rose answered heatedly.

'You're casting aspersions where you've no right,' said Mrs Bridges and Miss Roberts nodded her agreement. 'I'd give him a good whipping if he were mine.'

Ivy choked into her cup at the thought of Mrs Bridges whipping Mr Bellamy and provoked an angry glare from the cook.

'A fine old tory family like the Southwolds let down like that,' Mrs Bridges went on. 'It's wicked or worse.'

'But if it's his conscience that's bothering him,' Rose argued.

'If you're a Tory you don't need one,' said Mrs Bridges crushing Rose. 'You know you're right.'

Mr Hudson came back to resume his tea and the ladies lapsed into silence. They knew that the butler did not approve of political talk in the servants' hall, holding a firm opinion that politics were for gentlemen, and when common people became involved it invariably led to trouble and strife.

Unfortunately there was no such restraining influence upstairs. Lady Marjorie as usual had gained the upper hand.

'One stupid, unnecessary—you admit that yourself—unnecesary gesture, and you will ruin your chances of cabinet rank forever. People don't forget you know . . . and when we get back into power you'll be put aside. You won't be forgotten or forgiven.'

She might have been dressing down a servant; Mrs Bridges would have thoroughly approved.

'I don't see it that way,' Bellamy answered rather weakly.

'Well I do,' Lady Marjorie pounced on the lead he had given her. 'And so will they.'

She sat down looking thoroughly disgruntled. 'After all that's been done for you, Richard,' she said in a hurt, cross voice. 'It's so . . . so disloyal.'

The door opened and James Bellamy breezed in quite unaware of the relief he was bringing to his father. He had a friend with him, Captain Hammond of the Khyber Rifles, who he described as a 'real frontier Wallah' and asked his parents to entertain the young officer while he changed.

When Captain Hammond was introduced he presented a perfect picture of the Indian Army officer of romantic fiction; sunburnt, handsome, strong and silent.

As good manners dictated the Bellamys hastily buried their private hatchet and combined to try to put their guest at his ease. It was hard going.

Bellamy seemed on the way to success with a question about the Afridis and the seige of Chitral but it came to nothing.

'It must be very . . . very bleak out there,' Lady Marjorie suggested.

'Oh no,' Captain Hammond replied. 'It's really very jolly.'

Luckily they stumbled on the subject of opera and the gallant captain began to emerge from his shell. In India he had some records by Caruso but he had to admit that the Peshawar Amateur Operatic Society fell well short of Covent Garden. This reminded Lady Marjorie that she and her husband were going to a Royal Gala Performance of Tristan and Isolde the very next week. It also reminded Bellamy to his horror that a special meeting of the Ways and Means Committee had been called for that evening and he had forgotten to tell his wife.

Lady Marjorie was caught unaware.

'Really, Richard,' she said, how could you be so inconsiderate?'

They were all embarrassed by this unexpected outburst.

It was Richard Bellamy, ever the diplomat, who thought of the solution. He begged Captain Hammond to take his place and accompany his wife to the performance.

Captain Hammond readily agreed, indeed it would have been very difficult for him to refuse in the circumstances as Lady Marjorie pointed out to her husband later.

'He should be pleased as punch,' said Bellamy, rather proud of the neat way he had got himself out of a hole. 'Asked to take one of the most beautiful women in London to hear some of the greatest singers in the world.'

'He seemed rather nice,' said Lady Marjorie smiling at the compliment. 'Good for James.'

'Salt of the earth, men like Hammond,' said Bellamy. 'I sometimes wonder why we waste them leaving them to kick their heels on the far-flung frontiers of the Empire."

Lady Marjorie nodded thoughtfully.

'I wonder why they go out there in the first place,' she said.

A few days later when Captain Hammond escorted her to Covent Garden to hear Tristan and Isolde Lady Marjorie found out the answer to her question. He told her that from his earliest youth he had never got on with his father who, from his son's account, was a selfish brute. His parents' marriage had broken up when Hammond was still at school; his mother had died when he was up at Cambridge in the first year of a promising scholastic career. Utterly miserable and lost, he had pulled a few avuncular strings to obtain a direct commission in the Indian Army. In India he had found happiness and adventure and peace of mind.

Lady Marjorie asked him what it was like.

'On the frontier each step is on the brink of eternity.' He said.

The phrase appealed to Lady Marjorie, and listening to Charles Hammond talking with such enthusiasm about the wonderful places he had been to and the exciting times he had had fighting beside his beloved Pathans, simple loyal men after his own heart, she felt what a boring useless life she had led and what a shallow, worthless and spoilt society she lived in.

She soon discovered that Hammond knew a great deal about music and far more about the great singers of the day than she did herself. He had a strange original way of putting things.

He compared the soprano's voice to dawn on the frontier. 'You can see from Kabul in the West right round in an arc across Kashmir to the great Himalayas, blinding gold in the first light of the sun, the nearest three hundred miles away,' he said. 'Clean, hard, pure. That's what's important in life. Like the naked blade of a kukri, or the voice of a bird.'

A phrase from a poem learnt in the schoolroom came into Lady Marjorie's head.

'The same that oft-times hath charmed magic casements,' she quoted. 'Opening on the foam of perilous seas, in faery lands forlorn.'

Rather pleased with herself she looked up and saw his eyes. They were illumined by some inner light, the eyes of a visionary, searching her own with a desperate intensity.

Later that night in her boudoir as Miss Roberts undressed her and prattled some silly gossip about the King and Mrs Kepel, it was those eyes she remembered more than anything else of that strange exciting evening.

The next day a sheaf of red roses arrived for her and with them a little card in an envelope.

'Thank you for the happiest evening of my life. C.H.' it read. Lady Marjorie locked the note in her dressing table drawer.

The roses didn't go unnoticed in the servants' hall.

'From an admirer,' Rose explained.

'That's nice isn't it, at her age,' Edward remarked.

'It's only good manners—a token of esteem,' said Rose.

'Roses are symbolic, I've heard say,' Mrs Bridges hinted darkly from the basket chair beside the fire.

It was unusual that Lady Marjorie should insist on arranging the flowers herself but when Miss Roberts also saw her light the fire on a warm June day and burn the card in it the servants concluded that the little piece of pasteboard conveyed more than a formal token of Captain Hammond's esteem.

CHAPTER TEN

A few weeks later Lady Marjorie was in the book department of the Army and Navy Stores trying to find a suitable present for James's birthday. The assistant had just produced the latest novel by the Baroness Orczy, an adventure story about the French Revolution, when Lady Marjorie noticed a man with his back to her who seemed vaguely familiar. With a slight shock she realised it was Charles Hammond. He turned as if he could feel someone looking at him.

'I think you've been sent by Providence, Lady Marjorie,' he said. 'I've been searching for that quotation.'

For a moment she couldn't think what he was talking about; then she remembered. Together they found a copy of Keats's poems.

'Would you do me a great favour?' Hammond asked her. 'Would you read the poem to me?'

'Not here,' Lady Marjorie laughed rather nervously.

'No. Not here.'

If anyone before this day had told her that she would be asked to make one of the most important decisions in her life in the book department of the Army and Navy stores, Lady Marjorie would never have believed it. Yet she hardly hesitated.

'Yes,' she said. 'All right.'

For his stay in London Captain Hammond had taken one of those nondescript solid mahogany suited sets of bachelor's rooms that commonly abound in Ebury Street. Here, sitting on a worn easy chair, Lady Marjorie read aloud 'An Ode to a Nightingale'.

When she had finished Charles Hammond knelt beside her and taking her hand kissed it and told her that he found her the most beautiful and desirable woman in the world.

Nobody could accuse him of originality in his amorous approach nor could Lady Marjorie be said to have been completely taken by surprise; nevertheless she burst into tears. Tears of happiness.

Hammond dried her tears and guided her into the little bedroom with the conveniently large bed. There he undressed her and made love to her with an unexpected expertise. His bedroom skills had been acquired in the houseboats of Srinagar where his prowess as a lover was a byword among the ladies of the hill stations. Hitherto Hammond had despised his conquests in a game played with counterfeit currency and with a second-class sort of woman; now it was something close to worship. He was thrilled by the fierce passion of Lady Marjorie's response.

For a long time neither spoke a word and Lady Marjorie clasped his hard, lean body to hers. Far away in another world the traffic rumbled round Victoria Station. Then a clock struck four.

'Tea.' Said Lady Marjorie, suddenly restored to the world of reality. 'I must go or I shall be missed.'

'Not yet,' Hammond replied holding her tight. 'Oh my love, I am dazed by your beauty. How can a dingy set of rooms in dirty old London turn into Paradise?' he asked. 'Everything in this room will forever be unique. Just because of you.'

'It's our own private world,' Lady Marjorie whispered. 'Here we are safe, nothing can touch us. No one must ever know about it except us. If they do it will crumble and turn to dust.'

The delusion that their activities are wrapped in a cloak of invisibility is common among lovers. Normally Lady Marjorie would have realised that by dismissing her carriage and walking each afternoon from Eaton Place to Ebury Street 'on her own flat feet' as Edward put it, she was bound to cause comment among the servants. Nor would she have written a note to her lover at the desk in her boudoir and blotted it when it was still wet. But this was exactly what she did.

Miss Roberts changed the blotting paper daily and any piece that was clearly marked with ink she retained for further investigation.

In the servants hall Edward examined it in a mirror he kept for the purpose.

'Charles, my love,' he read, 'you are the light of my life.'

The younger servants had been excluded from such confidential and delicate business but Mrs Bridges, Miss Roberts and Rose now crowded round to read the exciting words for themselves.

'Well I never,' said Mrs Bridges, putting on a pretence of being shocked. 'She's nearly old enough to be his mother!'

'Passion strikes where it pleases,' said Miss Roberts. 'It's in the blood—look at Lady Helena, the one they call the Bolter. She was her aunt, wasn't she?'

'That was before your time, Rose,' said Mrs Bridges. 'And it's best to draw a veil over it.'

'You can't blame her, can you? You only live once and she can't be getting much from Mr B.' said Edward reasonably. 'It's only human nature. Twenty-seven years always the same pudding . . .'

Sensing that something was going on Mr Hudson came pussy footing in from his pantry.

'Edward!' he scolded. 'How dare you speak like that. Disgusting. Dirty. I thought as much from . . .'

He broke off at the sight of the blotting paper and the mirror and walked slowly over to examine them as if they were clues in a particularly distasteful crime.

'I'm shocked,' he exclaimed in a low voice, looking round accusingly. 'I am deeply shocked.'

'We're all shocked,' said Mrs Bridges. 'It's about time this all came out in the open. I don't hold with shovelling muck under the carpet.'

'And dirty minds find muck where there is none,' Mr Hudson reproached her.

'I'll thank you to listen to me, Mr Hudson. Not half an hour ago I was coming back from my friend in Pimlico when I happened to catch sight of Lady Marjorie alighting from a hansom cab outside a certain house in Ebury Street where there is suites of gentleman's rooms.' Mr Pearce had confirmed that they were Captain Hammond's rooms. She had it all chapter and verse.

'You lot ought to set up an agency for minding other people's business,' was all Hudson could find in reply. 'You'd have Sherlock Holmes beat any day.'

'We don't like it, Mr Hudson,' said Rose. 'None of us do. But you've got to face facts. Lady Marjorie's gone off the rails, and there's likely to be the hell of a crash. Mr Bellamy's a mild enough mannered man but he won't stand for this; nor will Society. It will be the scandal of the year, and this house and this family will be blown to bits and us with them. And we're frightened.'

'And we've cause to be,' added Mrs Bridges nodding her approval.

Mr Hudson stood at the end of the table.

'Now listen to me all of you,' he said. 'What Lady Marjorie or Mr Bellamy choose to say or do in their private lives is absolutely no business of ours. We should not enquire into it, far less question it. Our duty is to do our jobs as best we can and be loyal to our employers. We work for a fine family, people of quality, high up in the world, and no breath of scandal has ever touched this house in my time.'

He was forgetting the Royal Academy affair but in the circumstances it was understandable.

'If it does,' he went on, 'if it does, it is not going to be through the servants. Not while I'm still here.'

He took hold of his lapels and looked at them over his glasses.

'Chattering, whispering servants spread scandal like rats with the plague. It is mischievous, wicked, evil. I'm surprised at you.

He looked at them again, each in turn, and they lowered their eyes.

'If disaster comes to this house through the chattering of your senseless loose tongues,' he thundered, 'we'd all better be dead for the shame of it.'

He picked up the blotting paper and tore it into small pieces.

Unlike those happy lovers trapped forever in the marble of a Grecian urn, Charles Hammond and Lady Marjorie soon found it was not enough for him to love and she be fair. The realisation of this cruel fact led to their first quarrel.

'Our love is such an all-embracing thing,' said Hammond pacing restlessly round and round the sitting room. 'It can't live and breathe forever within these two little rooms.'

'Outside it would be destroyed,' Lady Marjorie replied. 'Burnt like a moth in a candle and left charred and dying.'

There was an unhappy silence.

'Charles you know the rules.'

'Damn the rules,' he cried impatiently. 'We make our

own rules.' He pressed his hands to the window like a caged animal. 'Oh I know the rules all right. Your rules. It's all right if you're not found out. Your friends would know about it of course, and snigger and gossip behind our backs. We should be asked to the same weekend parties, given adjoining rooms . . .'

He suddenly ran to her and knelt beside her. 'That's not our sort of love, my darling, a beastly furtive humbugging society sort of thing.'

'I don't think I could face divorce.' She said weakly.

'Divorce is only for vulgar people,' Hammond quoted bitterly. 'Another of those previous rules.'

'Don't be cruel, Charles.'

Lady Marjorie felt for her handkerchief in case she was forced to resort to tears. But they weren't necessary; as her lover begged her to forgive him and then asked her to listen carefully. He explained that he had been spending every waking moment thinking and planning their future. He had decided that he would leave the army and they would go abroad somewhere and start a wonderful new life. They would see the world, have great adventures and together open magic casements. Taking her hand he dedicated his life to Lady Marjorie then and there; she was his love, his life, his inspiration.

Lady Marjorie was deeply moved by Captain Hammond's devotion but even though her head was in a whirl of excitement, somewhere at the back of her mind she could hear that cool, calculating, spoil-sport voice of commonsense telling her that this was the stuff that only dreams are made of.

'Let us stay a few more hours in our secret paradise,' she begged. 'Just a little more time.'

She had her way, but they both knew that they had gone too far to turn back and the events of the next few hours or weeks or days would surely change both their lives.

It was the day of the Guards Boat Club Regatta at Maidenhead and James Bellamy had told his parents that he was taking a party, including his friend, Charles Hammond.

In the late afternoon Bellamy left the chamber and went into the Member's smoking room to have a drink and a cigarette. He was glancing at the evening paper when his eye was caught by an announcement in the stop press.

'Tragic accident mars Guards Regatta. Canoe goes over weir. Officer feared drowned.'

Bellamy knew that Mr Hudson always brought up the evening paper with his wife's tea and that she would immediately take the victim to be her son.

Having made enquiries and found out that the officer in question was alive and well and not in any case in James's regiment, Bellamy rushed back to Eaton Place to put her mind at rest.

On entering the morning room he found Captain Hammond apparently on the same errand of mercy as himself and his wife in a state bordering on collapse in that officer's arms.

At that time it seemed perfectly understandable that in her relief after the shock Lady Marjorie had nearly fainted and Captain Hammond had been giving her support to save her from falling. Later in the evening when Bellamy met James he took him to task for his behaviour.

'Your mother was terribly upset when she heard the news—very upset indeed. It was very thoughtful of Hammond to come so soon to put her mind at rest but not very thoughtful of you. You could have rung up at least.'

'But father, I didn't go near the Regatta,' James replied with righteous indignation. 'The adjutant got the colly-wobbles and I had to take his place on a blasted court of enquiry. I telephoned mother all about it before lunch.'

It was only then that the truth, or something like it, dawned on Richard Bellamy.

Like the pieces of a jigsaw puzzle small things that up till now he had taken for granted built a picture in his mind. The new hats, the sudden lack of interest in the Education Bill, the far away smile with which his wife had been greeting him on his return from Parliament.

These signs which Richard Bellamy had welcomed as an indication that the cloud which had been casting a shadow on their marriage had at last blown over now appeared in a more sinister light. His wife's interest had indeed been elsewhere—with Captain Charles Hammond.

After breakfast the next day Lady Marjorie was opening her letters at her desk when her husband came into the room.

'Aren't you going to the House this morning?' she asked brightly, more for something to say than anything else.

'Yes,' Bellamy replied. 'Yes I am—later.' He seemed ill at ease.

'Have you a few moments, my dear?'

'Yes of course.'

'I want to talk to you. Very seriously—about us.'

Lady Marjorie gasped. How had he discovered? She wasn't ready. She had no explanation prepared. Now she couldn't escape. She went and sat on the sofa beside her husband, feeling quite dazed, hoping he wouldn't notice her dismay.

'The House will be voting on the Education Bill tomorrow, sometime after tea,' said Bellamy.

'Oh,' she replied. The subject was so unexpected that she could hardly take it in.

'The next bit I find very difficult to say,' Bellamy continued, and Lady Marjorie's heart sank again. 'Even though I've been rehearsing it for days.'

She braced herself for the worst.

'I have been pigheaded, obstinate, ungrateful,' Bellamy said slowly and his wife again stared at him in disbelief. 'Ungrateful to you and to your father and your family. After all the party and Arthur Balfour have done for me it was a monstrous impertinence even to think of abstaining. I shall vote against the Bill like the good Tory and the good husband I hope I am!'

Lady Marjorie put her hand on her husband's arm in relief.

As you put it yourself, Marjorie,' he continued, 'it is a simple question of loyalty. That is the most important thing in our lives. Much more than our passing whims.' He smiled gently. 'Or passions.'

He got up and kissed her gently.

'Will you be back for dinner?' she asked as he went.

'Afraid not. We'll be at it hammer and tongs till all hours.'

Lady Marjorie spent the rest of the day walking in the Park. In the afternoon she delivered a note to Ebury Street. It was an invitation to Charles Hammond to meet her at the opera; by chance it was again Tristan and Isolde.

He didn't appear till the last act and when he arrived Lady Marjorie took him to the back of the box.

He held her in his arms in the dark.

'I can't go on with it, Charles,' she blurted out.

Hammond dropped his hands, quite stunned.

'What . . .! Has your husband found out? I was an idiot to come to your house. I knew it.'

'No,' Lady Marjorie answered quietly. 'I've found out, Charles. About myself.'

Hammond shrugged his shoulders in irritation. 'But only two days ago you said you couldn't live without me . . . ?'

'Poor darling. I don't know that I can. But I must try.' She held him tight. 'I still love you as much as ever,' she said. 'If only I didn't have to hurt you so. I'm a weak cowardly woman. I haven't your courage. I could never follow you. I'd pull you down into those perilous seas forlorn. My roots are too deep. And the cruellest thing, Charles, is that it is only through your love that I have come to see what a selfish useless person I really am. I have a husband who has been unfailingly faithful, thoughtful to me for twenty-seven years. Children to love me; loyal devoted servants who work out their lives to please my slightest whim.' She looked up at him. 'I haven't given much back in exchange.'

The sad dramatic music of the last act rose in a crescendo.

'I'm sorry that I've been so thoughtless . . . it's a silly word, but I can't think of a better one.'

When he tried to protest she shook her head.

'Charles, when . . . when you fall in love with the girl you will marry,' she began.

'No. Never again,' Hammond protested vehemently.

'Yes. You will. She will be a lucky girl. But don't put her on a pedestal. We are all frail, uncertain, hard to please. None of us are near perfect. It won't be fair on her—or on you.'

He nodded sadly understanding that in trying to excuse all womankind she was really trying to excuse herself.

Lady Marjorie was near to breaking point. She had planned her speech to the last word but it now seemed more difficult than she had thought.

'I have loved you as I have never loved a man before,' she whispered. 'You . . . you have fanned the dying embers of my heart to flame.' It was a phrase she had read somewhere in a poem and had written in the little book she kept for such things.

'These few weeks spent in our secret world have been wonderful . . . wonderful days.'

'The most wonderful days.' He forced a smile.

'They are our treasure,' she continued. 'Ours for always, locked away inside us. Nobody else knows of it.'

'Only we have the key to open that magic casement. And when things are bad, I shall open mine and look out and see your dear face and all my troubles will vanish.'

She pressed her head into his shoulder to conceal her tears. Hammond kissed her hair.

Taking a small box from his pocket, he pressed it into her hand.

'This is for you.'

Lady Marjorie stood back and opened the box. Through her tears she saw a little pendant brooch made of a single ruby in the shape of a heart.

'Goodbye, my only love,' she said and fled from the box.

The last act of the opera was coming to an end and Isolde was singing the Liebestod over her lover's dead body.

Charles Hammond remained where he was standing for

a full minute, then turned and sat in one of the chairs facing the stage. As Wagner's great aria to love and death swept over him, the tears began to stream down his cheeks, falling onto his stiff white shirt.

Richard Bellamy's intervention in the Education Bill debate on behalf of the Conservative Party has gone down in history as one of the greatest successes of his political career and was one of the factors that would eventually elevate him to full Cabinet rank. Messages of congratulation poured into the house in Eaton Place and when James came in before lunch to add his own plaudits, he had another piece of news to tell his parents.

'You remember old Charlie Hammond,' he said to his parents. 'Most extraordinary fellow. Suddenly decided to dash back to his Pathans at half an hour's notice. We just got him on the Liverpool train by a whisker.'

Bellamy glanced at his wife. There seemed no reason for comment.

'Ivor Finlay had a story he'd been jilted by some girl,' James laughed at the thought. 'Of course none of us believe it. If you'd ever seen old Charles with a girl—so frightened he could hardly open his mouth!'

Richard Bellamy went over and took his wife's hand.

'You look rather tired, my dear,' he said. 'It's this stuffy old London. Why don't you go down to Southwold for a week or two; the roses are at their best just now.'

'I think perhaps I will,' she replied gratefully.

Time and the restful beauty of Southwold soon combined to heal Lady Marjorie's wounded heart. At the end of July Richard Bellamy and James came down to join the house party for Goodwood; then there was Cowes and Scotland; Lady Marjorie immersed herself again in the usual round of social activity.

When things were upsetting her or when some piece of news disturbed her peace of mind she would take out the little ruby heart and remember Charles's dear face and all her troubles would vanish. As time passed she took out the heart less and less and the memory of the dear face became more difficult to place in focus. But one aspect of her affair would always please Lady Marjorie: no one except herself and Charles Hammond would ever know about it; not even her husband or her servants had ever suspected.

A few years later she happened to see in The Times that Major Charles Victor Hammond, V.C., The Khyber Rifles, had been killed in a border incident near a place called Landi Khotal. He had never told her of his decoration. How typical of him, she thought with a fond smile, but the pangs were no more than the bitter sweet memory of a summer's day long ago.

CHAPTER ELEVEN

The Bellamys, like many families in that year of 1906, were split on the subject of the motor car. Lady Marjorie took the old fashioned view that the new machines were dirty, noisy and continuously breaking down, but her husband was inclined the other way, pointing out that many constituency agents strongly believed that the preponderence of mechanised Liberal candidates had substantially affected the outcome of the general election. In his support for the internal combustion engine Mr Bellamy was strongly backed by Mr Pearce, who was after all, the head of the transport department.

Motor cars were expensive. To be precise the sort of motor car Mr Pearce considered worthy of his employers was expensive—at least seven hundred pounds—and Lady Marjorie held the strings of the money-bags.

Already once that summer the money-bags had to be opened wide, for in August and September the house had been wired for electric light from attic to cellar: even the bells had been electrified.

In the late autumn the Bellamys went to a levée at Buckingham Palace and the Duchess of Portland who was in waiting, told Lady Marjorie that the King had just purchased a motor made by Renault Frères of Billaincourt near Paris. It seemed appropriate that the Bellamys should follow this royal example and by doing so make a further gesture of their confidence in the 'Entente Cordiale'.

Mr Pearce was delighted; he had spent his half day at the Motor Show at Olympia and he too favoured the Renault, but for different reasons. He liked the water-cooled vertical cylinders and the high tension magneto ignition, not to mention the four forward gear speeds capable of propelling the machine at an incredible forty-five miles an hour.

One day in November, to the disgust of Mr Hudson and Mrs Bridges and the delight of Edward and Rose, Mr Pearce arrived outside the house in Eaton Place dressed in a brand new chauffeur's livery, sporting goggles, gauntlets and black leggings, at the wheel of a magnificent shiny royal blue three-litre twenty horse-power Renault limousine.

The Royal Family soon gave another indication that it was determined to keep up with the times when Queen Alexandra herself began to take an interest in the welfare of domestic servants. An eminent duchess was heard to announce that because the Queen had the misfortune to be a foreigner she would never learn the manners of the British.

As an example to ladies in society Her Majesty gave a tea party for four hundred maids in Regents Park. Unfortunately it rained so hard that the guests had to take shelter under the tables and the Bishop of London's speech on behalf of Her Majesty was all but obliterated by the collapse of the banner of welcome; but it was the thought that counted.

Ladies began to come together in groups and committees to discuss how they could best follow the Queen's lead without either spending to much money or giving their servants too many of the wrong ideas.

Lady Marjorie arranged a meeting in Eaton Place made up of her friend Lady Prudence Fairfax, old Lady Templeton who was too mad to organise anything herself, and a Mrs Van Groeben. Mrs Van Groeben's presence in the Bellamys house could be said to be yet another sign of the changing times and changing standards, for Mrs Van Groeben was really a very common vulgar sort of a woman and it was said that Mr Van Groeben had found her behind a bar in Capetown. The reason that Richard Bellamy had asked his wife to receive her in the first place was not only that Mr Van Groeben was a friend of Sir Ernest Cassel who in turn was a great friend of King Edward, but also he was very rich and especially generous in his support of the Conservative Party.

The ladies of Lady Marjorie's committee met every Wednesday for tea. Their arrival was quite a treat for Emily who could just see up into the street by leaning across the sink in the scullery and screwing her neck. Most of all she loved to watch the arrival of Mrs Van Groeben's beautiful carriage with its fine pair of matching chestnut horses.

'She must be awful rich,' she said to Rose one day. 'Will you look at those feathers? They must be twice as long as my arm.'

'You don't measure a lady by the length of her feathers, Emily,' Rose answered primly.

'I'd say she has a dress for as many days as there are in the year,' Emily went on dreamily. 'And Rose, look at that boy. Isn't he the most handsome one you've ever seen?'

Emily was referring to William, Mrs Van Groeben's footman who wore the most colourful uniform and always sat on the box when Mrs Van Groeben went out in her carriage.

Emily began to spend half the week longing for Wednesday to come round and she became so besotted with the thought of William that it began to affect her work. One dreadful day in her forgetfulness she put salt in the sugar jar, with the result that one of Mrs Bridges special puddings was completely ruined.

'That's what comes of staring out of the window all day at the carriages and that,' Mrs Bridges raged. 'Day-dreaming.' And she told Emily to scrub the whole kitchen floor anew although she had only half finished the washing up.

To make matters worse Ivy had had to go home to look after her sick mother and Emily was supposed to help Rose with the fires and the beds in addition to her normal duties.

'I can't manage it all, Rose,' she complained. 'I don't know if I'm coming or going. What with Mrs Bridges getting at me an' all.'

'You'll just have to learn to put up with it,' Rose replied unhelpfully. 'And just stop your dreaming or you'll find yourself in real trouble.'

But Emily continued to dream of William every day and on Sundays at Mass she prayed that she might meet him.

One day it came on to rain very hard while the ladies were in session and William was brought in to shelter. The servants were having their tea and he sat down at the end of the table opposite Emily.

The object of her admiration was so close that she dared not look up.

At the other end of the table Mr Pearce and Mr Harris, Mrs Van Groeben's aged coachman, were engaged in a long discussion on the respective merits of the carriage and the motor car.

Emily screwed up all her courage. 'Would you ever pass me the sugar, please?' she said to William. He actually smiled at her as he gave her the bowl.

A few moments later they both put their hands out for the same biscuit and they touched. Again he laughed and this time Emily smiled back. The ice was broken.

Before he left, William suggested to Emily that if she had nothing better to do on her next day off she might like to have a cup of tea with him.

Nothing so wonderful had ever happened in her life before and Emily could only put it down to the power of prayer.

William met Emily the following Friday at the corner of Eaton Place and Belgrave Place. Emily had never even seen Buckingham Palace, so at her suggestion they walked completely round it before going to a tea-shop in

Victoria kept by a friendly woman who understood the needs of impoverished young servants.

Emily had made a great effort with her appearance. She had big brown eyes and a beautiful clear complexion and when her long thick hair had been arranged by Rose she really looked very presentable.

After they had finished their first two cups of tea and had eaten the hot scones, William read aloud from True Life Stories. When he came to a very exciting bit, Emily found his hand under the table and gripped it tight. When he finished she sighed contentedly.

'You've awful good luck, William,' she said.

'I suppose I have,' he admitted.

'Being able to do both the reading and the writing,' Emily explained. 'I can't manage the writing at all, 'tis a terrible disadvantage. Now if my dada could have read and writ, I don't know what he couldn't have done.'

'What did he do? Your pa?' William asked, curious because he had never known one himself.

'He went and died on us, that's what he did,' said Emily sadly.

'Oh I am sorry,' William replied. 'How did he die?'

'He died from living,' said Emily. 'That's how he died.'

And she went on to tell William all about conditions in Ireland and about all her starving relations out there.

'We're the lucky ones,' she said.

'Lucky? What's lucky?' William asked indignantly. 'I do my job well, I please Mrs Van Groeben. She likes the way I look.' He said this because he knew it made Emily jealous. 'What's the luck in that?' he asked her again.

'The luck is—it was you she took from the orphanage,' she said. 'The bad luck would have been if she had not. Was it herself who taught you all the reading?'

William shook his head.

'The orphanage,' he admitted. 'Mind you, she's teaching me other things. Things she thinks I ought to know. How to get on. How to behave. She's a proper lady.'

And here William demonstrated just how ignorant he was of the ways of proper ladies.

'They say she thinks the world of you,' said Emily

rather sadly and William preened himself. He liked flattery. He was really rather a dull, stupid conceited young man but he was all the world to Emily and as spring came she fell more and more in love with him.

The days grew warmer and they took to walking in the park. One evening in early May they were sitting on a bench and Emily explained that her name wasn't really Emily, but Aoibhill, and that she had been named after an Irish Queen.

William had been taught to take the Irish with a pinch of salt.

'I didn't know they had kings and queens in Ireland,' he said sceptically.

'Ah sure you hardly know a thing, William,' Emily replied. 'You never even knew you were to meet me.'

'Meet you?' he asked blankly.

Quite often William didn't understand what Emily was talking about.

'That it was destined. Preordained,' Emily explained. 'I was always certain of meeting you. When I saw you that day in the kitchen, I knew, I knew you. You're more to me than my love, William, you're my need, you're my very self.'

When Emily went on like this William always felt ill at ease.

She took his hand.

'Ah William,' she said fondly. 'Everything that I do, I do it for you. Everything that I have to do in the house I imagine that I do it for you. Each fire that I lay, each floor that I scrub, each spoon that I polish is yours. I have you imagined all day.'

'If it wasn't for Mrs Van Groeben, I'd run away with you tomorrow,' said William anxious not to disappoint.

'Sure where would we run to?' asked Emily. 'The world's full of running people.' She thought for a moment. 'Maybe you could get a job,' she said hopefully. 'You can read and write and you're strong.'

Even as she said it she knew it was a hopeless idea. There was terrible unemployment in London and William had told her that Mrs Van Groeben had promised to make him her butler one day. More and more Mrs Van Groeben seemed to her to stand like a great colossus in the path of their happiness.

'Do you love me, William?'

Emily had never dared to ask this before, but suddenly it seemed terribly important to her to know exactly where they stood.

'You know I do,' he replied. 'I think you're the prettiest girl I've ever seen.'

'But do you have a passion for me?' she asked, 'Or do you just think I'm the prettiest girl you've ever seen?'

William thought quite hard.

'Yes,' he said. 'Yes. I really do love you.'

They were both uncomfortably aware of the lack of conviction in his voice.

'I have a passion, William, a passion for you. And I never thought I would ever know such a fine thing as this passion I have for you. There was nothing in my life before you, William. Really nothing. And now it hurts me because it is so fierce.'

'We'll be all right,' William said weakly. 'I'll look after you, Em.'

'How?' Emily asked bleakly. 'How would you do it? What can we do, Willy, sure there's no place for us.'

William shrugged. Emily seemed to delight in looking on the black side of things.

'You're a sad little thing sometimes, Emily,' he said.

'Wouldn't you be?' she asked him. 'I have nothing in the world but you. My mama's dying in the poorhouse. Phelim's in America and me other brother was killed in the African war—God keep him. Two of my sisters died before they could walk and of the two that did survive one is in orders and the other's ran off with a horse-dealer. The dada's dead these two years. There's precious little to write down on the slate.'

It was getting dark and he put his arm round her to comfort her and she nestled tight into his shoulder.

After a while he asked her if he might kiss her.

'We shouldn't do it. It's wrong,' she said. 'But I have such a passion for you, William.'

And for the first time they kissed.

Mrs Van Groeben had been taught in South Africa to look upon servants as household goods and she was consequently very possessive in her attitude to them. She had also developed a very effective secret service in her house based on the usual combination of fear and bribery.

Thus the bootboy first told the head housemaid about William and Emily in the hope of getting the footman's place and the housemaid told Mrs Van Groeben in the hope of being given a rise.

Mrs Van Groeben wasn't over concerned. She knew William too well. She sent for him when she was in her boudoir and made him stand near the dressing-table while she combed her hair.

She knew that he worshipped her and was at his most manageable under such susceptible and intimate conditions.

She pointed out quite kindly that there were more important things in life than a kiss and a cuddle with a scullery-maid. She made him understand that it wasn't very sensible behaviour from someone who wanted to get on; then she changed the subject to that of William's uniform

She reached out a slim bare arm and felt the lapel of his tail coat.

'This uniform is rather frayed and worn,' she said looking up at him and letting her wrap fall open just a very little.

'Yes, madam,' William replied. They both knew it was nothing of the kind.

'You're such a smart boy I think we'll have a new one made for you,' she said in her rather thick Cape-Dutch accent. 'You could help me choose the material and the colour. Would that be nice, do you think?'

William smiled back like a cat who has been promised a saucer of cream.

'Poor old Mr Harris, he's getting on. He can't do as much as he would like, so I think the person who's going to help him deserves a nice new uniform, don't you, William?'

'Yes,' madam,' Wiliam replied dutifully.

'And that other thing. There's no need to think about that anymore. It doesn't amount to anything now, does it?'

Mrs Van Groeben turned and gave the footman her special smile.

'No, madam, nothing,' William assured her. 'Just a bit of fun.'

Lady Marjorie didn't approve of interfering in her servants' private lives in the usual way but after Mrs Van Groeben had talked to her on the telephone about her footman and Emily, she decided that it would be kinder to make the position quite clear to Emily herself.

It was an agonising interview. As Lady Marjorie explained as kindly as she could that Emily mustn't see William again or he would be sacked without references, Emily stood stiff as a ramrod with fists clenched, bewildered and shocked.

'You are both very young,' Lady Marjorie said. 'You have your whole lives ahead of you.'

Emily managed to blurt out, 'Yes m'lady.'

'It will heal, that hurt I am sure you are feeling now,' Lady Marjorie went on. 'You will learn to put it out of your mind. A passion spends itself very quickly. Believe me.'

It should have been of great comfort to Emily that her mistress was so kind and sympathetic and had indeed been through something of the same agony herself but unfortunately she couldn't put William out of her mind and her passion for him refused to spend itself. It anything the ache in her heart grew worse until it became so unbearable that she decided that in spite of everything she must make some sort of contact with her beloved.

Rose, trying to comfort her, agreed to write a letter.

'What do you want me to write, Emily?' Rose asked, when she had the paper and pen ready.

'Dear Mother of God, I can never think of letters,' said

Emily. 'I have no mind for the written word, Rose. Put "William".' But try as she might she couldn't think of a single other word.

'Dear William,' Rose suggested, beginning to write. 'We have been forbidden to see each other, but I still love you and think of you every day.' How is that for a start?'

She pursed her lips in thought.

'Then "If you love me . . . '

'No Rose,' said Emily and touched Rose's arm to stop her. 'Just write these words,' she said. 'You are all that's left on the slate. Say you love me. Aoibhill.'

'What's that?' Rose asked. 'Your name?'

Emily nodded.

'How do you spell it?'

Emily hung her head. 'I don't know,' she admitted. 'Then you'd better put "Emily", so.' She looked away. 'I just want to know he's still there,' she said.

And now, when Emily needed her svmpathy most, Mrs Bridges seemed to take a delight in giving the wretched girl the rough edge of her tongue, harrying and bullying her from morning to night.

'Still no sign of your fancy boy,' she taunted one morning when Emily was scrubbing the kitchen floor. 'He won't turn up now, you know, they never do once they've had a sniff. They're all alike every man jack of them—only wanting one thing—thev want to tamper with you—that's what they want to do. They want to put their nasty red hands all over you. All over. Did Willy want to do that? Eh, Emily?'

And when Emily tried to escape to the scullery Mrs Bridges followed her.

'Of course it wasn't like that was it? We were going to get married weren't we? And live happily ever after?'

Mrs Bridges put her hands on her hips and came close to Emily.

'And where was you going to go Emily? Employers don't approve of their servants wanting to get married you know. And with no references who's going to want an ignorant little Irish waif like you? A girl who can do nothing right. Nothing.'

And in the end Emily ran out of the room in tears straight into Rose's arms.

'You been at her again, Mrs B,' Rose asked sharply.

'Just trying to teach her the facts of life, Rose,' Mrs Bridges answered with a shrug. 'A few facts of life.'

'Leave me be that's all,' Emily sobbed. 'Leave me be.'

Lady Marjorie and her committee had decided to hire a horse-bus and send their servants to Hampstead Heath for a picnic. The evening before the great day the food and drink contributed by the other three houses were delivered to 165 Eaton Place which was to be the starting place for the expedition.

Imagine Emily's joy when she saw her William actually carrying a hamper down the area steps helped by old Mr Harris. She waited while they put the hamper in the kitchen and then ran out into the passage and stopped in front of William. He walked past her without a single word. At first she thought that he hadn't recognised her in the dark passage but just as she was about to run after him Mr Harris stopped her.

'No point in rushing out there, lassie,' he said kindly and explained as best he could that William had new responsibilities which gave him very little spare time, in fact so little spare time that he hadn't even been able to read her letter.

Mr Harris produced the letter and gave it to Emily. It was unopened.

While the house was full of the excited chatter of the other servants preparing their finery for the outing Emily just sat on her bed staring at the letter on which had rested all her hope for the future.

Half the night she spent weeping and praying until at last she fell into a fitful uneasy sleep with the letter still clutched in her hand.

The next day the horse bus was due at one thirty so servants' hall dinner was early. Emily didn't eat a thing but this didn't surprise anyone as they were all too excited thinking about the tea to do much eating. Emily and Rose had hardly cleared the table before the bus arrived and with it servants from the other three houses and suddenly all was hustle and bustle. Although he was not himself going on the expedition. Mr Hudson as host butler supervised the male servants in loading the food and drink onto the top of the bus. The various housemaids, kitchen maids and scullery maids clambered inside and immediately began to chatter like jays and sing songs.

At the last moment when all was ready Mr Hudson couldn't find Emily and Rose was despatched to hurry her up.

She found her hanging dead from a beam in her attic room.

Mr Hudson rose to the tragic occasion magnificently. Within seconds of Rose telling him the terrible news he had extricated the Bellamy servants from the bus and sent it on his way. Wisely Lady Marjorie left everything in his care. It was Mr Hudson who set the other servants tasks to keep them occupied and prevent them chattering together; it was Mr Hudson who arranged with his friend Sergeant Williams from Gerald Row police station that the necessary report was handled with the minimum of fuss and publicity. It was Mr Hudson who identified the body in the absence of known relatives and it was Mr Hudson who saw to it that the men whose business it was to deal with the bodies of such unfortunates came with their plain van early in the morning when the inhabitants of that most respectable neighbourhood would be least disturbed.

It could be argued that Mr Hudson performed all these tasks so swiftly and tactfully because it was his duty to do so and because the suicide of one of the staff cast a slur on the household and especially upon its butler; but he was not a man lacking in humanity.

Mr Hudson had been very fond of Emily and it grieved him deeply to discover that such a good and devout girl would not be buried in consecrated ground and that like as not after the autopsy her body would be sent to a hospital for the doctors to use in their researches. The argument put forward by one of the undertakers that in this way Emily might benefit humanity did not appeal to Mr Hudson.

A great depression settled over the servants hall and although they tried not to talk about her, Emily seemed present in everything they said and did much more than she ever had been when she was alive.

The servants condemned William to damnation and Lady Marjorie severed all contact with the Van Groebens but the real cause of Emily's tragic death was her own nature being too sensitive to cope with the hard world in which she lived. If William had agreed to marry her they would have stood no chance of being employed in London either together or as a couple even with good references and if he had followed Emily's suggestion to try to find other work outside service, William would have found unemployment at one of the highest levels in history; a third of the nation were living below any normal human level of subsistence, destitution was commonplace and as yet there was no proper relief for the unemployed.

In the London of 1907 Emily's love for her footman was doomed from the start.

CHAPTER TWELVE

Emily's place was taken by a girl called Doris. She was a bright, tough sixteen-year-old cockney, the eldest of nine. Her father was a docker so that Mrs Bridges' scoldings and tantrums slid off her like water off a duck's back.

November was even foggier than usual and one morning when you could hardly see your hand in front of your nose and the oily yellow air was creeping everywhere into the house, Doris reported to Mr Hudson that she hadn't been able to give Mrs Bridges her early morning tea as her bedroom door was locked.

Mr Hudson sent Rose up to investigate and she reported that there were noises in Mrs Bridges' room but she could get no reply.

It had been Mrs Bridges' afternoon off the day before and, as she had been known to drown her sorrows in gin on occasions, they left her in peace and got on with upstairs breakfast themselves.

Ten o'clock came and time for Mrs Bridges' daily conference with her mistress.

At a quarter past ten when there was still no sign of the cook, Lady Marjorie sent for Mr Hudson to make some positive move in the matter.

It wasn't the first time Mrs Bridges had been late and for some time Lady Marjorie had endured the old cook's shortcomings because they in no way seemed to affect her cooking. This time she decided she would have to speak her mind.

As he was going up the last flight of stairs, Mrs Bridges passed Mr Hudson without saying a word. She looked rather tousled but otherwise none the worse for wear, so the butler decided to leave well alone.

When Mrs Bridges went into the morning room she was greeted by Lady Marjorie with a very curt, 'Good morning, Mrs Bridges.'

The cook didn't reply or bob-curtsey or give any indication that she had heard her mistress speak.

'I understand from Hudson that you've had no breakfast,' said Lady Marjorie.

'I'm not hungry, m'lady,' Mrs Bridges replied rather thickly. 'And it's no business of Hudson's.'

'I beg your pardon?'

'I said it's nothing to do with Hudson what time I come down in the morning.'

Lady Marjorie visibly stiffened.

'I'm afraid I don't agree, Mrs Bridges,' she said firmly. 'Hudson is responsible for the smooth running of this house.'

'And I'm responsible for the meals,' the cook grumbled.

'I know you are, Mrs Bridges. I expect you to be punctual in the servants' hall and set an example to the other servants.'

Mrs Bridges looked sullen.

'And I expect you to obey my rules. One of which is that I will not have the servants locking their doors, as you well know.'

Mrs Bridges didn't reply.

'Why was your door locked when Rose tried to rouse you?' Lady Marjorie demanded.

'I've a right to my privacy, m'lady, without the under servants poking and prying into my affairs,' Mrs Bridges said angrily, and sat down, without permission, in the presence of her mistress.

'Everyone's against me,' she moaned, 'talking and whispering behind my back. Saying as it's all my fault Emily did herself in. I know what they're saying. They're all against me.' She sniffed twice. 'I know I'm not wanted in this house, nor appreciated neither, so I'd best give in my notice and clear out. That's all I've got to say, m'lady, thanking you.'

Thoroughly persecuted and upset Mrs Bridges got up and began to shuffle towards the door.

'Mrs Bridges,' Lady Marjorie called sharply. 'Come back here. At once.'

Force of habit made Mrs Bridges stop and turn.

'I'm giving in my notice,' she repeated without conviction.

'You're doing nothing of the kind,' said Lady Marjorie. 'Now sit down and tell me what is the matter?'

Mrs Bridges sat down again and crossed her hands.

'I really can't say, my'lady, I'm sure,' she said.

Lady Marjorie waited, knowing that Mrs Bridges would pour out her troubles in her own good time.

'It's like this m'lady,' she said at last. 'I get these headaches. Sharp pains in my head. Everything seems to get on top of me. I can't seem to stop crying and I can't sleep for thinking of that poor dead child. If I scolded her some times it was only to teach her how to get on in service. I was trained by your mother's cook, m'lady, Mrs Arkwright.'

'I remember,' said Lady Marjorie.

'Well, she was strict enough,' Mrs Bridges went on. 'You've got to be firm with them. Then when little Emily . . . did away with herself, it was like I lost my own daughter . . .'

Overwhelmed with remorse Mrs Bridges burst into floods of tears.

'Would it surprise you to know that I too lie awake thinking about Emily?' said Lady Marjorie when the worst of the storm was over. 'It was a shock to us all and we must all try to forget about it,' she continued. 'You are among old friends here and certainly no one blames you in the least. So dry your tears and try to cheer up, Mrs Bridges.'

After Mrs Bridges had left the room clutching her menu Lady Marjorie sighed to herself. The cook was clearly undergoing the change of life and the next few months were not going to be easy for any of them. She thought with some trepidation of all the dinner parties she had planned and she wondered if she should ask Doctor Foley to see Mrs Bridges. She knew from experience that it was dangerous to bring a doctor to servants; they were very apt to imagine themselves worse than they really were.

Her reverie was interrupted by the entrance of Alice to attend to the fire. Ivy had never returned from her bed-ridden mother, so Lady Marjorie had engaged Alice in her place; she was a large cow-like girl with chilblains and impeccable references and very little charm.

Later in the morning the new under houseparlourmaid came into Mr Hudson's pantry in quite a state.

'There's a bumping coming from Mrs Bridges' bedroom,' she said breathlessly, 'and the door's locked. Do you think it can be thieves, Mr Hudson?'

Mr Hudson had had quite enough of Mrs Bridges' bedroom for one morning. He took the master key from his drawer and went upstairs. Alice followed him.

Sure enough there was a strange bump, bump, bump, coming from inside the room.

Mr Hudson was no coward. Telling Alice to stand well back, he borrowed her broom and quietly unlocked the door. Then, broom at the ready, he burst into the room ready to do battle.

A little baby was sitting on the bed bouncing happily up and down and banging on the wall.

The strange news sent a shiver of anticipation through the basement. Never before in anyone's memory had Lady Marjorie sent for Mr Bellamy to come back from the House of Commons; and now Mrs Bridges was in the morning room, and the baby in the servants hall, the centre of female attention.

'Fancy a baby at her age,' said Edward.

'Really, Edward,' Alice replied quite shocked. 'It's not humanly possible, surely you know that?' She wasn't yet used to Edward's idea of a joke.

'Well my mum's expecting her tenth,' said Doris.

'If you're anything to go by she can't be hardly human herself,' said Edward.

'Now you just mind your tongue,' said Rose, coming in with a baby's bottle full of milk.

'I expect it's some relative asked Mrs Bridges to mind it for her,' said Alice, who always went for a respectable solution. 'Poor little thing look how thirsty it is!'

The baby was gulping down the milk like a calf.

'I don't know why she didn't ask us to help in the first place.'

'Because it's not been honestly come by,' said Rose with conviction. 'That's why her door was locked. She's stolen that baby.'

'What'll happen to her?' Alice gasped.

'They'll shut her up same as they did my auntie,' Doris answered, wise in the ways of the criminal world. 'She did away with hers,' she added.

In the morning room Mrs Bridges was sitting in a crumpled heap by the fire, making her confession.

'I'd been visiting my friend in Pimlico, sir,' she said

to Mr Bellamy. 'The one who was cook to Lady Wallingford. Retired now. When I come across this pram outside a greengrocers. Such a lovely baby laying there, smiling at me, nobody minding it. I stooped you see, and touched its little hand.'

Mrs Bridges smiled at the memory.

'I couldn't help but touch it,' she continued. 'When its tiny fingers curled round mine, I felt I wanted to pick it up. Well, no harm after all, there was no one there.' She shrugged. 'I knew it was wrong, but I just had to do it, sir.'

She had taken the baby and wrapped it in its shawl and brought it straight back to Eaton Place. She couldn't remember the street. She couldn't remember the shop. Even the colour of the pram.

'What in Heaven's name made you do a thing like that?' Bellamy exclaimed. 'Have you thought of the parents of the child, what they must be going through at this very moment. The terrible anxiety?'

Lady Marjorie frowned at her husband. Shouting at Mrs Bridges wouldn't do any good in her condition. She rang for Mr Hudson and told him to escort the cook to her room.

'Of course the police will have to be informed,' said Bellamy when the door closed behind them.

'Richard, no!'

'But how else can we trace the child's parents?' asked Bellamy.

'I can't allow Mrs Bridges to be carted off to a women's prison or more likely a lunatic asylum, with the Curzons coming to dinner next week!'

Bellamy stared at her for a moment. 'How can you think of dinner parties at a time like this?' he asked flabbergasted.

'Because I have to, Richard,' his wife replied. 'I have to run this house and entertain important guests for your sake. How am I to do that without my cook?'

'I am trying to be patient with you,' Bellamy answered with maddening calm. 'A child has been stolen. By Mrs

Bridges. The parents have got to be traced and the child returned. That's all that matters.'

Lady Marjorie shrugged her shoulders. 'If we could find where it came from, we could send it back. With no fuss . . . with some kind of explanation of course.'

'Have you quite lost your reason?' Bellamy demanded. 'You're asking me to by-pass the normal course of the law in order to shield a person who is guilty of a criminal offence.'

Although it is generally agreed that women are less respectful of the laws of the land than men, in Lady Marjorie's case there was some excuse. Her family had been a law unto itself for many generations. As far as she was concerned, laws were made for people who broke them. Renegades and criminals. Not for her cook.

During Mrs Bridges' confession Lady Marjorie had been turning over a plan of action in her mind. She remembered Mr Hudson's friend, Sergeant Williams of Gerald Row Police Station, who had been so cooperative over Emily's death. Now was a chance for him to co-operate again. Mr Bellamy was very strongly against such an underhand course but when he found that his butler sided with his wife in the matter he reluctantly agreed to the plan.

Mr Hudson was away all the afternoon; the fog had turned to sleet and rain and it wasn't till nearly time to change for dinner that he returned, wet but triumphant. Sergeant Williams had let slip over a pint of beer that there was a report of a baby being kidnapped from a pram outside a greengrocers in Lupas Street the night before and Lupas street was on Mrs Bridges' route between her friend and Eaton Place. The baby belonged to people called Webber, lower middle class and quite respectable according to Sergeant Williams. They lived at 96a Vauxhill Bridge Road.

Abandoning all thought of dinner Lady Marjorie asked Mr Hudson to tell Mr Pearce to bring round the Renault immediately.

96a was the ground floor flat in a desolate newly built

charity block. When Mrs Weber opened the door Lady Marjorie swept inside carrying the baby.

'We've come to return your baby,' she explained with a gracious smile. 'He is quite unharmed. May we come in?'

Lady Marjorie in her sable coat and huge hat and veil and Richard Bellamy in his black coat with the astrakhan collar seemed oversize people from another world in the dingy room.

Mrs Webber was confused by the suddenness of it all, and the obvious importance of her visitors.

'We're not very tidy,' she said unhappily, then suddenly becoming aware that it really was her lost baby the beautiful lady was proffering to her, she rushed forward and took it in her arms with a little squeak.

Lady Marjorie smiled rather proudly at her husband.

A small pale young man came into the room from the back, hastily putting on his coat.

'Is that the baby back?' he said. Something was wrong with his adenoids.

'He's safe,' said Mrs Webber sobbing. 'Safe, Arthur. This lady and gentleman brought him back not a moment ago.'

Mr Webber turned to greet his guests.

'Well, we're very grateful I'm sure,' he said. 'Where was the child found?'

Lady Marjorie looked at her husband. Mr Bellamy produced his card. Webber studied it and nodded.

Bellamy then explained that one of their domestic staff had had an unfortunate lapse and that she regretted her conduct very much.

'What was her name? The woman who stole our kiddie?' Webber enquired very pointedly.

'I hardly think that is relevant, Mr Webber,' Lady Marjorie told him with a gracious smile. 'There is of course the question of compensation. After all we do appreciate that you and your wife must have suffered a great deal of anxiety.'

'We both feel you are entitled to some sort of restitution,' Bellamy added.

But Webber was one of those tiresome men who don't know when they are in luck. The sight of the considerable sum of money that Bellamy produced from his note-case in offer of compensation merely made the little man bristle like an angry dog.

'If people like you think you can buy your way out of having your underpaid and overworked servants had up in court you're very much mistaken,' he said aggressively.

'Who said anything about court?' asked Bellamy, with a conciliatory smile.

'The woman who stole our infant, Mr Bellamy,' Webber went on, 'is either a criminal or a lunatic. In either case, she ought to be behind bars, where she can't snatch any more babies from their prams. As for your offer of compensation, sir, I see from your card that you're a member of parliament. You should know better than to try to bribe a man to keep his mouth shut and impede the law.'

There was nothing really more to be said after that.

That the Bellamys should have run up such a determined troublemaker was pure bad luck. He was probably a Socialist in which case the offer of money in compensation had been a mistake, as those sort of people were notoriously touchy.

Nevertheless the Bellamys considered that when Mr Webber had got over the considerable shock of the whole affair he would be persuaded by his wife that on the whole it had been very lucky that the child had fallen into such good hands and he would be sensible enough to leave well done.

The next morning Rose and Alice were cleaning the morning room before breakfast using a new self-styled wonder of modern science 'The Aspirator Air Suction Cleansing Machine'. Alice pumped away at a pair of big bellows contained in a large wooden box on wheels while Rose directed a nozzle at the end of a pliable hose-pipe.

'What I can't understand is why Mrs Bridges hasn't

had the push. I mean, causing all that trouble,' said Alice.

'They can't afford to lose her, that's why. She's too good a cook,' Rose replied. 'Besides they took the kiddie back and that's the end of it.'

'It was a lark having it to care for. Dear little thing,' said Alice fatuously. 'I'd love to have a baby.'

'I expect your turn will come, one day. When it does, let's hope it's intentional.'

Alice was the most inoffensive of girls but some mornings she really got on Rose's nerves.

The front door bell rang. It was ridiculously early for visitors but Rose wasn't going to be caught cleaning whatever the hour. She and Alice rushed the heavy equipment out of sight down the backstairs just as Mr Bellamy came down and Mr Hudson answered the door.

It was Inspector Cape of Gerald Row demanding to speak to Mr Bellamy.

Inspector Cape was one of those keen aggressive modern officers who achieve success and promotion by their ruthless application of every letter of the law.

'On the evidence laid before me, it is my duty to take the woman calling herself Mrs Bridges in charge under the Offence Against Young Persons Act Of 1861,' he said, standing with open notebook in front of the morning room fire. It was quite clear from his manner that if Mrs Bridges had been cooking breakfast for King Edward himself it wouldn't have diverted the Inspector from his duty. Bellamy had no alternative but to tell Mr Hudson to withdraw Mrs Bridges from the stove as tactfully as possible and prepare her for the police station.

'May I ask you a question, sir,' said Cape. 'How did you know where to return the infant, seeing as how you failed to report your discovery to the police?'

'I don't care for your tone, Inspector,' Bellamy retorted, now thoroughly nettled as well as hungry.

'Don't you, sir?' Cape replied with something like a sneer. 'Well, I must remind you that failure to report the discovery of a felony can be taken as an accessory after the fact.'

In this case, however, the Inspector, having achieved the primary object of his visit, was prepared to treat Mr Bellamy with magnanimity and overlook the offence.

Mr Hudson produced Mrs Bridges in the hall and she was escorted out of the front door by a uniformed officer and the Inspector. 'The poor wretched woman, she might have been going to the guillotine,' the butler said later describing the pathetic scene to Rose.

As he made his way slowly into the dining room Richard Bellamy reflected that it was as well Inspector Cape had called to do his deed and departed before his wife's descent to break her fast.

Lady Marjorie was indeed extremely angry to find that one of the best cooks in London had been abducted from her house before breakfast with a large and important dinner party looming only two days ahead. The fact that her husband had been right about the police and she had been wrong did nothing to improve her temper.

Her first idea was to go straight to the Lord Chief Justice who was a friend of her father's and have the impudent Cape taken to task. Her husband was able to deter her from this Draconian method by the sensible suggestion that he himself would abandon his business in the House of Commons for the morning and go instead to see Sir George Dillon, their legal adviser and put the matter of Mrs Bridges' defence in his capable hands. Sir George briefed a young advocate called Mr Perry who came round to Eaton Place later in the day, having spoken to the cook. He was not very optimistic.

The Bellamys were most surprised when Mr Hudson craved an audience and offered himself as a witness for the defence and even more surprised when Mr Perry accepted his offer with alacrity.

The next morning Mrs Bridges was brought before the magistrates. In her best coat with the speckled fur collar and her brown Sunday hat she looked exactly like a flustered thrush.

When Mr Perry had made it clear to their worships that the plea of 'Not Guilty' put forward on Mrs Bridges' part was based on the momentary loss of responsibility on behalf of his client, he lost no time in calling on Mr Angus Hudson to take the stand.

Having taken the oath in a loud clear voice Mr Hudson looked round the court with composure. It may be remembered that he was no stranger to the Courts of Justice and that it was his firm conviction that had the circumstances of his birth been more propitious he could have been numbered among the stars of the legal orbit. Here was his chance to shine in that sphere and he siezed it with both hands. He began by explaining the unfortunate effect on Mrs Bridges of Emily's suicide.

'Being a very lonely person with no relatives or dependants, she had come to regard the dead girl as her own daughter,' Mr Hudson began. 'They were very close. I believe that Mrs Bridges is badly in need of affection and a sense of being wanted,' he went on warming to his theme. 'She is a brilliant cook, Your Worship, and most highly regarded in that capacity by my employers. But in the personal sense, she has no one to care for, and nobody to care for her or advise her or look after her.'

It seemed sensible to Mr Hudson for the sake of the case to ignore Mrs Bridges' elderly friend in Pimlico.

'For that reason,' he continued, taking both lapels, 'For that reason I have offered her my hand in marriage.'

He paused and looked round the court, pleased at the surprised gasp from the public gallery and the look of amazement on Mr Bellamy's face. Mrs Bridges stared hard at the brass rail in front of her nose. Mr Perry allowed himself a smile of satisfaction; he knew a good defence witness when he heard one.

'We are both single persons, Your Worship,' Mr Hudson continued when order had been restored, 'and it occurred to me that, if I could undertake to keep the accused lady happy and cared for in the future, during our continuing service with Lady Marjorie Bellamy and in later years, when we shall have perhaps retired, Your Worship might see his way to overlooking this unfortunate lapse and be assured that, with me by her side to help and guide her, such a thing would not occur again. Furthermore ...'

Mr Perry was on his feet trying to stop the flow of oratory before it drowned the case.

'Thank you, Mr Hudson,' he called. 'Thank you. You may stand down now.' Turning to the Magistrate he asked for the case to be dismissed and dismissed it was. Mrs Bridges was bound over for three months on a promise of good behaviour.

Lady Marjorie's pleasure at the outcome of the proceedings was only tempered by the news of Mr Hudson and Mrs Bridges' intended nuptials. When a cook and butler were married the alliance invariably caused trouble. It might be all right in the country but not in London.

The happy pair were able to reassure her on this point.

'We have agreed to reserve ourselves for each other,' Mr Hudson explained. 'Whilst continuing in your ladyship's service as before.'

When the subject of the dinner party came up Mr Hudson asked if he might intervene.

'As Mrs Bridges has been through a good deal of anxiety and distress lately, m'lady,' he said, 'I was planning for her to spend a few days with my sister in Eastbourne if you would consider allowing her the time off. In the meantime I've found an excellent cook . . .'

Mrs Bridges puffed out her chest. 'You never said none of this to me, Mr Hudson,' she cried indignantly.

'The idea was to surprise you with a little holiday.'

'I don't want to be surprised by no little holiday, thank you very much,' Mrs Bridges replied, very much back to her old form. 'Begging your ladyship's pardon.'

She took a pace towards her intended. 'Do you think I'm going to run off to Eastbourne and leave my kitchen to an outside cook when there's important people to dinner. I'm very grateful to you for the thought Mr Hudson, I'm sure, but . . .'

Bellamy was quick to intervene in this first lovers' quarrel.

'You're not her husband yet,' he remarked. 'Are you Hudson?'

'So it would seem, sir,' the butler replied ruefully.

'No, he's not,' said Mrs Bridges.

The dinner party was a great success and the Italian ambassador congratulated Lady Marjorie on her French chef, not suspecting for a moment that it had actually been a middle-aged spinster from Bristol who had cooked the dinner.

CHAPTER THIRTEEN

Elizabeth Bellamy was twenty in February 1908. She seemed to take less and less interest in the things that ought to have occupied a young lady of her age and class. Perhaps because of the unhappy outcome of her romance with Baron Klaus Von Rimmer she showed not the slightest desire to meet members of the opposite sex, however charming or eligible, and her mother despaired of ever getting her only daughter to the altar.

Lady Marjorie had always taken a keen interest in charity work and was on numerous committees of ladies who organised such admirable fund raising activities as jumble sales, bazaars, whist drives and even ping pong tournaments. She was delighted when Elizabeth actually volunteered to help with the handiwork stall at one of these affairs in aid of the poor.

A girl called Henrietta Winchcomb was also serving at the stall and by the end of the evening she and Elizabeth had become friends. Henrietta was a practical, down to earth kind-hearted sort of girl, the daughter of a broad minded solicitor from Leeds; broad minded, because he had allowed Henrietta to come to London by herself after she had matriculated to take an Arts course at one of the Women's Colleges attached to London University. She had a room of her own in a boarding house in Holland Park, which seemed to Elizabeth the height of emancipation.

Elizabeth had long been worried about the condition of the poor in a vague sort of way, and now she found that Henrietta was actually doing something about it; every evening she was free she went down to Bethnal Green to work for the Destitute Children's Dinner Society.

Henrietta was delighted to find another enthusiast and took Elizabeth with her on her next visit.

The state of the houses and the people, especially the children, were worse than Elizabeth had ever imagined and she immediately volunteered to join the society. There was more than enough to do and Elizabeth began to spend every afternoon and evening dispensing soup and old clothes to the poor and needy. At last she felt she was doing something useful with her life.

The Bellamys considered Elizabeth's new found vocation a mixed blessing. While no one could deny that it was admirable work and it certainly kept the girl occupied, on the other hand it was hardly a suitable job for such a young and inexperienced girl and the East End of London was known to be a hotbed of disease. Lady Marjorie was also dismayed that her daughter would be cut off even more from people of her own age and class but she took no action hoping that it might be just a passing phase.

When Elizabeth brought Henrietta to tea at Eaton Place, Lady Marjorie was relieved to find her daughter's new friend a serious girl with plenty of commonsense; she was not Elizabeth's class, of course, more like a governess, but in the circumstances what could be more suitable?

August arrived and the usual migration to Scotland. Lady Marjorie took Miss Roberts with her and Mr Hudson went with Mr Bellamy to act as his valet and loader. As James was now stationed at Windsor he was using the house more and more when his duties and his pleasures brought him up to London, and as Elizabeth refused to join her parents until the end of the month because of her work, the remainder of the staff was left in Eaton Place.

One evening James came down from Windsor feeling rather jaded, after a week of polo and gay parties, hoping to spend a quiet evening at home. To his dismay he found the morning room occupied by his sister and Henrietta Winchcomb and maps spread all over the floor.

'Hullo, said Elizabeth, looking up from the floor. 'You have met Miss Winchcomb haven't you?'

James had met Miss Winchcomb and considered her a very typical example of the dreary sort of woman his sister seemed irresistably drawn to. He picked up the evening paper and made his way through the maps to a chair.

'So let's see,' said Elizabeth turning her attention back to her notebook. 'If we let Penny Martingale and her group have Hoxton.'

'Yes,' Henrietta agreed. 'It's in a dreadful state, Hoxton.'

'Then Angie Wilkinson can take Stepney and we can have Whitechapel,' Elizabeth suggested.

'With deevy Miss Pinkerton,' Henrietta agreed enthusiastically. 'I do think she's a brick.'

James put down the paper with a sigh. These two chattering females could well go on all night. He wondered about his evening. The Guards Club was shut for the summer holiday but there was always White's or the Cavalry.

'Are you dining here?' he asked.

'No,' said Elizabeth, rolling up a map. 'We've got work to do. Don't worry, we're just going out.'

James helped himself to a whisky and soda. 'The trouble is that this is the only habitable room in the house,' he explained to Henrietta. 'When my parents go away the whole place goes to pot.'

The drawing room and the dining room were undergoing their summer cleaning.

'I've got no complaints,' said Elizabeth.

'What are you doing with all those maps?'

'It wouldn't interest you.'

'It might.' James was hurt at being snubbed when he had made an effort to be interested. 'You never know.'

'We dish out soup in draughty church halls,' Henrietta explained. 'Want to come and help?'

'Well. I haven't really . . .'

'I thought so,' said his sister.

'It's really awfully worthwhile. P . p . . people are starving,' Henrietta sometimes had trouble with her consonants.

'Even I know that,' James replied, sitting down again. 'I don't mean to imply any criticism of the Destitute Children's Dinner . . .'

'We've changed,' Elizabeth snapped. 'It's the Young Women's Christian Fellowship now . . .'

'Well whatever it is,' said James blandly, 'it's splendid. Keeps you out of those tedious ballrooms. It satisfies the current craze for young women everywhere to be something more than frivolous and decorative, which is my dear sister's constant theme. It acts as a marvellous moral purgative. That's all it achieves and it's foolish to pretend otherwise. The poor will always be with us.'

''That doesn't st . . . st . . . st . . .'

'Don't waste your breath,' Elizabeth advised her. 'He takes delight in provocation.'

But Henrietta's blood was up and she gave James quite a lecture on the condition of the poor and the moral duty of the beter-off to help them.

'Has it ever occurred to you,' James retorted rather enjoying himself, 'that these people mightn't want your interference. They might find it just a trifle patronising. Little middle class misses from the West End pushing their well-meaning noses into problems that don't concern them. Adding insult to injury?'

'We at least fill their bellies.'

'And take their pride.'

'We give them hope.'

'They despise you.'

'Oh come on Henrietta,' said Elizabeth impatiently. 'Come and see for yourself, dear brother, before you judge us.'

James had nothing else to do, so thinking that it might be rather amusing he accepted Elizabeth's challenge, and informed Rose that he would be out to supper. Mrs Bridges was furious. She had made a hare pie especially for Mr James just how he liked it and now it would be wasted for none of the servants would ever think of eating vermin.

When the party arrived at a draughty church hall in a dingy, ill-lit garbage strewn street, other ladies were busy preparing soup in huge iron tureens over coal stoves. The grey faces, the coughing men, and above all the unwashed smell of the crowd outside shook James more than he would have liked to admit. The whole scene was like something out of a novel by Charles Dickens; he had really no idea that such things existed in the enlightened age of Edward the Seventh.

'Hello, Mr Bellamy. Nice to have you aboard,' said Miss Pinkerton cheerily. 'Now you can fill this hod for a start.' She indicated a large coal hod.

'He's only come to observe,' Elizabeth said sweetly, getting a little of her own back.

'Nonsense,' said Miss Pinkerton. 'Better take your coat off. Dirty work.'

It was good advice as James was not dressed for coal heaving. The coal was at the back of a long low cupboard and the ladies had already opened the gates for the hungry hordes when James reappeared to fight his way across to the stove.

It was for this reason that he failed to observe Sarah in the queue. As it was they almost bumped into each other, and Sarah fainted clean away. James put down his coal and went forward to help but two ladies had already lifted her up and were reviving her. Sarah looked thin and ill, her hair was upkempt and her clothes patched and torn.

Elizabeth had noticed the incident and when James reached the stove she asked him about the strange ragged girl.

He was suspiciously vague and evasive. 'She used to work for us,' he said. 'Long ago.'

'I don't remember.'

'I think it was when you were away in Germany.'

'Why did she leave?'

'Oh look,' said James with a shrug. 'Why do servants

leave? Either they steal things or they're unsuitable or . . . I don't know . . .'

'Why did this one leave?'

'I told you. I really can't remember.'

Elizabeth gave her brother a curious look and went over and introduced herself to Sarah.

'What are you doing here?' Elizabeth asked. 'Have you no job?'

'Oh yes. I'm not here for the reasons you think. I was just . . . just looking for a friend of mine.'

She smiled at Elizabeth. Rose would have known what to expect next.

'Yes, she's an actress, and I'm a bit worried about her. You see, she was appearing in this show, the Merry Widow it was with Lily Elsie and she took up with this gentleman, a Lord of the Realm, but he got called away to Australia—on business . . . Her name is Mercy Proudfoot,' she added.

James had been listening to the familiar cockney voice and when the ladies set about enquiring after the imaginary Mercy Proudfoot he came over.

'Hello, Sarah,' he said with a smile.

'Oh Mr James, sir,' Sarah answered with a little of her old cheek. 'Didn't expect to see you here.' She was overcome with a fit of coughing.

'I'm sorry to see you here,' James replied.

'No, I was explaining to your sister, I'm looking for a friend,' Sarah said quickly.

'Mercy Proudfoot?'

Miss Pinkerton came back to say that no one had ever heard of the missing lady. 'I'm sorry,' said Sarah. 'I must have been mistakenly informed.'

Sarah got up to go but as she made for the door was overcome by another fit of coughing. Elizabeth went over to her and began to question her about her present position and her prospects. Sarah evidently had neither and Elizabeth immediately proposed that she should come back with them to Eaton Place. James protested strongly to his sister but Elizabeth insisted that no servant who had ever worked for the family should be left in Sarah's woeful condition without help and she reminded her brother that she was trying to help the poor and needy and that kindness began at home.

When Elizabeth brought Sarah into the servants' hall later that evening, Doris and Edward were playing cards, and Mrs Bridges was dozing by the fire.

'Mrs Bridges,' Sarah exclaimed, 'Don't you remember me?'

'Well, bless my soul, little Sarah,' said Mrs Bridges, standing up. 'What have they done to you? Grown so thin . . . Come and sit by the fire, there's quite a chill these summer evenings, and you in that flimsy frock.'

Sarah started to cough again.

Mrs. Bridges clicked her tongue. 'And that cough,' she scolded. 'Doris, brew some cocoa, quickly girl.'

Sarah looked around at the familiar room.

'Where's Rose?' she asked.

'Gone to the bioscope,' Mrs Bridges explained. 'She's taken Alice. They'll be back soon.'

'Who's Alice?' asked Sarah suddenly jealous. It was Sarah who had first told Rose about the bioscope.

'She's the under house parlourmaid, what you used to be. She's a good girl, clean and punctual,' Mrs Bridges explained.

When Elizabeth suggested that Sarah might be found a temporary position in the kitchen at Eaton Place, Mrs Bridges became flustered; it was usually Lady Marjorie and Mr Hudson who made decisions of that sort.

'Well,' she said. 'I don't know. Doris has her faults but she's improving. I couldn't hardly throw her out.'

Elizabeth suggested there should be two kitchen maids, just for the time being.

'I'm trained for upstairs,' Sarah explained. They ignored her and came to a compromise. Not to put Doris' nose out of joint Sarah was to be given the lowly title of scullery maid.

'But I've got sensitive hands,' Sarah protested. Elizabeth frowned at such ingratitude. 'It won't be for long,' she said firmly and bade them good-night.

'Where's she going to sleep,' Doris asked when she returned with the cocoa. 'There's no room with me.' She didn't trust other girls from the East End.

'She'll have to have Emily's room,' said Edward.

'Oh yes. I remember Emily. What happened to her?' Sarah asked, sipping the hot cocoa. Doris made a face behind Mrs Bridges' back to indicate that it wasn't a subject that could be discussed in front of the cook.

Later, when she had escorted Sarah up to Emily's old room, she explained about Emily.

'Hanged herself?'

Sarah could hardly believe it.

'From that very beam. Love, they say,' said Doris. 'A footman from another house let her down. 'Course, I wouldn't know not being here at the time.'

When Doris had gone, Sarah sat thinking about Emily. 'Poor little soul,' she murmured to herself and shook her head; she just couldn't imagine there was a man in the world worth killing herself for.

Her reverie was interrupted by the sound of Rose's familiar voice outside in the passage.

'She's in there now? Sarah?' Rose sounded really amazed and Sarah smiled to herself.

'Yes, in Emily's room.'

'All right Doris,' said Rose's voice. 'You go to bed.'

'I don't think it's right,' said another voice. 'Employing someone without consulting you, Rose. After all, Mr Hudson put you in charge, and anyway, we don't need a scullery maid.'

Sarah's eyes narrowed; she didn't like the sound of Alice.

She went out into the passage. Rose and Alice were at the old familiar bedroom door.

'Rosie!' Sarah ran down to greet her friend. 'I'm back.'

Rose stared at her coldly. Alice sniffed and went into the bedroom.

'Hullo Sarah!' said Rose.

'Aren't you coming?' Alice called. 'You promised to do my freckles.'

Rose turned and shut the door in Sarah's face.

The duties of scullery maid consisted almost entirely of washing up the dirty dishes and scrubbing the floors and Sarah didn't take at all kindly to them. Mrs Bridges was for ever nagging at her for not cleaning in the corners and the other servants treated her like dirt which was of course only right and proper for a servant in her position.

She found Alice's superior bossy manner especially infuriating and was deeply hurt when Rose continued to ignore her almost completely.

Sarah had no idea how much her previous departure from Eaton Place had upset Rose; she knew nothing of the sleepless nights, the near breakdown and the desperate fruitless searches in Ilford. If only she could have half an hour alone with Rose, Sarah felt, she could put everything right. She waited until it was Alice's afternoon off and then crept along to Rose's bedroom and opened the door quietly.

Rose was sitting on the bed sewing.

'What do you want?' Rose asked coldly.

'To talk to you, Rosie,' Sarah answered softly and persuasive. 'Alice about?'

'You know she isn't or you wouldn't have come here,' Rose answered and for a long time in spite of Sarah's persuasions and excuses she stayed silent.

'You could have written at least,' Rose said at last.

'I know, I meant to,' Sarah replied apologetically. 'You know me when it comes to writing, how difficult it is. And I was always so busy.'

'Busy were you?' Rose replied sniffily. 'Doing what? Did you find all that excitement you was looking for? Or was it mostly down on your luck in Whitechapel?'

She really does want to know, thought Sarah, and that's a start.

'It wasn't bad all the time. Some of it was quite good,' she said.

'Oh yes,' Rose replied.

'I joined a fair to start with. I was with them almost two years. We travelled all over the country. I was assistant to a clairvoyant.'

Rose looked up sharply.

'It's true,' Sarah protested. 'Madame Sophie. She could do all sorts of things and she had a parrot called George who she said was her husband in another life. She could tell the future and predicted all sorts of things that came true, including the fair running out of money and having to close down.'

Rose smiled. 'Your stories,' she said.

'Cross me heart about the fair,' Sarah answered. 'I met so many interesting people.'

'Including men,' Rose asked with a hint of the old jealousy.

'Of course, what do you think? I fell in love with one of them.'

His name was Benito, she explained, and he was an escapologist. He used to get shut in a trunk and put in a tank of water and he always escaped. His problem was that although he could easily escape from all the ropes and chains binding him, he couldn't escape from his wife and six children in Naples.

'You are awful,' said Rose and when both the girls began to laugh Sarah knew that she was well on the way back to her old place in Rose's heart.

They talked for hours about all the things that had happened in the four intervening years since they had met, about Alfred's dramatic departure and poor Emily and Mrs Bridges' baby, and Sarah embroidered her own adventures in her very best style and had Rose in fits of laughter.

'My big ambition,' Sarah confessed, 'my big ambition is to go on the stage.'

'What's stopping you?' Rose demanded.

'It's hard to get started,' Sarah confessed. 'You have to do favours for people. You know.'

'And you won't?' Rose asked, ever curious about men and their ways.

'No but I'm seriously thinking about it.'

'You mustn't, Sarah. Ever.'

'Why not?' Sarah replied seeing her chance. 'I mean, look where forbearance has got me. Back in the bloody scullery. You got to get me out of there, Rose. I'm desperate.'

But Rose was not yet ready to take up the cudgels on Sarah's behalf; as always the wretched Alice stood in the way.

'But you don't like her,' Sarah demanded. 'That snooty great ox?'

'Now watch your tongue,' Rose warned.

'You tell her to watch hers. Giving herself airs and telling me what to do. You can't like her as much as me, Rose. You can't.'

Alice opened the door; they had forgoten how late it was.

'Oh, sorry,' she said very sarcastic. 'Am I interruption?'

'Oh sorry am I interrupting?' Sarah mimicked. 'Yes, you bloody well are,' she went on in full-blooded cockney. 'You're interrupting a conversation I'm having with my friend, Rose.'

'All right, Sarah, we've said all we have to say. You can go now,' said Rose, quick to turn her coat.

'You bet I'll go,' Sarah spat out the words. 'Wouldn't stay in the same room as her.'

'Oh why is she always so unpleasant to me?' Alice complained.

'Because you have that effect on me, dearie,' Sarah said sweetly and banged the door.

'I'm sure I've never done anything against her,' Alice went on. 'Rose, how could you sit there and let her insult me like that?'

'Oh stop moaning,' said Rose.

Alice shrugged sulkily. Really one didn't know what to do or say for the best with some people.

From then on Sarah determined to get rid of Alice and get back into Rose's bed by hook or by crook. Days went by and no handy hook or crook appeared; she seemed to be getting nowhere. One night as she was getting ready for bed, she suddenly seemed to feel Emily's presence in the room.

'Oh Emily, I can't stay here with you, love,' she said out loud. 'I got to make up my mind. Either to get on in this house or get out. But not the way you did, not me.'

Alice heard the voice coming from Sarah's room and woke Rose up.

'She's got someone in there talking,' said Alice. The two girls listened. Nothing more was heard.

'Go back to sleep,' said Rose.

Next morning Alice spread the story round the servants hall. Mrs Bridges and Doris were fascinated.

'Was it a man's voice?' Doris asked, and Alice shrugged. They accused Edward of visiting Sarah as they suspected he rather fancied her. He denied it hotly. 'You wouldn't catch me with a scullery maid, a dead or alive one,' he said haughtily.

Mrs Bridges had a brainwave. She sent for Sarah. 'Now girl,' she said to Alice. 'Repeat what you just said.'

'I only said I thought I heard voices in your room last night,' Alice explained in a non-commital voice; she was rather frightened of Sarah.

'They think you and me is up to no good,' said Edward.

'Voices?' Sarah asked puzzled.

'That's right,' Alice replied, more aggressively.

'Well is it the truth or isn't it?' Mrs Bridges began to bully. 'Come on girl, speak up. No use denying it.'

Rose came into the servants hall. 'I'm glad you've come, Rose. Alice has just accused me of having a man in my room,' said Sarah, cunningly twisting the charge.

'I only said voices . . .'

'Oh that's all is it? Voices,' Sarah mimicked.

'Don't be so stupid, Alice,' said Rose. 'You were dreaming, I told you.'

'No she wasn't,' said Sarah suddenly.

There was a silence. Sarah waited till they were all looking at her. 'She was quite right. She did hear voices,' she confessed.

'Yours?' asked Mrs Bridges.

'Yes.'

'Who else?' said Rose.

'Can't you guess. Can't any of you guess?'

Sarah looked round, keping them on tenterhooks. You could have heard a pin drop in the room.

'Emily's,' she said with quiet sincerity.

'She's been in touch,' she added. 'I wasn't going to tell you, but I have these powers, not given to many.'

They didn't believe her.

'Want me to prove it?'

'Yes, go on prove it,' said Rose. Sarah promised she would prove it that very evening after supper.

One of the most useful lessons Sarah had learnt from Madame Sophie was the art of good stage management; after supper she took elaborate care instructing the other servants exactly where the table and the chairs and the candles should go. She classed Mrs Bridges and Doris as potential believers and Rose and Edward as doubters with Alice an unknown quantity so that when she put them in their seats she mixed doubters and believers alternately.

When the main lights were turned off, Sarah made quite a ceremony of lighting the candles.

'I don't like it. I don't like it,' Doris whimpered.

'You be quiet or you'll go to bed,' said Mrs Bridges.

'What would Mr Hudson say if he was here?' Alice remarked.

'Well he's not here, he's in Scotland. So he can say what he likes,' Mrs Bridges snapped. It was clear she was all of a dither.

'You can't do it,' said Rose.

'You wait,' Sarah retorted.

'Don't you need something from the departed one,' Edward asked with elaborate innocence hoping to catch out the medium.

'I've got a button,' said Sarah producing one and holding it up. 'I found it in her room.'

'Bless my soul. She really can do it,' muttered Mrs Bridges and advanced Sarah's cause considerably thereby.

'Link hands,' Sarah commanded. They did so in silence.

"Too much light,' said Sarah after a while.

It was one of Madame Sophie's favourite ways to increase tension.

'That's so we won't see her tricks,' said Alice nastily.

Doris turned out the gas bracket by the fireplace. When they were all settled again, Sarah suddenly banged the table three times which made them all jump. After staring upwards for a while she flopped back into her chair in a trance. They watched her carefully.

'Look her lips are moving,' Doris whispered. 'She's trying to say something.'

'Sssh,' Mrs Bridges hissed.

'I am Albert Moffat,' said Sarah faintly.

'Who's Albert Moffat when he's at home?' Edward asked irreverently.

'A psychopathetic personality,' Mrs Bridges whispered angrily. She had been very much taken with spiritualism at one time.

'I am Albert Moffat, Sarah's father in another existence,' said Sarah. 'I shall bring Emily to Sarah.'

'Mercy God,' sighed Mrs Bridges. They were all very tense now. All except Rose. Sarah began to have minor convulsions.

'The table's moving,' squealed Doris.

'Levitating,' Mrs Bridges corrected. And it was. There was the sound of bells.

'Mercy on us,' moaned Mrs Bridges.

'It's the morning room; we're wanted upstairs,' said Rose.

She was right. It was James ringing for more soda. Rose got up. Mrs Bridges threw her down into her chair.

'Keep your mouth shut, Rose,' she hissed violently.

'I, Albert Moffat, through my one time earthly daughter, Sarah, I am bringing you Emily,' Sarah continued rather quicker. 'Can you hear me, Emily?'

'Yes I can hear you, Albert Moffat.'

Emily's exact voice came faintly across the table and Sarah's mouth hadn't moved.

'She spoke,' Mrs Bridges gasped. 'Oh Mercy God, she's there.'

'Have you any messages for the people round this

table?' Sarah asked calmly. And Emily's voice replied, 'I have some messages.'

'Tell us your messages.'

'I am happy where I am, so help me.' It was Emily's County Clare lilt exactly. 'And I forgive him. I forgive him.'

'She means William,' said Mrs Bridges. 'She forgives William. Oh Emily, forgive me too, child. I could have helped you with a kind word. Oh take the load off my heart, child.'

There was a deathly pause.

'I forgive you, Mrs Bridges. I forgive all of you,' said Emily's voice.

'Bless her. Bless her,' cried Mrs Bridges and broke down weeping. Emily spoke no more. After a while Edward dared to switch on the light. Sarah was huddled in her chair unconscious and on Mrs Bridge's instructions nobody touched her till she came round some minutes later.

The strange thing was she couldn't remember a thing about it. They even had to tell her about Albert Moffat and Emily. And that was a sure sign that Sarah was a genuine medium—according to Mrs Bridges.

CHAPTER FOURTEEN

The effect of the seance on Sarah's reputation was immediate. All the other servants except for Rose treated her with a sort of fearful awe.

After breakfast the next day Alice came up to her and humbly asked her if she would help her get in touch with her mother who had passed over two years before. Sarah graciously promised to do her best.

Not a minute later, somewhat to Sarah's surprise, Edward, the unbeliever, came up and asked in a whisper for a word in private.

'Who's dead in your family? I'll have to start charging soon,' said Sarah.

But Edward was still an unbeliever; in conspiratorial tones he admitted that it was he who had moved the table, and now he suggested an alliance. In plain terms he wanted to get in on the act.

Sarah was righteously indignant. She didn't hesitate to call all the other servants together and inform them of Edward's monstrous suggestion.

Mrs Bridges led the cries of outrage. To clear her good name Sarah offered to hold another séance and get in touch with Emily again on condition that Edward was excluded. She felt that this would finally bring Rose down on her side.

The strange news from the basement soon emanated upstairs to the morning room. Elizabeth was intrigued, her brother not at all.

'I don't care if she is your protegé,' said James that evening. 'She must leave.'

"Why?' asked Elizabeth, prepared to fight.

'Because she's disrupted the entire staff, that's why. They're in an uproar down there. You can ring till you're blue in the face and no one comes. That's why.'

'It's only a little harmless fun for goodness sake.'

'Harmless!' said James in mock amazement.

'Oh I'm sorry. I didn't realise she was a *genuine* medium,' Elizabeth answered with heavy irony.

'Of course she's not genuine.' Nothing annoyed James more than when his sister was deliberately silly. 'The harm lies in the effect she has on simple minds like Mrs Bridges and those other young maids.'

He never could remember their names.

'Last time she was here,' James continued on another tack, 'she upset mother, father, Hudson, everybody.'

'What about James?' Elizabeth asked innocently. James looked up sharply and Elizabeth saw that she had caught a fish.

'Yes. What about James? What did he do to Sarah to make her faint at the sight of him years later. Eh?' Elizabeth wasn't going to let him off the hook.

'Do stop being childish,' said James.

'You had an affair with Sarah, dear brother,' she went on. 'Admit it.'

'Absolute rubbish,' James blustered.

'Admit,' Elizabeth was relentless. She knew her brother only too well.

'All right, I admit. Once, a long time ago, something almost happened between us. Now are you satisfied?'

'Well you're not, clearly.'

'Don't be cheap.'

'I'm not being cheap, just simply helping you to face yourself. "Something almost happened" whatever that means. What about now?'

'All finished. Nothing.'

Elizabeth looked her brother in the eye.

'What's all the fuss about then . . . If you're in love with the girl why not be honest about it?'

James said nothing.

'Or aren't officers in the Household Cavalry allowed to fall in love with housemaids?'

James wasn't in love with Sarah, not in the least, but the renewal of their acquaintance under such strange and sordid circumstances had had an effect on him. He felt guilty that somehow it was his fault she had fallen so low and that it was some trick of fate which had deliberately brought him face to face with her again.

He dreaded meeting her in the house and on several occasions had avoided coming back to Eaton Place in case that should happen.

'It's really none of your business,' he said to his sister. 'I want Sarah out of the house. By the end of the week.'

'And I refuse,' Elizabeth retorted.

'I'm in charge while our parents are away,' James answered. 'I make the decisions.'

'Not in domestic matters. You assume father's role, I assume mother's. Sorry James.'

The second séance was very much a repetition of the first except that Elizabeth was present by special request and Edward was specifically excluded and retired sulkily to the butler's pantry muttering that he had better things to do than wasting his time on fakes.

Everything went exactly according to plan until Sarah came to the words, 'I, Albert Moffat, through my one time daughter, Sarah, am bringing you . . .'

At that moment Doris stood up with a scream and pointed at the door. Framed in it stood the black figure of a man in an old fashioned bowler hat and cloak.

'Albert Moffat!' moaned Mrs Bridges. 'Lord have mercy!'

The figure moved and there was a crashing of overturning chairs. The light went on suddenly and Mr Hudson was revealed.

He had come back unexpectedly to collect the fishing rods and escort Elizabeth back to Scotland with him.

As soon as some sort of order had been restored the butler held a court of inquiry into the chaotic state in which he found the household on his return. Lights burnt late in Mr Hudson's pantry as each of the senior servants in turn produced their evidence.

Taking advantage of Rose's preoccupation with Mr Hudson, Sarah informed Alice confidentially that she had been in touch with Emily earlier in the day. The spirit of the little kitchen maid had suggested that she might be able to bring Alice's mother back that very night if her daughter would spend it in Emily's old room. Sarah generously offered to swap rooms with Alice. The exchange having been accomplished Alice sat nervously on the bed in the little room wondering when something would happen. Sarah had told her to turn out the light but she hadn't dared to.

Suddenly she became aware of a faint voice.

It was the same Irish accent she had heard in the seance, Emily's voice.

'Alice,' the voice asked. 'Alice, are you there, Alice? It's Emily. Can you hear me? If you'll be patient now, I'm after bringing your mother to you. I'm looking for her in the celestial halls . . .'

Alice was a very literal girl; whether it was the fact that Emily who had never known her addressed her by her Christian name or that the words 'celestial halls' seemed a little too good to be true, she began to have doubts.

After a moment spent in deep thought she tiptoed out of the room and along the passage to her own bedroom and opened the door. Sarah was kneeling on the bed, hands cupped, talking to the wall.

'I think I see her, Alice,' she was saying in Emily's voice.

'You beast,' Alice screamed, and fell on her.

Alice was a big strong girl and although Sarah had been the terror of her streets in her youth, she was giving away at least four stone. It was a hair-pulling, scratching, clothes-tearing sort of fight, as dirty as you could find.

Alice had at last pinned the screaming, kicking Sarah to the floor and was punching her face when Rose came in.

'Alice!' she shouted.

She picked up the ewer and poured the contents of it over them. It had a most immediate satisfactory damping effect.

'It was her started it,' Sarah gasped. 'She jumped on me, Rosie.'

'You tricked me,' Alice shouted. 'You and your voices ... Fake!'

'Alice!' said Rose, trying to quieten her.

'No, don't you touch me. You're in it with her. You want to get rid of me, so you can be in this room together,' Alice shouted tearfully. 'Well, all right you can have it, because I don't want it. I'm not stopping in this house a minute longer.' She ran out of the room.

'What have you done to her?' asked Rose suspiciously.

'Nothing,' Sarah was the picture of innocence.

'She said "fake" didn't she?' Rose asked. 'Didn't she?'

Sarah smiled winningly. 'Well you know,' she admitted. 'It's ventriloquism, that's what they call it. It's still a gift.'

Rose put her hands on her hips.

'There's no harm in it,' Sarah went on. 'Made Mrs Bridges happy. Could have made Alice happy too, if she hadn't found out. Silly cow.'

'Well, I don't know what to think I'm sure,' said Rose.

'I had to get back with you, Rose. You're pleased, aren't you?'

'Much good it'll do you. I'm off to Scotland with Miss Elizabeth in the morning, and Mr Hudson wants to see you first thing.'

'Well he'll be needing a new houseparlour-maid now, won't he?' Sarah said cheekily.

'You've got a nerve,' said Rose.

Sarah snuggled down under the sheets.

'Goodnight now, Rosie,' she said in Emily's voice.

Rose shook her head. What could one do with a girl like that!

Mr Hudson had found himself unable to take the strong disciplinary measures he thought proper to bring the house to order because he was hamstrung by Miss Elizabeth's unfortunate participation in the séance. Confronted with the sudden departure of Alice he had little alternative but to allow Sarah to stay until the return of the Bellamys from Scotland, just as she herself had prophesied. But he gave Mrs Bridges explicit instructions that at the least sign of trouble he was to be telegraphed in Perth.

One morning a week later James had come in to collect his letters and was standing in front of the morning room fire when Sarah opened the door and came in. They were both surprised to see each other. Strangely they were standing in exactly the same positions as on the fateful night four years earlier.

'Excuse me, sir,' said Sarah. 'May I do the fire?'

'Yes, Sarah,' James answered. 'I didn't know you were still here.' He was surprised to see what a change good food and care had made in the girl.

'Yes, sir,' Sarah answered, looking straight at him. 'You didn't want me back in the first place, did you sir? Done your best to get rid of me?'

James frowned. 'Look, I'm not going to . . .' he began.

'What have you got against me, sir?' Sarah went on boldly before he could finish his sentence. She had nothing to lose.

'Well,' James replied. 'I just think you are a . . . a disturbing influence.'

'Well you won't be "disturbed" much longer, Mr James. I'm going Tuesday. I'm just working out my notice.'

'I see. I hope my sister's given you a good reference.'

'She would've done. She's a nice girl your sister,' Sarah replied, not making any effort to go near the fire and putting down her box. 'I'm not going on with this job, thank you.' James shrugged. He didn't in the least want to get into a long discussion about Sarah's future. This time her departure was nothing at all to do with him.

'Back to Whitechapel?' he asked, for something to say.

'Hope not,' Sarah replied. 'Might be going to go on the stage.'

James nodded. 'Well,' he said, folding up his letters and preparing to leave. 'I gather you've shown considerable histrionic talent just lately. Good luck.' He went to the door.

'Thank you, sir,' said Sarah. When James had gone out of the door she put out her tongue at it.

James couldn't put his encounter with Sarah out of his mind; just when he thought he had exorcised the memory of the girl for good, here she was coming back to haunt him.

'What have you got against me, sir?' she had asked and he couldn't answer truthfully, even to himself. He felt he would like to make amends in some way for his unfairness and one morning when he was inspecting his troop horses he suddenly remembered Corporal-of-Horse Fox.

Mr Fox had been James's Troop Sergeant for several years and on his retirement had set up as a theatrical agent with an office in Seven Dials. James, knowing him to be an able and efficient fellow, had lent the ex-corporal-of-horse some money to help him start up the business. Now Mr Fox might do something in return.

After talking to Fox, James wrote to Sarah at Eaton Place enclosing an introduction to the theatrical agent and wishing the girl the best of luck with her future.

Mr Fox was a huge jovial man with a black curly moustache and a rose in his button-hole. In his limited experience of the theatre he had never come across a female ventriloquist before but, as he was fond of saying, you have to make a start somewhere. He was impressed by Sarah's spirit and her delightful figure and reasoned with himself that if the ventriloquism was a dreadful failure at least she would fit very neatly into the back row of a West End chorus. To Sarah's great delight he agreed to put her on his books and give her a start in her chosen profession, and at the same time salved his old troop leader's conscience.

CHAPTER FIFTEEN

'The fact that we are having to scrape the barrel for Elizabeth is nobody's fault but her own,' said Lady Marjorie to her husband one day. 'She was born clever, poor child, without the wit to disguise it.'

They were planning to take Elizabeth away for the weekend where she would meet a very dreary young man whose only claim to fame was that he was rich and the second son of a Marquis.

'She'll learn in time,' said Bellamy. 'We must be tolerant.' But Elizabeth's twenty-first birthday was only days away and even he was getting worried about the almost monastic life his daughter was leading.

Before the weekend Elizabeth told her mother that she wouldn't be able to go away after all. She had been asked to a party, a very important party with new friends. Lady Marjorie hadn't seen her daughter so animated for months.

'Who are these new friends?' she asked suspiciously. 'What sort of people are they?'

By that she meant, were they respectable people of Elizabeth's class.

'They are intelligent people, mother,' Elizabeth explained. 'People who talk about things that matter. I feel elated and happy when I'm with them.'

She didn't mention the fact that she hadn't actually yet made the acquaintance of these exciting new friends. 'I'm honoured to be asked into their circle,' she continued. 'They're mostly poets and painters and people who write books. Friends of Henrietta Winchcomb,' she added cunningly.

Lady Marjorie asked her husband to adjudicate in the matter of the weekend.

'She is old enough now to choose her own friends,' he declared.

'Not if they are unsuitable,' Lady Marjorie retorted.

'That's for Elizabeth to decide.'

Elizabeth was dtlighted to be given her freedom and, blessing her father, she rushed out to Liberty's and spent a sizeable part of her monthly allowance on a gold and sliver djibbah. As she explained to Rose when she unwrapped it, the djibbah was the very latest thing.

'Women wear them in the East. I'm going east on Saturday evening towards Bloomsbury. So I must dress as the natives do,' Elizabeth explained. She put her arms in the air. 'Undo me, faithful handmaiden. Release me from these horrible whalebones. I am twenty-one on Monday and would be freed from their tyranny.'

Rose raised her eyebrows and began to unlace her young mistress. The loose lines and the bright colours of the djibbah didn't appeal to her.

'What's the use of having a body, Rose,' Elizabeth asked, 'if it's to be all twisted out of shape.'

'Talking of bodies now, is it?' said Mrs Bridges when she heard about the djibbah. 'We all know what that means. The colonel's lady and Judy O'Grady.'

If Elizabeth had told her parents that the person giving the party was none other than the notorious political extremist Miss Evelyn Larkin, they would undoubtedly have forbidden her to go to it.

The truth was that even Miss Pinkerton's enthusiasm for feeding soup to the poor had begun to pall on the two younger women. The air of 1908 was humming with new ideas and new theories and they grew impatient for change. They read countless pamphlets and studied Mr Bernard Shaw's Prefaces and went to a Fabian lecture at the Caxton Hall on 'The Distributive Mechanism in State Finance', but even Mr Webb's obvious enthusiasm failed to inspire them. Everyone admitted the country was in a mess and all they ever seemed to do was to write and talk about it. Henrietta and Elizabeth wanted action, not words; Evelyn Larkin promised a new world, not in the future, but now. When she was first introduced on the night of the party Elizabeth thought Miss Larkin looked like a beautiful black witch. She was the daughter of a Midland schoolmaster and had a flat hard accent; her coal black eyes seemed to penetrate Elizabeth's and when she shook hands she had the grip of a man.

'We are special people,' Evelyn Larkin told her disciples, 'brought together from the wilderness. We have thrown off all the stupid conventions of our forefathers. We can be utterly frank, unshackled by cant or convention. We are in the lead. Together we can make a new world. We must fight the evil of commercialism. Not only with words but with deeds.'

There was an excited growl of enthusiasm. Elizabeth thought she had never heard such a splendid speech in her life. If only people like her father would try to understand people like Evelyn Larkin.

At first Elizabeth had been dazed and bewildered by the dark smoky atmosphere in the long bare room with its beaten copper fireplace and extraordinary lithographs from Vienna on the white walls. It was full of people sitting on cushions and talking and smoking and drinking. Never in her life had Elizabeth seen such a strange collection in such extraordinary clothes. Henrietta was able to point a few of them out to her. The man in the French workman's overalls and the Russian cap was Gustave, a self-styled anarchist, but also, according to Henrietta, a perfect pet. The very large lady smoking a cigar whose many coloured chiffon dress seemed to be held together by row after row of amber beads was the once famous novelist, Perdita. Henrietta pointed out the fellow student who had first introduced her into Evelyn Larkin's circle. She was lying entangled with an intense looking young man with thick glasses, a fluffy tweed suit and a red tie; his name was Stanley and the couple were engaged in an experimental liaison.

Lawrence Kirbridge completely exceeded Elizabeth's expectations. He was reclining at full length on a couch by the fire, the centre of attention. Although the poet was simply dressed in a white open neck shirt and grey flannel trousers, Elizabeth thought she had never seen anyone so beautiful. He had the aura of a Greek god. When he actually beckoned to her to come and sit on a cushion near his feet she blushed with pleasure and went quite dizzy for a moment.

Evelyn Larkin sat in the shadows and watched. Perdita came swaying over to her. 'A neophyte eager for action, an unsullied page,' she croaked. 'Whose harem have you robbed of that little odalisque?'

'Now don't you corrupt her, Perdita my dear,' Evelyn warned.

'Me corrupt her!' Perdita laughed hoarsely. 'One for the barricades if you ask me . . . they're tougher than they look these little patrician maidens.'

'She's very young,' Evelyn replied and her eyes hardened suddenly, as she watched Lawrence Kirbridge's hand stray to Elizabeth's shoulder.

'Poetry is as natural as eating or making love,' the young poet announced to the room. 'It is life, the spirit of gloriousness in things.'

He waved his fine hands in the air as if to evoke that same spirit.

'Do you read poetry, Elizabeth?' he asked.

'Yes,' Elizabeth replied nervously. 'I admire your poems enormously, although I must confess I don't always understand them.'

'My poetry isn't to be understood,' the great man explained. 'Let it flow over you like the great spumy waves over the body of the naked swimmer.'

He began to recite one of his own poems and Elizabeth lay back and tried to do as she had been commanded.

Conversation flashed and rumbled round the room like summer thunder.

'Mr Bernard Shaw is living proof that a teetotal vegetarian diet produces the perfect mind,' Stanley cried enthusiastically. 'And bicycling the perfect body,' Henrietta's friend chipped in, not to be outdone. 'The Webbs frequently bicycle forty miles.'

Hentrietta stood up. 'In the ideal state only the physically and mentally perfect should be allowed to procreate,' she proclaimed with absolute centainty. Elizabeth was amazed to see Gustave give her a lusty kiss on the mouth.

'Nonsense, Henrietta,' Lawrence Kirbridge retorted. 'My father was a professor of physics married to the seventh dull daughter of an even duller Dorset baronet. Look at me. Brilliant and forty times more sensitive than my parents.'

'That is where free love comes in,' Henrietta replied triumphantly. 'A true friendship with a man is not possible without physical intimacy as his beloved and lover.'

Gustave leaned forward and pulled her into his lap. 'If a woman cohabits with twelve different brilliant men,' Henrietta continued quite unperturbed, 'then her life will be twelve times . . .'

'My dear innocent children,' Perdita cut in, 'listen for a moment to the voice of experience. If you could imbibe wisdom like hot soup simply by sleeping with a genius I ought to be the wisest woman in Christendom. Rodin once did my torso—but all I remember about him are his strong hard hands.'

They looked at her in admiring wonder; even Henrietta was reduced to silence.

Someone announced that Lawrence Kirbridge was kindly going to give a poetry reading on the next day which was a Sunday.

'Oh Lord,' said Henrietta, 'I'm terribly sorry, I forgot to tell you; the beastly Bible readers have bagged the hall.' Lawrence was rightly furious and Elizabeth suddenly had a wonderful idea. Flushed with excitement and rather over anxious to please her new friends, she suggested that the reading should be read in her house in Eaton Place. Her parents were in the country and there was plenty of room.

'It would be deevy if you could all come.' She said.

'Bless you my child, you are a true friend of Art,' Lawrence rewarded her with a formal kiss. 'To mark the occasion, I shall write a piece to my lady of the Kasbah.' He drew Elizabeth to her feet and held up her hand. 'Something in the style of the Rubaiyat. It will consist of seven stanzas, each as exquisite and ephemeral and meaningless as the eyelash of a gnat or the first pale flush of dawn. It will be inscribed gloriously in red ink on gold vellum. There will be only one copy.' He knelt before Elizabeth. 'We shall read it together a stanza each day,' he promised. 'Then we shall die; for that is our tragedy.'

Everyone clapped and Evelyn Larkin took the poet by the hand and led him firmly away. Later, when Elizabeth wanted to find them to make her farewells, Henrietta explained to her that Evelyn and Lawrence were not available.

'They are communing with nature,' she said.

The next morning Elizabeth didn't get up till half past eleven. She was still tingling with the excitement of all the wonderful things she had seen and heard at the party the night before. When she eventually came downstairs she paced about the empty morning room pretending her parents were sitting in their usual places.

'Good morning, mother. Good morning father,' she said, giving each of them an imaginary peck. 'Yes. I had a wonderful evening, thank you. Such fascinating people. Sorry to be a little late down. I overslept owing to an excess of rum punch and intellectual conversation. They're all coming to tea by the way.'

Having reminded herself of the fact she went to the bell by the fireplace and rang it.

'There was a most charming young man there,' she went on. 'Such exciting eyes and a voice like a caress.

When he looked at me and spoke those beautiful sonnets he had composed . . . I felt as if I were almost undressed.' She felt her body luxuriously.

'Elizabeth!' she said sharply in her mother's voice.

'Sorry mother,' she apologised. 'You wouldn't understand.' Little did she really know her mother. 'I felt somehow as if he was penetrating right . . . right through to my innermost soul—possessing me. I was metaphorically seized and flung over the saddle of his white charger and so we galloped across the desert into the sunset of my maidenhood.'

'I beg pardon, Miss,' said Mr Hudson who had come in quietly.

Elizabeth jumped in the air. 'Oh Hudson,' she exclaimed, 'I was . . . was just memorizing some passages from a book.'

'Yes, Miss,' said Mr Hudson in his neutral voice.

'I'm expecting some friends to tea,' she said.

'Yes, Miss Elizabeth. How many?'

Elizabeth really hadn't the least idea. 'Oh six, seven, perhaps eight or nine.'

By four-thirty there were twenty-eight disciples draped casually all over the morning room floor listening to Lawrence reading Swinburne's 'Atlanta to Calydon'.

Rose and Edward climbed over the prostrate bodies with plates of tiny sandwiches and cakes which disappeared as if by magic.

The sudden demand for more food caused a flurry of activity in the kitchen.

'Where do I get a dozen loaves from on a Sunday afternoon?' Mrs Bridges complained. 'Has anyone thought of that. Not that I don't like to see young people with a nice healthy appetite.'

'The way they're gobbling them down,' Rose remarked, 'you wouldn't think any of them had had a square meal for a week.'

'Or a bath for a month,' Edward added screwing up his nose and causing Doris to choke with laughter.

'What are they like?' she asked.

'Like something from the zoo if you ask me,' Rose sniffed.

'I suppose they're all people Miss Elizabeth's picked up in the East End. She can't resist stray dogs; never could. Look at Sarah,' said Mrs Bridges.

Mr Hudson coming into the kitchen corrected her.

'No, Mrs Bridges,' he said. 'No working class person would come into this house dressed like that. They'd have more respect. Socialists if you ask me.'

'I don't know what makes Miss Lizzy mix with such people. I really don't,' Edward demanded.

'Tainted blood,' Mrs Bridges told him. 'I'll not forget the night her Aunt Helena danced naked on the lawn at Southwold. Bold as brass.'

Disapproving of this turn in the conversation, Mr Hudson hustled his forces upstairs again.

'Was she stark naked?' Doris enquired in wonder.

'Now you just go and wash your mouth out, Doris,' Mrs Bridges scowled. 'And get on with them dirty things.'

When Doris had gone she sat down with a sigh and passed her hand over her hair.

'The wickedness there is in this world,' she said to the empty kitchen.

Upstairs the party was gaining momentum. Someone had produced a guitar and was playing a Spanish love song, Perdita and Gustave had found the drink tray, carefully hidden away in a cupboard by Mr Hudson, and Stanley was holding forth by the sofa.

'I feel degraded even stepping into this mausoleum, this monument to extortion and oppression,' he shouted, rasing his fist, his eyes glinting with true revolutionary zeal.

'It should be pulled down and chucked on the dust-heap along with its inhabitants.'

'How can you be so ungrateful, Stanley,' Henrietta chided him, loyal to her friend. 'After Elizabeth has asked us here and given us such wonderful eats and everything.'

'They are all a bit mad if you ask me,' Rose reported coming down with more dirty plates.

'Chucked on the dustheap with its inhabitants,' Edward quoted indignantly. 'I nearly gave him dust heap, the little . . .'

He was silenced by a loud voice singing *'The Marseillaise.'*

Gustave appeared holding the whisky decanter. Mrs Bridges, Rose, Doris and Edward were transfixed.

'Poor slaves,' cried Gustave with a wild gesture of despair. 'So this is the galley where you sweat out your little lives without sun, without hope.'

He sank into a chair. The servants looked at each other. Rose was right. This one was certainly soft in the head.

'Do you require anything, sir?' Edward piped up gamely.

'I do,' Gustave answered, steadying himself on the pillar near the window. 'I require a bomb to blow out those prison bars.'

He pointed at the servants hall window which, like all servants hall windows in London, was barred against intruders.

'You were born free, mes enfants,' Gustave pleaded. 'Why stay forever chained to this dark basement?'

Edward made for the door.

'Tear off the uniform of servitude,' Gustave lunged at Edward's tailcoat in passing and missed.

By the time Edward returned with Mr Hudson and Henrietta, Gustave had Doris firmly by the arm.

'Why should you slave away all your life scrubbing floors,' he implored her, 'until you are a withered old hag.' Here he discourteously waved towards Mrs Bridges. 'One day I will lead you, the servant slaves of London, up, up into the sun. The gutters of Belgravia will run red with the blood of the tyrants.'

'Gustave!' Henrietta called furiously. 'I'm so sorry,' she apologised to the servants. 'Being a foreigner he doesn't quite understand our ways.'

'He needs deporting,' said Mrs Bridges, when they had gone. 'Locking up at the least.'

'I thought there was quite a lot in what he said,' Doris remarked thoughtfully and was immediately sent to bed.

Upstairs the party was rapidly getting out of hand and Elizabeth was bitterly regretting ever having asked anyone to tea. She wondered how on earth she could get rid of them all.

It was unfortunate that the news of the death of a distant cousin should have brought the Bellamys back early from the country that weekend; it was doubly unfortunate that when they came into the hall Gustave was just sober enough to welcome them to the guillotine in the name of the people and that when they opened the morning room door Evelyn Larkin was performing a Spanish dance on a valuable marquetry table.

Silence fell slowly on the room. Elizabeth ran across to her parents.

'Mother, father,' she said desperately. 'May I introduce . . .'

'I hardly think this is quite the moment for introductions,' Lady Marjorie answered in an icy voice and turned and hurried upstairs.

Elizabeth caught up her father in the hall.

'Father,' she said. 'Why shouldn't I have some friends to a party?'

'Do you call this a party?' Elizabeth had never seen him so angry. 'It's the most disgraceful exhibition I have ever seen. Turning the place into a cheap music hall and on a Sunday too. No thought for your mother. Or for the wretched servants who have to clear up after you.'

And because she well knew there was a lot of truth in his words, Elizabeth simply boiled with anger and humiliation as she watched her new friends file out in scornful silence.

Elizabeth's twenty-first birthday could hardly have started less propitiously. She had a row with Rose when she was dressing because Rose wouldn't take her side over the party and when her parents were equally unforgiving, she flounced out of the house in a temper, leaving her presents unopened, saying she was going to apologise to Evelyn Larkin for the ungracious behaviour the evening before.

When Elizabeth arrived at Evelyn's flat she was still in bed and Lawrence answered the door in his dressing gown.

'The horror of these primped-up semi-educated children of the rich, wearing their newly discovered Socialism like a hat,' Evelyn said to Lawrence when he told her who had called. 'Miss Bellamy bores me to death.'

'She enchants me utterly,' he replied.

'That has not escaped me,' Evelyn said with a mirthless smile.

'Well I'll send her away then . . .'

'No. Send her in. Let her find me warm in my lover's bed. It will advance her education. And talking of education I shall befriend the child, it is her birthday after all. I shall test the strength of her so-called political convictions.'

Lawrence was suspicious.

'She is not to be harmed,' he warned.

'Not her body, I won't touch that,' Evelyn explained sweetly. 'Perhaps her pride. Now fetch her to me.'

She had no difficulty in persuading Elizabeth that it would be a wonderful thing to spend her twenty-first birthday—the day of her emancipation—doing political work for the good of society.

Over lunch they discussed the plan of campaign and in the afternoon, about the time that Mrs Bridges was putting the finishing touches to her birthday cake, Elizabeth rounded up half a dozen shoeless dirty urchins in Paddington and taking them into a shoe shop, saw them equipped with the best stockings and boots money could buy.

When the shopkeeper produced the bill, Elizabeth refused to pay.

'You had boots upon your shelves you could not sell,' she explained to the goggle-eyed little man. 'The children for their part could not buy them. Now you have fewer boots to trouble you and the children are properly shod. Thus little by little we proceed to the just society.'

Evelyn Larkin, who had accompanied her pupil thus far, now gave her a nod of approval and took her leave and Elizabeth sat down alone for the shopkeeper to fetch a policeman.

The Bellamys were still waiting for their daughter to come back home for her birthday tea when the telephone rang to tell them that she was at Paddington Green police station.

Evelyn Larkin sat in front of her gas fire eating crumpets and enjoying the thought of Richard Bellamy, obliged to abandon his Tory conspiracies for the afternoon to rescue his ninny of a daughter from the hands of the law.

Unlike the aggressive Inspector Cape, the Paddington superintendant was a policeman of the old school and knew a gentleman when he saw one. He agreed with Richard Bellamy that by far the best course was to treat the whole thing as a childish prank and, when the shopkeeper had been suitably compensated for his trouble, Elizabeth was handed over to her father.

Back at home Elizabeth remained unbowed and unrepentant. 'I just want to say that I regard what I have done as totally justified, morally and politically,' she said. 'If people are not prepared to suffer for their principles, there's precious little hope for the world.'

'And who says so?' Lady Marjorie retorted. 'Your friend Miss Larkin I suppose?'

'Yes,' said Elizabeth belligerently. 'My friend Miss Larkin who is good and clever and cares about humanity.

She refused point blank to go down to Southwold as her parents insisted she should and she equally refused to give up seeing Evelyn Larkin.

Finally she turned on her heel and ran out of the house, slamming the front door behind her.

Richard Bellamy put his arm round his wife's shoulder. They were both deeply distressed.

'Richard, were we right to speak our minds?' Lady Marjorie asked, anxious to be assured that it was not their fault that Elizabeth was behaving in the way she was.

'Perfectly right, my dear,' Bellamy answered sadly. 'She has come under influences stronger than ours.'

When Elizabeth arrived again at Evelyn Larkin's flat in distant Bloomsbury it was already dark and beginning to snow; Elizabeth was cold and the row with her parents had left her rattled and in need of comfort.

Evelyn herself opened the door.

'What do you want?' she asked.

'I've left home,' Elizabeth explained.

'That was rather silly.'

'But it was because of you.'

'Sillier still.'

When Elizabeth begged that she might stay Evelyn told her to run away and find her own lodgings and then slammed the door in her face.

Elizabeth sat on the stone stairs for a full three minutes unable to grasp the fact that Evelyn meant what she said. Then, stunned and bewildered, she walked slowly down to the street like someone in a dream. Outside she began to wander in a westerly direction. When she reached the Tottenham Court Road the snow was turning to sleet, making the pavements slippery and mushy. It was a part of London that Elizabeth didn't know at all; there were street stalls lit by naked jets of flaming gas twisting and spurting in the cold north wind that howled down the street. The people were poor and rough and every hundred yards there seemed to be a pub and the sound of noisy drunken singing. Unlike the night of the Londonderry House ball no one offered to help her; rather the women she passed gave her hostile glances, drunken men swayed near her with obscene suggestions and when she took refuge for a moment in a doorway a policeman shone his torch in her face and gruffly ordered her to move on. The slush had penetrated her boots and her feet were beginning to lose their feeling. Her coat was soaked through and she began to whimper and then to cry, tears of misery and self pity running cold down her face. Why was everyone so cruel to her? What had she done to deserve it? She was passing a big hospital. Serve them right if I catch pneumonia and die, she thought to herself. There was a cab on the rank in front of her and the cabby stood warming his hands by a brazier. Elizabeth opened her purse with numb fingers; there was just enough money in it to get her to Holland Park.

Henrietta asked no questions; having pulled off Elizabeth's wet clothes, she put her in a hot bath with plenty of mustard in it and then sent her to bed with a bowl of hot soup. Minutes later Elizabeth fell into the deep sleep of utter exhaustion.

Not many young ladies could boast of such an eventful twenty first birthday.

CHAPTER SIXTEEN

The next day Elizabeth was still very exhausted and beginning to suffer a reaction from all the shocks of the previous week. Henrietta decided that she should stay quietly in the house until she was stronger.

After what happened Henrietta naturally broke off all relations with Evelyn Larkin and her group and when Elizabeth read in the paper that the Webbs were in need of people to distribute pamphlets in their fight for Poor Law Reform, the two girls decided to answer the call. While Henrietta was away at her lectures Elizabeth busied herself by addressing hundreds of envelopes, the names being taken from the London Street Directory. She was most surprised one morning when Lawrence Kirbridge drifted in to see her, having apparently met Henrietta in the street. He was lodging with old friends in St. John's Wood and was evasive on the subject of Evelyn Larkin. Henrietta told Elizabeth later that she had heard that Lawrence had parted with Evelyn on account of her treatment of Elizabeth, which made Elizabeth feel rather guilty but also proud that she had a friend noble enough to sacrifice himself for her sake.

The only other person Elizabeth had told of her hiding place was Rose. She knew that Rose would never let her down if she was in real trouble and sure enough on the next Thursday, which was Rose's day off, the housemaid appeared with a little valise with some of Elizabeth's personal belongings in it.

Later that night she was caught by Mr Hudson creeping up the backstairs.

'Isn't that Miss Elizabeth's valise you have there?'

Rose knew it was pointless to deny it.

'I took it to be mended for when she comes back,' she explained, as convincingly as possible.

The corners of Mr Hudson's mouth turned down and he adjusted his spectacles—bad signs, as Rose well knew.

'Don't lie to me, girl,' he said severely. 'You know where she is!'

Rose drooped slightly and put down the valise.

'Oh Rose. I wouldn't have thought it of you,' the butler continued. 'You know how upset her ladyship has been and you knew where Miss Elizabeth was all the time and kept it from them.'

Rose looked down at her feet and in spite of all Mr Hudson's persuasions refused to give away the young mistress's secret.

The butler told her to sit down on a chair by the big table in the servants hall.

'Now Rose,' he asked gently, 'why did you do it? All I want is a reasonable explanation.'

He sat down opposite her.

'Miss Elizabeth asked for my help,' Rose explained.

'She shouldn't have. It wasn't fair to you.'

'But I didn't mind!'

'You should have done,' said Mr Hudson gravely. 'Because it's your good name you'll lose and no one has the right to ask that of you.'

'I don't see that,' said Rose.

'Don't you, Rose?' Mr Hudson answered sadly, looking at her over his glasses like St Peter examining a fallen angel. 'I shall have to tell the master tomorrow that you know where Miss Elizabeth is, and that, for all you knew how upset her ladyship was, you didn't say anything. And he'll tell her ladyship, and then they'll both know that after all these years you've been with them, they can't trust you.'

He stopped and looked at Rose and shook his head slowly. 'They'll be sorry to know that. I know I am.'

Rose sat staring across the table for a long time; then she burst into tears.

'Oh Mr Hudson,' she moaned, 'I don't know what to do!'

Mr Hudson stood up and left her to the dictates of her conscience.

The next afternoon Elizabeth and Lawrence Kirbridge went to Herne Hill to deliver pamphlets. They went most of the way by tram and Elizabeth was amazed how cheap it was and what a strange and fascinating new view it gave her of London.

When they got back it was dusk and she knelt to make up the fire. 'Henrietta will be back soon,' she said. 'You'll stay to supper, won't you?'

'I can't,' Lawrence replied. 'I'm going to the opera.'

'Oh.' Lawrence had other friends, many many friends, Elizabeth knew that, but she couldn't hide the disappointment in her voice.

She blew the fire into flame with a little pair of wooden bellows decorated with poker work.

'You shouldn't sit in the firelight,' said Lawrence.

'Shouldn't I?'

There was a tiny crack in her voice when she replied. He had never spoken to her quite like that before.

'There is something about a woman and firelight. I suppose it makes us think of childhood,' he went on. 'Nanny, mother, familiar things. It makes us feel safe when really it's the most dangerous thing in the world.'

He jumped up suddenly as if he had caught himself in the act of being serious.

'I must go,' he said. He took a newspaper from his

pocket and threw it across to Elizabeth. She picked it up and opened it. It was The Westminster Gazette and one of Lawrence's poems was printed in it.

'Your poem,' Elizabeth exclaimed in delight. 'You mean you've been carrying this about all day?'

Lawrence was embarrassed.

'I'm sorry I sent it now.'

Elizabeth was reading the poem.

'Oh no, it's wonderful!'

'Oh, do you really think so?' He sounded really pleased. Elizabeth looked up at him. What a funny shy diffident person he really was underneath, she thought, not a bit like the confident arrogant young intellectual lion he pretended to be in public.

'The editor insisted on cutting out two verses. He said they were an attack on religion and marriage.'

'Were they?'

'Yes, of course. But I didn't think he was clever enough to realise it.'

They laughed together. Lawrence opened the door and Elizabeth straightened up on her knees. 'Lawrence!'

He turned.

'I think I'm falling in love with you. Would that be a mistake?'

'A terrible mistake for you,' he replied straight away and watched her face fall. 'But wonderful for me.'

He was gone. Elizabeth stayed a long time on her knees in front of the fire wondering what Lawrence really thought of her, words came so easily to him that she never could be sure if he meant what he said. She wondered if she had made a mistake in telling him of her feelings. It made her flesh creep with shame when she remembered the fool she had made of herself with Klaus Von Rimmer blurting out her love for him over tea at Gunter's. What a silly dreadful girl he must have thought her and no wonder he had run away. She hadn't really minded very much about Klaus but she minded very, very much about Lawrence. It would be absolutely dreadful if she frightened him off by being too possessive. She wondered if that had been the real trouble with Evelyn. She had been jealous and possessive all right and she had certainly been Lawrence's mistress; or was it the other way round? Had he been her—there was a word for it, an Italian word; 'Cicisbeo'. Elizabeth went over and looked it up in Henrietta's Concise Oxford Dictionary; *Cicisbeo: Recognised gallant of married woman.* It wasn't quite the right word but anyway Elizabeth didn't want Lawrence to be her recognised gallant, she wanted him to love her just as much as she loved him. But she was counting her chickens, as Rose would have said; Lawrence hadn't even kissed her yet.

Her train of thought was interrupted by a knock on the door.

'Come in,' she said vaguely.

She looked round and saw her father in the door. He looked out of place in the untidy little room in his morning coat and striped trousers.

'Hullo, Elizabeth.'

'Hullo, father.'

She stood up and kissed him just as if he had come into her room at home. She was pleased and relieved to see him. She had been worrying about her parents for days, especially when she woke up first thing in the morning. Now she was glad they had somehow found out about her and her father had come to meet her on her own ground.

'You've made your protest,' he said. 'I understand that. Now you can come home.'

'It wouldn't work,' Elizabeth replied. 'I can't live the way you and mother do—worrying about what you wear, and what you eat, and what you say. It would be like taking part in a perpetual charade. Lawrence agrees with me—it's exactly the same with his mother.'

'Who is Lawrence?'

'Lawrence Kirbridge, the poet. He's another friend of mine,' Elizabeth answered with a touch of defiance.

'That's the rather precious young man who writes poems against religion and marriage.'

'He writes poems *for* a lot of things too, but you wouldn't notice that,' Elizabeth shrugged angrily. 'He writes about truth and honesty, and about being young and knowing that the world belongs to you.'

Richard Bellamy resisted the temptation to throw Miss Larkin back in his daughter's face.

'But Elizabeth, you won't always be young,' he said quietly.

'All the more reason not to betray youth while I have it.'

For a while they continued the time-honoured dialogue of parent and child across the gap of the generations, and Bellamy was interested to note that almost every argument Elizabeth put forward was supported by the opinion of Mr Lawrence Kirbridge, the poet.

Richard Bellamy had not been a member of Parliament for half a century without learning the lesson that to put over a convincing argument it was essential to know your facts. He spent a very profitable afternoon in the House of Commons reference library and thereafter began to drop the name of Lawrence Kirbridge into conversation with his wife; gentle hints, not strong enough to alarm Lady Marjorie, but intriguing enough to rouse her curiosity.

One day at teatime he remarked casually that there was a poem by the young poet in The Westminster Gazette; he was quick to add that he neither approved nor fully understood the work in question.

'At least he gets them published,' said Lady Marjorie. 'I suppose that's something.'

Bellamy knew that his wife was very apt to judge success in life by the tangible results.

'He's getting quite a name you know,' he ventured carefully.

'Really!'

'Yes. A lot of people seem to think he's very gifted. Hugh Cecil was talking about him only yesterday.' He glanced at his wife over the paper to see if she was paying attention.

'His uncle J. G. Kirbridge was Tory Member for Bristol North for years.' He hoped he hadn't overdone it.

'I think father knew him quite well,' Lady Marjorie replied.

'Of course the Kirbridges are all Wykehamists,' Bellamy added casually. There was a considerable pause during which he concentrated on the stock market prices.

'I suppose we *could* ask him to lunch,' said Lady Marjorie.

Elizabeth was extremely suspicious of the luncheon invitation, by the same token that the Trojans suspected the Greeks most of all when they proffered gifts.

She was genuinely surprised when Lawrence seemed delighted with the idea and decided that the only way to show him what impossible people her parents really were, was to agree to go with him.

There was great excitement in the servants hall when Mrs Bridges came down from the morning room to announce the return of the prodigal to lunch. There was also considerable speculation about Miss Elizabeth's young man.

'This Mr Lawrence Kirbridge is a poet,' Rose told them, pleased to be the source of confidential information.

'He's a poet and he don't know it,' said Mr Pearce with his usual vein of humour.

'He speaks lovely,' Rose went on, 'and he's the handsomest gentleman I've ever seen.'

'Handsome is as handsome does,' said Mrs Bridges.

'And who says he doesn't!' said Edward giving Doris the giggles.

'Out,' shouted Mrs Bridges. 'I'm sure I don't know why Mr Hudson tolerates that boy in this house.'

'And I'm sure Miss Lizzy couldn't find a finer gentleman. I'm sure she couldn't,' Rose avowed loyally.

'If he's one of them riff-raff that came to tea before her birthday you can have him,' said Mrs Bridges, reserving her judgment.

The whole visit was a nightmare for Elizabeth. Before lunch Lady Marjorie cross-questioned Lawrence on his family and their connections in such an embarrassingly snobbish sort of way that she was forced to exclaim. 'Oh Mother, what does it matter who is related to whom?'

Lawrence, strangely enough, seemed to think that it did, and boasted about his important relations for what seemed like hours until Mr Hudson came in to announce that lunch was ready. During the meal Elizabeth sat in agonised silence, listening to Lawrence holding forth in his most facetious show-off manner on a great number of subjects he really knew very little about.

It annoyed her still more that her mother seemed to find all this nonsense highly diverting and when her father actually congratulated Lawrence on his fine flow of oratory and told him that he would one day make an excellent politician, she felt forced to intervene.

'We don't believe in politics as they exist today,' she said defiantly. 'Any more than we believe in religion—or marriage.'

It was an awkward moment but Lawrence soon had them laughing again with his description of a mad uncle who had been eaten by cannibals in the South Seas.

When it was time to go Richard Bellamy asked Lawrence if he would like to come to a luncheon he was giving for some literary alumni at the Atheneum.

'That's very kind of you, sir,' Lawrence replied. 'I'd like to very much.'

It gave Elizabeth the chance to get in the last word.

'You'll know where to find him,' she said smiling sweetly as she guided Lawrence out of the room. 'Henrietta has gone down into Wales and Lawrence is coming to share her lodgings with me.'

She was pleased at the stunned look on her parents' faces as the door shut behind them.

'They liked him!' Rose remarked triumphantly to Mr Hudson as they went down the backstairs.

'He's not quite what we're used to,' the butler replied. 'But I must admit he has quite a pleasant easy way with him.'

In the circumstances Lawrence Kirbridge's debut at Eaton Place was something of a triumph.

At Easter Elizabeth and Lawrence went on a camping holiday in the New Forest where they joined some of Lawrence's old Cambridge friends. They were charming, gay and intelligent, the children of doctors or professors or parsons, and Elizabeth enjoyed their company. The girls slept in one tent and the boys in another and most of the day and half the night they talked endlessly about Life and Death, and the Mystery of Beauty and Love.

Elizabeth had expected that in the free gipsy atmosphere of the open air there would be plenty of making love as well as talking about it, but as far as she could see they were all as chaste as nuns. One day when they were lying on a bank and Lawrence was stroking Elizabeth's hair something must have touched his memory.

'You don't have to worry about me and Evelyn, you know,' he said out of the blue.

'I don't,' Elizabeth replied, rather surprised.

'It wasn't a great success, Just as well perhaps or she wouldn't have let me go so easily.'

He laughed. 'She cares about that sort of thing.'

'Don't you?'

'Of course I do.'

'I'm sure I shall.'

But although he must have known that she would willingly have given herself to him then and there he merely laughed again and pulled her to her feet.

Having taken such trouble to make it clear to everyone that she was living in sin Elizabeth felt rather cheated.

Lawrence's father was dead and his mother lived near Ringwood and at the end of the holiday they went to pay her a visit; Lawrence warned Elizabeth not to mention the camping trips as it might upset the old lady. Mrs Kirbridge was much older than Elizabeth expected, quite as old as her grandparents, in fact, and charming and gentle with Lawrence's twinkle in her eyes. She lived in a very old house with a lovely garden surrounded by generations of fierce brown terriers. After tea Mrs. Kirbridge took Elizabeth to see her roses and they talked about all sorts of things including Lawrence and his mother mentioned quite casually that she thought it was high time he got married. It wasn't the first time Elizabeth had heard that same idea brought up that spring. One day when she was visiting Eaton Place to collect some things her mother told her very frankly that her immoral behaviour was damaging her father's career and that she was being spoilt and selfish and childish and making them all miserable. She also made it quite clear that Lawrence had made a good impression and that if he was to ask for Elizabeth's hand paternal approval would almost certainly be forthcoming.

Rose for her part made no bones about her wish to see Elizabeth being led up the aisle all in white, but that was only to be expected from a servant. It was when Henrietta, that apostle of free love, asked Elizabeth when she and Lawrence were going to name the day, that she really did start to feel that the whole world was blind to all reason and fettered by convention.

She said as much to Lawrence one evening when she was sitting leaning against his knees in Henrietta's room.

'Well why not marriage?' he said. 'I mean if it will make your parents happy, why not?'

'Because it's against our principles,' Elizabeth replied fiercely.

'Oh if we were just doing it because we were afraid of conventions, or afraid of people who were afraid of conventions, I agree. But what harm will it do us to say a few meaningless words in a rather ugly pseudo-Gothic barn, and then forget about it?' Lawrence reasoned.

'A great deal of harm to us,' Elizabeth replied firmly, 'and to the things we believe in.'

'But how can it change us when we don't believe in it?' Lawrence shrugged.

'Oh it isn't just getting married,' Elizabeth stood up and went to the window. 'It's joining their world, their fat comfortable world. It will make us fat and comfortable too.'

Suddenly a mischievous awful thought came into her mind, the thought that Lawrence would be quite happy in that fat comfortable world. She dismissed the thought immediately.

'Don't ask me to do it!' she begged him. 'Please don't ask me!'

He didn't ask her and afterwards she remembered his words, 'How can it change us, when we don't believe in it?' and they seemed reasonable enough. If the only way she was going to achieve fulfilment and happiness was by going through a form of marriage it seemed ridiculous not to accept the fact. She told herself it was nothing more than a huge tribal charade to amuse their families and their relations and of course their servants, and after it was over she and Lawrence could go off and lead their lives just as they wanted.

A white wedding in June! When it was noised abroad in Eaton Place that Elizabeth was to be married and an announcement to that effect was actually printed in the Times, great was the rejoicing both upstairs and downstairs and it seemed to her parents that an unhappy period in Elizabeth's life was really coming to an end and that at last she had come to her senses.

CHAPTER SEVENTEEN

One day James Bellamy noticed a pink envelope among his mail addressed in a very childish hand. Inside was a card with a wavy edge.

On the front was printed the words

'MISS CLEMENCE DELICE!

Song and Dance. Speciality Ventriloquism'

On the back the same childish hand had scrawled:

'Empire Stretam next week. Sarah.'

For a moment James thought it was a practical joke then he realised that it was a sort of invitation. He smiled feeling rather pleased that his introduction to Mr Fox had at least got Sarah as far as the Empire Theatre, Streatham, then threw the card into the fire.

The next week James found himself at a loose end one evening and instead of sitting down to play cards in his club he decided that it might be quite a lark to go and have a look at Sarah's act.

When James arrived at the theatre the second house had already started but he was able to get a small box. It was a good old rowdy 'Friday night is pay-night' audience. Sarah's turn came on two items before the first interval. She sang a song called 'What shall we do with Uncle Arthur?; strictly in the Marie Lloyd tradition, about an old gentleman who in spite of his age still had an insatiable passion for the ladies. It was 'naughty' even by the standards of Edwardian music hall. Sarah not only sang but she danced; when she mimed ' 'Ave him doctored, like a tom cat?' it brought the house down. For an encore she had the whole theatre singing the chorus.

James was astonished; not because Sarah could sing or dance but because it was instantly clear that she had a real talent for the stage.

In the interval he sent his card backstage and was rewarded by its return with an invitation to come to Sarah's dressing room after the show scrawled on the back of it.

It was Sarah's first ever private dressing room and although it was barely six foot square and divided from a lady juggler only by a velvet curtain she was very proud of it.

When James came in she was taking off her make-up in front of a piece of looking glass propped up on the tiny dressing table.

'Hullo Mr James.' She looked round and smiled.

'Hullo, Sarah.' James suddenly wished he had never come. Backstage it was all so sordid and garish. 'Congratulations!'

'Thank you, sir.'

'None of that,' James forced a laugh and the tension eased very slightly. 'I say you were really splendid. I've never heard more applause.'

'Always like that Friday nights,' said Sarah modestly. 'Mind you, if I was to go out there and recite the Lord's prayer in Dutch, they'd still yell their bloody heads off.

Sorry I haven't got nothing to offer you in the way of refreshment.'

'Oh don't worry about that. Perhaps if you're free we could go out somewhere,' he suggested.

When he came to the theatre it was the last sort of thing he had had in mind.

Sarah turned and looked up at him.

'You don't have to ask me you know,' she said. 'When I sent you that card, I didn't think you'd actually ever come. It was just to sort of thank you for all the trouble you took.'

James nodded. 'Well I'm very glad I did come, Sarah, or should I say, Miss . . . I'm sorry I can't remember.'

'Sarah will do.'

'Look Sarah, James went on. 'I . . . er . . . I really mean it. I mean about taking you out.'

'All right, Mr. James, if you really mean it,' Sarah replied with a touch of her old cheek. 'If you'd just undo the two top hooks and then wait outside the stage door, I won't be a couple of jiffies.'

They found a place that catered for supper and James insisted on buying a bottle of champagne. It loosened Sarah's tongue and over their meal she told him of her surprising and meteoric success in her chosen profession. Modestly she gave most of the credit to a mixture of good luck and Mr Fox.

The agent had heard of trouble with a dog act in Wolverhampton and had hurried Sarah up there and pushed her in at the bottom of the bill as assistant to a professional ventriloquist. He had turned out to be a terrible old drunk but Sarah had stayed with him on the Midland circuit until one night at Stoke on Trent he had been quite incapable of going on stage and in desperation the manager had allowed Sarah to have the act to herself. To fill in she'd improvised some songs and they had caught on.

Another of Mr Fox's clients had composed 'Uncle Arthur' and it had been such a success that she had given up ventriloquism to concentrate on singing. Somehow the song had just clicked with the public and here she was in the dizzy heights of Streatham.

After supper James escorted Sarah back to her lodgings and afterwards in the cab on the long journey back across the Thames, he began to hum the tune of 'Uncle Arthur' and suddenly realised he hadn't enjoyed an evening so much for months.

Life in the army had become stale and unprofitable for James Bellamy; most of his friends had left or gone abroad or were on the Staff and although he was now a captain he had no real military ambition. He was bored with the monotony of public duties and parties and the mess was always full of noisy young puppies behaving exactly as he had six years before.

Opportunities for men of James's class and age and experience in civilian life were strictly limited. He had no interest in politics and although he liked foxhunting the thought of taking on a pack of hounds of his own didn't appeal to him. Anything to do with commerce or trade or the city of London was quite out of the question. So James had begun to drift, drinking too much, gambling too much, becoming bored, lonely and bad-tempered.

Sarah's success acted on him like a tonic. As Mr Fox was careful to arrange that her engagements were always in the London area where managers from the West End could easily spot her and where her cockney humour was most appreciated, it became a habit with James to go to whichever theatre she was playing in and to take her out to supper at some local hotel every Friday night.

At about the time of Elizabeth's dramatic twenty-first birthday Sarah was performing at the Old Bedford in Camden Town on the same bill as the great Dan Leno. At the end of the performance James was waiting in her dressing room with a bottle of champagne already half empty.

Sarah eyed him critically when she came in.

'Thought you wasn't coming tonight,' she said. 'I thought you was on duty at the barracks.'

'I've managed to get out of it,' James explained, pouring her out a glass of the wine. 'I say I've found rather a jolly place in Hampstead for supper—quite near.'

'Where nobody will recognise you as the son of Mr Richard Pemberton Bellamy M.P.?'

'That's not the point, Sarah.'

'It is the point,' said Sarah standing over him. 'It's always some "jolly place in Hampstead". All right then, if that's not the point, we'll go to the Ritz, that's a jolly little place, isn't it? Show me off to your mother and father's friends. "There's Lady Marjorie's boy"' she mimicked, '"with his new lady friend who's nothing but a little music hall artiste wot sings risque songs on the stage." "Dear, dear",' Sarah held up an imaginary lorgnette, '"What a little trollop she looks; all them feathers and jewels. I do hear she was under house parlour . . ."'

James cut her off.

'Shut up,' he exclaimed. 'You know I'll take you to the Ritz if you want. I don't care what my parents say; what anyone says . . .'

'Well I do,' said Sarah very seriously. 'I care, Jimmy. I don't want you to take me to the Ritz or any other posh place not till you're sure you want to. Till we know where we are. Whether I'm a bit of your guilty conscience or just good for an evening out and a giggle, or something more serious. You know what I mean.'

'Sarah I assure you,' James began, but Sarah stopped him.

'You don't have to assure me about anything, Jimmy. but there's one thing you've got to promise me.'

'Anything within reason . . . I mean, a necklace . . .'

'I don't want nothing like that from you, Jimmy. I just want your promise to go easy on this stuff.' She pointed at the champagne. 'Too many bottles of this and you'll go all bloated and depraved And I wouldn't want that.'

She put her arms round James and looked at his face. 'My brave Captain to go all depraved.'

She kissed him and went over and dropped the empty champagne bottle into her waste paper basket. Then she laughed and turned her back to him.

'Now then Captain, if you'll kindly undo me, I'll get changed then we'll whistle up a cab and drive back to my place for a cup of cocoa.'

Sarah's place was a little apartment she'd taken near King's Cross, She cooked James some supper and afterwards he insisted on helping her to wash up.

'I shouldn't have come here this evening you know,' said James.

'That's what Hudson always says,' Sarah replied, and they both laughed in sudden memory.

'Damn Hudson,' said James, and took Sarah's hand and then let his fingers go slowly up her arm.

'To hell with the regiment?' asked Sarah.

That night they completed the scene that Alfred had interrupted five years before in Lady Marjorie's boudoir.

Once she had taken the plunge, Elizabeth found to her surprise that she was really enjoying all the ridiculous process of getting married.

To everyone's delight she moved back into Eaton Place and mother and daughter got on better than they had done for years. There were lists to write and invitations to send out and visits to make to St Paul's, Knightsbridge, where the marriage was going to take place and where the Bellamys went to church every Sunday, and dresses to be made for Elizabeth and Henrietta, who was to be her only bridesmaid. Presents poured in daily and Elizabeth really began to feel it was one great glorious charade.

One day Mr Hudson came into the morning room to tell her that she was wanted in the hall. She found all the servants lined up at the bottom of the stairs and Mr Hudson presented her with an engraved travelling clock on their behalf. Elizabeth was completely taken by surprise and deeply moved. When she thanked Mr Hudson she kissed him impulsively and then she had to go right down the line kissing them all until she reached Doris. Doris got the giggles and they all started laughing, even Mr Hudson.

'Why is everyone so kind when one is getting married?' Elizabeth asked her mother afterwards.

'They remember their own love,' Lady Marjorie replied, 'and happiness suddenly seems very vulnerable. They want to cherish it.'

As the great day grew closer the hustle and bustle of preparation in the house increased until at last the awning was put up outside the front door, the sign that all was ready. Inside the house every piece of silver and glass the family possessed was ready polished and on display. The presents were all laid out for inspection in the dining room and the little gilt chairs and tables and cases of champagne had been carried in from the caterer's van. The morning room and the drawing room had been half emptied of furniture and decorated with great vases of flowers and finally the three-tiered wedding cake which had taken Mrs Bridges and Doris a week to make, was taken upstairs in secret and locked away in a drawing-room closet, safe from prying eyes.

When the bells started the crossing sweeper in Belgrave Place had been commissioned to warn Mr Hudson. It was the signal for James, who was best man, to set off with his mother in a hired carriage while Mr Hudson led the servants in crocodile fashion across the wastes of Belgrave Square and along Wilton Crescent to the church.

Outside Mr Pearce gave a final polish to the gleaming brass of the Renault's bonnet and inside the suddenly silent house Richard Bellamy waited for his daughter, remembering his own wedding day and knowing just how she must be feeling.

Elizabeth was beginning to feel the butterflies flapping about inside. She looked round the familiar room that she had slept in since she could first remember and she had a sudden sharp pang of regret. She looked at herself in the long mirror and thought that she looked quite ridiculous; all she needed was a pair of wings and a wand and she would do for the top of the Christmas tree.

'Don't let me forget my bouquet,' she said to Rose.

'No,' Rose replied. 'And remember what her ladyship said about how to hold it.'

'Not over my stomach as if I was concealing a baby and not in my arms as though I was nursing one.'

'Miss Elizabeth,' Rose exclaimed, and they both laughed.

Rose lifted the veil high and lowered it over Elizabeth's head.

'Just think, a honeymoon in Vienna!' she said, mouth full of pins.

'Yes,' said Elizabeth. 'Rose.'

'Yes Miss Elizabeth.'

'In case you have any doubts about it, I am still . . . still quite pure you know.'

'Yes, Miss Elizabeth.'

'You had doubts, didn't you Rose?'

'Well, Well, with all your talk about not believing in marriage . . . anyway I'm glad to hear it.'

'I'm not,' said Elizabeth in sudden despair. 'If it wasn't for you, Rose, I wouldn't be standing here now in this ridiculous dress.'

Rose was horrified.

'Oh Miss Elizabeth. I did it all for the best.'

Elizabeth smiled sadly. 'Everyone's done everything for the best, and now I'm so frightened.' She shivered and all her nerves tightened. Rose didn't dare hug her for fear of crushing the cream silk of the dress.

'But you love him, don't you?' she asked.

'I wish I knew,' Elizabeth replied. 'I wish I knew . . . how fond he was of charades.'

Seeing Rose's worried puzzled face Elizabeth smiled again and kissed her.

'I do love him, oh I do! Perhaps it is all for the best.'

'I'm sure it is,' said Rose firmly.

Whatever happened Rose was going to see to it that Elizabeth didn't run away from her own wedding.

As James showed her to her pew in the front of the church Lady Marjorie had the same dreadful thought.

'Don't worry,' her son assured her. 'Father will get her to the post.'

Lady Marjorie turned and surveyed the rapidly filling church. She was just thinking how dull and undistinguished the Kirbridge friends and relations looked when her eye was taken by the peacock figure of a very pretty girl coming up the aisle. The face seemed vaguely familiar and to Lady Marjorie's horror she suddenly recognised her erstwhile under house parlourmaid. Sarah had stopped in the middle of the church and was waving up at the Bellamy servants in the gallery, and the bride was due at any moment. Catching his mother's eye James hurried to the rescue and pushed her quickly into a vacant seat.

'Don't worry, Jimmy,' Sarah whispered to him with a wink. 'I wouldn't spoil an entrance.'

Looking back on her wedding Elizabeth could remember only an impression of smiling faces and cheering people in the sunlight and the mass of huge hats in the church looking like a sea of coloured umbrellas. Henrietta, her only bridesmaid, cried a great deal and Mr Balfour kissed her and made a speech.

After the cutting of the cake Sarah made her way through the familiar green baize door down the dark stone stairs to see her friends in the servants hall.

They were very excited to find such a celebrity in their midst and Edward opened a bottle of champagne while Sarah sat on the table and told them stories of her life behind the footlights. They asked her to sing and autograph her portrait which had the place of honour over the fireplace beside the one of James Bellamy at the Coronation. Then she sang 'Uncle Arthur' and they all joined in, even Mrs Bridges.

'Terrible time he gives to Auntie Martha!—they sang,
'Chasing the ladies'
'Whenever he can,'
'After the birds from morning to night,'
'A truly amazing appetite.'
'Oh what'll we ever do with such a man!'

Singing and dancing Sarah led them in file round the table; when she reached the door through to the kitchen passage, she narly bumped into Mr Hudson.

'Sarah!' he said in a voice of thunder, then remembering their relative positions in society, he added with elaborate irony, 'Begging your pardon, Miss Delice!'

'Yaas, Hudson,' Sarah answered in Lady Marjorie's voice and Edward and Doris had to hold themselves up for laughing.

'The other guests are assembling in the hall for the departure of the bride, Miss,' Mr Hudson observed with dignity.

'And I'm assembling down 'ere,' Sarah replied.

Ignoring her Mr Hudson ordered those still subject to his discipline to take their places on the pavement and as they filed past he issued each with a ration of rice and confetti.

There was a call of 'Sarah!' from the top of the stairs.

'Down here, Jimmy!' Sarah called back and put out her tongue at Mr Hudson who contented himself with one final glare of disapproval over his glasses before turning and following the others up the area steps.

When James found her Sarah was alone in the kitchen.

'What on earth are you doing down here?' he asked her. He was in a gay excited mood.

'Reliving old memories.'

'You hated every minute of it.'

'Not every minute,' Sarah answered with a wistful smile. She shrugged. 'I don't really belong anywhere now, do I? Not downstairs or upstairs . . . or in my lady's chamber.'

James swung her round and placed her on the dresser like a doll.

'You belong to me,' he said.

'Do I?' she asked doubtfully.

For a long time they looked at each other before James kissed her.

'We must go upstairs,' he said. 'Elizabeth's ready to go.'

'I wish we could go away.'

'Where to—Vienna?'

'I'd rather go to Paris.'

'Paris,' said James considering it. 'All right,' he cried suddenly with a wide cavalier sweep of his arm. 'Let's go!
'No?' Sarah's eyes opened very wide in amazed delight. 'Why not?'
'To hell with the theatre,' she said.
'To hell with the regiment!' he replied.
'Vive La Republique,' they both shouted together, and James picked her up in his arms and carried her upstairs.

Later that evening Richard Bellamy came into his wife's boudoir for the ritual removal of his cufflinks.
'I really thought Elizabeth looked rather nice today,' said Lady Marjorie.
'She looked quite, quite ravishing,' Bellamy answered. 'If that is the right word for a bride. Even your Aunt Kate said so.'
'I do hope they'll be all right,' Lady Marjorie went on in a vague motherly sort of way. 'She has really been quite different lately. Of course the first baby is so important.' She added, thinking ahead.
'Lawrence is nobody's fool,' said Bellamy. 'I had quite a long talk to him the other day. I think if we were to dangle a nice safe seat in front of him—with another general election coming along next year . . .'
'Poetry and politics?' Lady Marjorie smiled and tucked the cufflinks into her husband's waistcoat pocket.
'I used to write poetry at his age,' said Bellamy thoughtfully. 'Rather good poetry.'
'Richard!' said his wife in disbelief.
Bellamy smiled at her. 'You didn't catch me until I was twenty-five, my dear,' he said. 'I'd sown my wild oats by then.'
Lady Marjorie sighed.
'James is twenty-eight. I wish he would get married.'
Richard Bellamy went to the door.
'Don't be long, darling,' said Lady Marjorie. 'We're both tired.'
'I won't,' Bellamy promised. 'I really think James is the least of our worries.'

Downstairs in the Butler's pantry, Mr Hudson and Mrs Bridges were sharing a bottle of Mr Bellamy's best vintage port and considering the possibilities of boarding houses by the sea.

THE END

There's no putting down

Hand-Me-Downs

RHEA KOHAN

Marilyn's mother loves him. Her father loves him. Even her grandmother loves him. Everyone loves Marilyn's husband except Marilyn!
After eight deadly years with the kind of creep who folds his socks at night Marilyn wants out, fast. As Hollywood's sharpest glamour lawyer she fixes million dollar palimony for the famous and the flashy, but when it comes to her own life she can't even fix a stiff drink – until she takes the plunge. Singles bars, jacuzzis, group therapy, live-in companions, luscious bodies and lying eyes . . . there's a dazzling sunset strip of total pleasure for Marilyn as soon as she trashes the family hand-me-downs and gets her glad rags on!

'Very funny, exceedingly moving and extraordinarily sharp.' *Cosmopolitan*

GENERAL FICTION 0 7221 5246 9 £1.75